M000206128

MIDNIGHT REVELATIONS

Karen M. Bence

The Dark Whispers Series
Volume One

★ **SterlingHouse Publisher, Inc.** Pittsburgh, PA

Other titles in
The Dark Whispers Series

MIDNIGHT
REVELATIONS

Crow Books

ISBN-10: 1-56315-414-5
ISBN-13: 978-1-56-315414-0
Trade Paperback
© Copyright 2008 Karen M. Bence
All Rights Reserved
Library of Congress #2008924345

Requests for information should be addressed to:
SterlingHouse Publisher, Inc.
7436 Washington Avenue
Pittsburgh, PA 15218
info@sterlinghousepublisher.com
www.sterlinghousepublisher.com

8th Crow Books
is an imprint of SterlingHouse Publisher, Inc.

SterlingHouse Publisher, Inc. is a company
of the Cyntomedia Corporation

Cover Design: Brandon M. Bittner
Interior Design: Kathleen M. Gall

All rights reserved. No part of this publication may be reproduced,
stored in a retrieval system, or transmitted in any form or by
any means…electronic, mechanical, photocopy, recording or any
other, except for brief quotations in printed reviews…without prior
permission of the publisher.

This is a work of fiction. Names, characters, incidents, and places
are the product of the author's imagination or are used fictitiously.
Any resemblance to actual events or persons, living or dead, is
entirely coincidental.

Printed in U.S.A.

ACKNOWLEDGEMENTS

I would like to thank everyone who has supported me on this project: Barbara Green, Carol McCabe, Karen Caine, Dr. George Zitnay, Marty Haggerty, Valerie Clark, and my wonderful family. I couldn't have done it without the kick in the butt from Bob, the never-ending encouragement from Ricky, or the inspiration from my mom.

PROLOGUE

1972—Virginia

The mahogany haired woman clutched the blanket tightly to her chest as she opened the door and stepped out into the dawn. It was bitter cold out, and a thick layer of snow had settled overnight. She wouldn't have chosen to try to drive in these conditions had the circumstances been different. Making her way carefully down the slick stone steps, she heard her father's booming voice behind her. She crossed behind the station wagon and came around to the passenger side. Looking across the roof of the car, she could see that life had started stirring at the farm, even at this early hour. A man near the barn saw her and waved. She would have waved back but her arms were full.

"You take her out of here," her father growled from the top step. "Don't you ever bring that child back into my house. I don't ever want to lay eyes on her again. If it was up to me she would go the way of those damn feral cats. She has branded and disgraced our name."

With eyes locked on her pursuer, she quickly opened the car door, afraid he might try to rip the baby from her arms as he had in the house. It took the strength of two women to wrestle the small, crying infant from his beefy arms. She looked down at the small, perfect face while carefully placing the swaddled infant into the wicker clothesbasket that was wedged on the front seat. The baby cooed softly.

"Shush, it will be all right," she said.

She closed the car door and quickly ran around to the driver's side. He met her as her hand reached for the handle.

"It never ends. A damned curse hovers over us, nothing but a black cloud. That girl has only brought agony and torment to this family, ripped the beating heart from my chest," he said, incensed. The older man's face was beet red, and he reeked of whiskey.

"Pa, please, just let me go," the dark haired woman cried.

"Conspirator, that's what you are!" he bellowed.

The veins in his neck stood out and he spat as he talked. He had morphed into this angry, drunken monster more than a decade ago. She was afraid that he would lose what little control he had left and strike her. The memories of fleeing from his rage years before washed over her, making her wonder how she ever had the courage to come back. They both turned when they heard someone rapping on a window. An older woman with red swollen eyes and tears on her cheeks was looking down from an upstairs window.

"See what this has done to your mother. Destroyed her!" he said, turning back to look at his terrified daughter.

"Please, she wants me to leave and take the baby. Please, Pa," she begged, her gaze rising up to meet his bloodshot gray eyes.

She realized she was shivering, but wasn't sure if it was from the bitter cold or fear. It was doubtful as to whether she could get the baby out of there alive. She heard it then. A voice was drifting up from the barn, calling to him. The man that had waved to her had been watching. She looked over her father's shoulder now, praying for intervention so she could escape with her precious little one. The man had captured her father's attention long enough for her to open the car door and jump behind the wheel. She had the car started and in reverse before he realized what had happened. The intoxicated old man grabbed for the car door, but she had locked it. She looked ahead, put the car into gear and stepped on the gas. He was left standing there, cursing her and the baby.

"If you ever come back here, it will be the last thing you ever do. Dead, that's what you'll be, you and that child of the devil. You hear me? Dead!" he screamed. He started to chase the car down the drive but he lost his balance and fell hard on one knee.

Glancing back, she thought it would be a cold day in hell before she would venture to set foot anywhere near her childhood home again. When the gravel of the driveway met the macadam of the main road, the realization that they had made it overwhelmed her. She took a deep breath before turning the heater dial to high and double-checking that the baby was wrapped securely. The infant girl looked up at her and peacefully yawned.

"Don't worry," she whispered. "You're safe now. Everything is going to be fine. It's all arranged. You'll be in your mother's arms by this time tomorrow. You are a gift from God, my precious little one. And you're in his hands now."

She pulled away, leaving the large stone house behind her. When she glanced in the rearview mirror, the peak of the rooftop disappeared from sight.

"May God save you too," she whispered under her breath as her eyes refocused on the road that lay ahead.

CHAPTER ONE

2008

Sara caught sight of the mirror out of the corner of her eye. It was tucked into a far back corner of the antique store. Drawn to it, she reached out to run her hands along the outer edge. Peering at her reflection, she could have sworn there was an instant when it looked oddly distorted, like a camera lens trying to come into focus. It was only a second, but it would stay with her. Sara's eyes followed the detail around the entire edge. At the top was the face of a god, or perhaps the devil. Down each side were two arching naked women. It was clearly very old. The gold leafing was worn and chipped in several places. Standing back, she cocked her head as she admired its beauty. What was it about this mirror that seemed to hypnotically possess her? She felt compelled to buy it, justifying the purchase as a birthday present to herself.

"Excuse me, how much is this mirror?" she asked the old man who was busy refinishing a rocking chair.

"Seven hundred and fifty dollars," he said without looking up.

"You're kidding," said a white-haired old woman who materialized from around the corner of a large armoire. "That ugly mirror—it's awful. Why on earth would you want such a thing?"

"Be quiet, Madeline. It's none of your business. If the lady wants it, she can have it. It's yours for 750 even. I'll cover the tax as a bonus for having to listen to my wife," he said, winking at Sara.

"I don't care what you say," the older woman chimed in. "I'm telling you, that thing is creepy. It's given me the shivers ever since you hung it up in here."

"Madeline! Go back in the other room!"

She gave him a dirty look, then turned on her heels, disappearing into the back of the shop.

"That's okay," Sara said when his wife was gone. "We all have our opinions. I'll take it." Sara pulled out her checkbook and pen.

The shop owner watched as she neatly wrote out the blue rectangular bank slip for seven hundred fifty dollars. "I see here that you moved into the old McHugh place," the man commented as he read the address printed on the top of the check.

"Do you mean the decrepit old farm on Standish Lane?" she kidded. He nodded that she was right. "Then I guess so," she replied. "I didn't know who lived there before. We bought it directly from the bank."

"This mirror came from that estate sale. We ended up with it in the auction. How about that? It's going back to where it came from." The man's smile was brimming over with delight as he handed Sara a receipt for her purchase.

"Huh, I'll be darned. I can't wait to tell my husband."

"Great old place. It was a heck of an estate years ago. Glad to see people back in it. Place sat empty for a long spell. You know how gossip can start swirling when a house sits on the market for a long time."

"Really?" she asked with a wrinkled up nose. "Like what?"

The weathered man hesitated for a moment as he studied her face. "When you live in a small town, people need something to talk about. Nothing but tall tales made up by little children and old maids."

"Oh. Do you know why the bank had it?" Sara asked. "I mean, the place is a mess, but I would have thought someone in the family would have jumped at the chance to live there."

While sharpening the intensity of his gaze, he lowered his voice and shrugged. "Not sure. I guess the girls didn't want to be bothered. There was some kind of falling out between them and their parents a long time ago. Nothing worse than holdin' onto anger. It eats at your soul."

"Wow. They must have had one heck of a fight. I never would have sold it. I could barely contain myself when the realtor showed it to us. My husband had to keep me from jumping up and down. I swear, it's one of the most beautiful houses I've ever seen. Well…at least I can envision that it will be, once it's done being renovated. I feel like it was just waiting for us to come along and save it."

"Good luck with the place. Let me bring this out to your car. It's real heavy," the shopkeeper said as he lifted the mirror off the wall.

"Thanks a bunch."

Sara held open the front door. Leading the man over to the curb where her car was parked, she winced as a crisp winter wind whipped the hair across her face. The sidewalk covered with sand and salt crunched under their shoes. Sara opened up the back hatch of her SUV, allowing the man to slide the mirror's gilded edge across the cargo area's carpeting.

After guiding her find securely into place, he straightened up and gave her a warning. "Be careful taking this out. You'll need some help. Weighs a ton plus some, and it's hard to get a good grip on the darn thing." The man closed the door and started back toward the shop.

"I will. Thanks again," she called out, prompting the owner to pause and turn around.

"I was wondering," he said.

"Yes," Sara answered. She could feel the skin on her cheeks starting to tighten from the cold.

"If you don't mind me asking, how did you end up looking for a house way out here? We're not exactly what you would call a bustling city—a bit off the beaten track. Were you born nearby?" The man, wearing only a flannel shirt and jeans, looked unscathed by the cold.

"Gosh, no! Born and raised in New York, although I've lived in Pennsylvania for more than ten years. I have a good friend who lives over in Leesburg. We visited last fall and fell in love with northern Virginia. My husband and I were looking for a change, a new start, I guess you could say. I think it was the house that clinched it for us. We were just toying with the idea until we found it. It also helps that this is some of the best countryside in the nation for riding horses—a big plus since we have six!"

"A horsewoman. I should have known," he said with a chuckle.

"Shoot! Look at the time. I really need to get going," Sara said as she checked her watch.

"I apologize. I didn't mean to hold you up. As I said before, good luck with your new farm." The shop owner cheerfully gave a little wave as they went their separate ways. The man went back in the building as the half-frozen woman hurried around the side of the car.

Once in the front seat, Sara put the heater on high, then pulled away from the curb. The air blew cold for the first few minutes before settling into the sub-sauna temperature she preferred. As she made her way through town, her mind drifted back to the man's last question. The painful truth was that she and her husband, David, were desperately trying to fix their marriage. Life as they knew it started to unravel after they lost a baby more than a year ago. Sara became emotionally paralyzed, while David wanted nothing more than to put the death of their daughter behind him. When the dust settled, they had forgotten how to be together, how to fit. This house was a way for them to escape from the memories that tore them apart.

Sara shook these thoughts from her head and focused on the mirror. It seemed so odd that it had come from the house. She wondered what other treasures could be found tucked away in the dusty corners of local antique shops. Sara's mind wandered through the various rooms, trying to figure out where it might have been hung in years past—the foyer, the parlor or possibly the landing at the top of the staircase.

Before Sara realized it, she was pulling into the long, gravel driveway. Not much of the house could be seen from the road, only the very tops of the chimneys. Rolling pastures were obscured here and there by a tree line or stone wall. The magnificent stone house, part of an old Virginia plantation, stood just beyond the crest of a hill. Centuries had witnessed the slow divorce of land from the original estate, leaving it now with a mere 100 acres in contrast to the thousands it once possessed.

Sara pulled the SUV in next to their truck. She could see David on the sun porch and motioned for him to come out as she climbed out of the front seat. "David, can you come here? I need your help," she called through cupped hands.

Sara and David were approaching their eleventh wedding anniversary. David had always been a patient, kind, and comforting man who her mother would frequently refer to as a saint. Sara was well aware that this was more often meant to be a criticism of her versus a compliment to him. However, secretly in her heart, she agreed with the description. The past year had stolen that person as he struggled to come to terms with his own grief. David towered over her at six-foot-five. With dark brown hair and matching eyes, he came from salt-of-the-earth Pennsylvania German-Dutch heritage. Hard-wired with strong analytical skills, he viewed the world through practical eyes. In contrast, Sara grew up in the midst of a loud and moderately neurotic New York Italian family.

From the moment they met in college, they were inseparable. They embraced one another because of their differences. Together they felt whole. He was a typical middle child who demanded little attention but longed to be the center of someone's world. She was an only child who desperately needed someone to belong to without question. Whereas he was even keeled and difficult to enrage, she was hot tempered with a tough exterior. After David had earned her trust, Sara opened up, exposing a soft heart accentuated by an acute vulnerability. The couple had a running joke that she was the red sauce on his vanilla. From the start of their relationship, David swore that she made him the happiest and angriest of anyone he had ever met, which she insisted was the only way love should ever be. They never anticipated how this theory was to be tested.

David walked down the stone steps from the house without a coat on. "Wow! It's cold out here! What do you need?" he asked.

"Some help," she answered. "I bought myself a present. It's something for the house, a mirror. And guess what?"

"What?" he asked suspiciously, as he squinted to peer through the SUV's tinted rear window.

"It was owned by the family that lived here before! Isn't that wild? I found it at an old antique shop in town. The fella said he picked it up at an auction. It's kind of different. I guess it sort of spoke to me. I couldn't resist," Sara rambled as she moved around her husband, whose nose was still almost pressed against the glass. She bumped him out of the way with her hip, then lifted the rear door.

"I can't see it very well in the car. Let's get it out," David said.

"Be careful. He said it was really heavy," she warned as he began inching out the mirror.

"The guy was right. This thing must weigh close to a 100 pounds. I'm gonna need help getting it in the house. I don't exactly have a free hand," David said, grimacing from the effort.

He struggled up the steps as Sara ran ahead to get the door. She had to fight the wind, propping her body against the wooden panel to keep it open for him. Once inside, he brought the massive mirror into the kitchen and laid it down on the table. "You liked this thing?" he asked arching his left eyebrow.

"Yes!" Sara said defensively.

"It looks a little…baroque to me, not exactly what I would envision in a Virginia manor house. Where are you going to put it?" His tone suggested that "out of sight" would be good.

"You don't like it," Sara said, pouting. "But it belongs here."

"I'm surprised, that's all. It's not your usual style. But I'm sure it will look amazing wherever you want it. Happy birthday, sweetheart," he said, backing down.

Sara smiled, acknowledging David's graceful retreat. Turning her around so they were face to face, David bent down and kissed her softly on her lips. Any lingering hint of defensiveness melted away instantaneously. She was lost in the security of his embrace. "I love you, and thanks," she whispered.

"I love you, too," he said, squeezing her tighter.

Their private moment was lost when Jack, their 7-year-old son, came bounding in the room with their three dogs, two massive Great Danes and one hyperactive Springer Spaniel. Jack wore a broad grin that was instantly infectious. The little boy had inherited his father's easy-going nature and height. Sara's influence was seen in his facial features and hair color. When he was a baby, his hair was almost black. Over the years it had lightened considerably to a honey brown.

"Hi, Mom. Whatcha get?" he asked.

"A mirror, one that used to live in this house. What do you think?" Sara asked, while still holding tight to David.

Jack looked down at it from the kitchen chair he had climbed up on. "Um, there are naked ladies on it, Mom," he commented without offering an opinion.

"Yes. I know that, sweetie," she said very delicately.

"Are we allowed to hang up naked ladies in our house?" he asked, turning to look at his amused parents.

"We can, if your mom says so, Jack," said David with a wry smile.

"Then I guess I like it," he announced. "How 'bout you, Dad?"

"I like whatever your mother does," he answered with the faintest hint of sarcasm.

"Good! I like it too! Another year and I won't be able to lift you, little boy. You're getting big and I'm getting old," Sara said, helping him off the chair.

"You're not old yet, Mom."

"Thanks, I think," she replied, bending to kiss him on the head.

"I'm hungry. Can I have lunch?" he asked, changing the subject.

"Me too, Mommy," David teased, squeezing the right cheek of his wife's buttocks as she walked passed.

Sara gave her husband a sideways glance that suggested that she would take care of his sexual appetite later. She recognized and appreciated the effort he was making to rekindle the dormant fire between them.

Jack ran off into the living room. Sara could hear him humming while she gathered together the fixings to make a peanut butter and jelly sandwich. She poured a glass of chocolate milk as David leaned against the counter, watching her.

"You had some phone calls, birthday girl," he said, stealing a potato chip from Jack's plate.

"I can't imagine who would call," Sara joked as she pressed the two sticky slices of bread together, then sliced them diagonally in half.

"Leila and your mom," he answered. "The usual suspects."

"Did you talk to them or did they leave a message?" Sara asked. Picking up the cup and plate, she walked over to the only available spot left at the kitchen table. "Jack, your lunch is ready. Come on."

David opened his mouth to answer but was interrupted by pounding footsteps. Jack came tearing through the kitchen, planting himself in the seat in front of his sandwich. "Thanks, Mom," he said.

"Try not to get food on the mirror, okay?" Sara cautioned.

"Okay." The little boy looked up to emphasize that he got her point.

Sara ran a finger around his cheek, silently noting how he had come to resemble her more and more as he got older. Their brief trance was broken when she heard David answer her question.

"I spoke to Leila," he explained. "She said she was going to come by tomorrow to check out how the house is coming along. She wants to go out riding if it's not freezing cold like today. Why don't you ask her to stay for dinner? She always brings exceptionally good red wine. I can pick up some steaks. What do you think?"

"Sounds like a great plan to me. I'll ask her when I call back. I'm so excited. I can't wait to show her my mirror," Sara said.

Leila and Sara had been friends since the third grade. They learned how to ride at the same barn, forging a lifelong love of horses and a friendship that spanned more than 25 years. It was a visit to Leila's last fall that spurred their decision to move. She had relocated to Leesburg a couple of years ago to open her own interior design shop. They were as close as any two sisters could be.

"And what about my mother?" Sara asked.

"She left a message to call. It was really strange. She said she needs to talk to you about something important, but doesn't want to do it over the phone. Sounds like she wants you to drive up to see her in New York," David said with a mixture of curiosity and concern. "What do you think that's about?"

"No idea."

"You may want to phone her first," David suggested.

"She hasn't been feeling very well lately," Sara said. "Bad headaches, I think. Maybe there's something really wrong with her."

Sara noticed David's attention shift as his gaze drifted past her. She spun around to find Jack kneeling on the kitchen table, his small torso hovering precariously above the mirror. Topping off this unusual sight was Jack looking up at the ceiling with a baffled expression.

"Jack! What are you doing? Get down before you fall and break the mirror and yourself!" she screamed in panic.

"But Mom, I saw someone," Jack replied.

"Of course you saw someone. It's a mirror. You see your reflection," Sara snapped.

"I know that, Mom. But it wasn't me," he explained.

"What?" David asked. "What do you mean you saw someone?"

Sara and David crossed the room. They stood next to Jack and stared down at the mirror.

"I was eating my sandwich and then I saw this lady's face in there," he said, pointing. "I sat up to have a closer look, but she was gone. Then I figured she must be on the ceiling looking down at it, so…." Jack's reenactment came to a quick halt.

"Get down. Get down," Sara chastised, pulling her son's body from the table. "There is no lady. It must be giving off a weird reflection from the light. The glass must have some distortion in its surface because it's so old. I noticed something odd about it in the shop."

"Mom, I saw a lady," he adamantly protested.

"I believe you, Jack. Apparently, your mom bought a spooky mirror. Don't worry about it," David teased, waving his hand as if Jack's experience were commonplace. Mother and son simultaneously turned to glare at him. "It was a joke. Come on! Both of you lighten up. I'm sure it's simply a distortion…which looked like a lady."

"Are you done eating?" Sara asked.

"Yes," Jack answered.

"Fine. Then clean up, put your plate and cup on the counter and go play," she said sternly.

Jack did as he was told and trotted out of the room without another word or glance at either of his parents.

"Relax, will you? He's just a little boy with a great imagination," David said, redirecting his attention to calm his agitated wife.

"I guess you're right. I overreacted, didn't I?" Sara realized with a slightly embarrassed smile. "I just didn't want him to get hurt. Had Jack slipped and fallen onto the mirror…I don't even want to think about it."

"He'll survive. Children are resilient that way. I worry more about you. Tell you what…how about we drop it, since you really need to return those calls. Come on. Here," he said, putting the phone in her hand as he pushed her through the kitchen. "Go. Your mom and best friend are waiting to wish you happy birthday."

"Ah, the art of distraction and redirection. Clever," Sara said with a wink as she walked out of the room and down the hall.

Sara opened the door to their bedroom. This was her favorite room in the house. She loved to linger in their king-sized bed, but sleeping in was a rare treat. A cozy sitting area, with an overstuffed loveseat, was nestled in the far corner of the room. Sara sat down in one corner, laying her legs across the remainder of the cushions. She closed her eyes and took a deep breath. As she exhaled, the fear of losing her one remaining child to a stupid accident dissolved away.

Sara looked out the French doors, over the private balcony, and down into the expanse of the pasture below. Two ponies were busy entertaining themselves by galloping and bucking. Sara noticed it was starting to snow. Easily entranced by the zigzagging lines of white, she was startled when a massive canine head propped itself on the back of the sofa. Buster, their two-year-old Great Dane, was searching for attention. The giant black and white dog, sporting a pair of mismatched blue and brown eyes, circled around Sara, taking up a position right next to her. While all the dogs followed Sara like a shadow, Buster was particularly attached. At the moment, he was towering over her, waiting to be acknowledged.

"What do you want?" she asked, rubbing his ears. "Lie down, Buster."

He obliged, stretching down next to the loveseat, the length of his body equal to hers. The large dog moved his head to the side, enabling him to rest it on her stomach.

She smiled down at him and stroked the fur on his neck. "Good boy."

Refocusing, Sara flipped open her cell phone. She wondered if her mom could really be ill. Joe, her father, had died about three years earlier after a prolonged battle with cancer. Sara, David, and her mother, Maria, had been in his hospital room at the end. Maria insisted that her husband would be fine up until his final breath. Sara's stomach still turned when she recalled how different her dad had looked after his heart stopped.

About a month later Maria sent further shockwaves through Sara's life. In tears, Maria told her that she and Sara's father had been keeping a secret from her, that she was adopted. Only now, with her husband gone, did she feel free to tell Sara the truth. Maria had explained that Joe had never wanted his daughter to know, stressing that she had always been against this decision, but never felt strong enough to oppose him. Sara winced at the memory. At the time, it seemed like everything moved in slow motion. She vividly remembered the urge to vomit and the look of disbelief on David's face when she told him the news.

The revelation helped to explain Sara's irrational fears. From the deepest part of her mind she always felt different, as if she didn't belong. She shook her head violently, trying to clear away the bad memories. It had taken a long time to work through her feelings of anger and betrayal. She had spent too much time and energy feeling lost. But time had an amazing way of distancing her from pain, and gradually Sara and her mother moved beyond the fact that Sara was not her biological daughter to the reality that she was just her daughter. Sara kicked around the thought of trying to locate her birth parents, but the idea of searching seemed like it would be a daunting task. She decided that it was better to move forward. There was no sense in trying to rewrite the past.

Sara brought herself back to the present and punched in her mother's number. The telephone rang six times with no answer.

By the seventh ring she had lost patience and was about to hang up when a woman's voice resonated across the line.

"Hello."

Sara paused a second, realizing that it was not her mother's voice on the phone, yet she vaguely recognized it.

"Hello. Is anyone there?" the woman asked.

Sara answered this time. "Hi, this is Sara. Is my mother there?"

"Oh, Sara honey, this is Aunt Donna. I'm here with your mother. Let me get her for you. Hold on one minute," she said.

Sara could hear her aunt calling her mother. Aunt Donna returned to the receiver and rattled out a list of questions without taking a breath or waiting for an answer to any of them. "Sara, how are you? How is the new place? Are you feeling well? Your mother is here, darling. Take care. Oh, I almost forgot. Happy birthday," she said handing the phone over to her sister before Sara had the chance to utter a single word.

"Hi, Sara, I'm glad you called me back. I know how busy you are with the new house," Maria said apologetically before clearing her throat.

"Mom, what's going on? Are you all right? Why is Aunt Donna there? You didn't tell me she was planning a visit," Sara blurted out.

"Well, first things first, happy birthday. Donna's visit was a last minute thing. How are you? How's Jack, my little doll? He must be so big."

Sara smirked into the phone with the growing suspicion that she was getting the run-around. She pushed on, hoping to get a straight answer. "Mom, Jack is fine. What's going on? You said in your message that you had to tell me something and you wanted me to come up. You're scaring me. Are you sick?"

"No, no…not really. I've just been feeling funny the last month. I can't put my finger on it. I went to Dr. Johnson and he told me that he couldn't find anything wrong with me. Well, nothing other than what's always been a problem. You know, blood pressure, cholesterol, and things like that. The usual ailments that plague us old folks," she answered.

"Okay. Maybe you should see someone else, and what exactly

do you mean by feeling funny?" Sara asked.

"I know this is going to sound, well…nutty, but I've been having the strangest dreams," her mother explained. "Sometimes I wake up screaming for you. I can't really remember what they're about. That's the funny thing. I mean, you would think if a nightmare were bad enough to wake me up, I would remember. I almost called you a couple of times in the middle of the night to make sure you were all right, but then I would have scared you to death." Maria's quivering voice couldn't hide her fear.

"What? You can't remember anything?" Sara asked, feeling goose bumps on her arms.

"No, not exactly. They're fragmented. Nothing seems to make sense. Dr. Johnson suggested keeping a notepad by my bed and writing down anything I recall as soon as I wake up. So far, I've only gotten an image here and there. I'm telling you, there is no sense to any of it. I have this overwhelming fear that you're somehow in danger. I told you it's crazy, but I can't shake it. That's why I'd like you to come home. I think it will pass if I can see you for myself. Please."

"Geez, Mom. I can't right away. The best I might be able to do is next weekend. I'll have to check with David and get back to you. Okay?"

"I guess that will have to do. I have to confess that I'm feeling a little bit better now that Donna is here with me. I was dreading going to sleep at night, but I feel safer now."

"I'm sorry I can't give you an answer right now. Try not to worry. I'm perfectly fine and everything here is, well…better. Really, the move has been good for both of us. Honestly, paint fumes have been the most dangerous things we've encountered thus far. I'll be sure to call you back as soon as we work out the details. I love you," Sara said, trying to be reassuring.

"I love you too, honey. I'll talk to you later."

Sara pushed the off button after she heard Maria hang up. "High maintenance. Simply high maintenance," she muttered to herself before yelling for her husband. "David! David, can you come in here a minute?"

Buster stirred at the sound of her raised voice.

"David, did you hear me?" Sara shouted.

"I'll be right there!" she heard David bellow from the other room. "What do you need?" he asked a few minutes later as he walked over to his wife.

"Can you come with me to New York next weekend?" Sara asked, letting her eyes plead her case. She followed this up with the condensed version of their conversation, topping off her appeal by conveying her heightened concern over the presence of her Aunt Donna in New York, which was highly unusual.

Donna, Maria's older sister, lived outside of Boston. After her husband died, she rarely ventured farther than the corner grocery store or church. It was at least 10 years since she took a trip anywhere.

"Mmm, so basically Maria has finally lost all her marbles. Let me see about switching a meeting at the end of the week. I don't think it will be a problem. You're a good daughter," David said as he moved over to the loveseat to slide himself under her finely sculpted legs. He grasped her hand and brought it to his lips.

Sara leaned forward and hugged him. David had a way of calming her fractious spirit, even in the most chaotic of situations.

"I love you," he whispered, the words floating like a soothing melody from his lips.

"I love you too," she cooed.

David leaned forward and kissed her softly on the lips. Their relationship was on the mend.

Over his shoulder, Sara could see the snow was really coming down. She lingered a minute, thinking about how peaceful it looked outside before sitting back. Their moment of connection had passed as her attention was drawn away from him.

"Have you gotten to Leila yet?" David asked.

"No, I'll call her now," she replied.

Sara picked up the phone and dialed. Staring out the window, she wondered whether the weather would interfere with the whole plan for her friend to visit.

"Hey Leila, it's me," Sara said.

"Hey, hi! Is it snowing in the boonies?" Leila asked.

"Yes it is. It started about thirty minutes ago. We probably have an inch or two already. David informed me that you're going to grace us with your presence tomorrow," Sara said.

"Yup. I want to see how the house turned out. I haven't visited since the painters were there. Is it gorgeous? I bet it is with the colors we chose. Also, I have a birthday present for the 'old fart' in the family; that would be you in case you're stuck in a state of delusion. I was going to bring my chaps but I doubt if it will be warm enough to ride, at least warm enough for me to ride," Leila said in what sounded like one long drawn out breath.

Sara would often tease Leila, saying that she got out of bed every morning going eighty miles an hour. If you didn't know her, you would suspect that she was in the habit of mainlining amphetamines. It was always a challenge to keep up with her, mentally and physically. She had an uncanny way of raising the level of energy and excitement whenever she walked in a room.

"Why don't you stay the night? David gallantly offered to run into town to get some steaks," Sara said.

"You got me. I'll pick up a few bottles of wine on my way over," she answered.

Sara gave a thumbs-up to David and blew him a kiss as he left the room. Then she turned her attention back to Leila. "Hey, I just got off the phone with my mom. She's been freaking out over some nightmares. My Aunt Donna is even there. Remember her? We stopped and visited her when we went to Nantucket that summer."

"Oh, yeah. I thought she never traveled. Your mom would always have to go up there. What's she doing in New York?" Leila asked.

"Precisely. Very weird."

Sara got up, crossed the room, and peered out the French doors. The ponies had settled down and were focused on trying to dust snow off the wilted blades of grass. She could see the show horses scattered throughout other paddocks. They were huddled under turnout blankets, their butts to the wind, their heads down.

"Sara?" Leila said loudly, apparently thinking they had been disconnected.

"Sorry. I was distracted for a second. I can't wait for you to get here. I want to show you the mirror I bought today. It has a very interesting…oh, what do you decorator people call it…provenance," Sara explained as she walked back out to the kitchen.

"Really?"

"Turns out it was part of this estate!"

"Okay, that's just too weird, even for you," Leila said.

"Can't argue with you there. What time should we expect you?" Sara asked.

"Probably about noon. I need to get my beauty rest you know. I'll see you then. Ta, Ta."

CHAPTER TWO

After hanging up with Leila, Sara found herself back in the kitchen, gazing down at the mirror. Picturing Jack balanced over the table, she longed to give him some "Mommy over-reacted" hugs and kisses and in the process tell him about their plans to visit his grandmother. Turning away from her reflection, it was there again. The corner of her eye caught it: some sort of distortion, as if two images were superimposed, one over the other, the same thing that had happened while looking at it in the shop. When she glanced back to look at it straight on, there was no trace of anything unusual. Sara chalked it up to the light coming in from a strange angle. She turned away again and this time kept going.

Trotting up the staircase, then down the hall, Sara passed two empty guestrooms. Rounding the corner, she came to Jack's bedroom at the far end of the hall. He chose the front room because it had a window seat that caught the afternoon sun and its own staircase leading up to a secret room in the attic. It was a little room with a single octagonal stained glass window. The only access was from a door cleverly built into a bookcase that swung out. The ring pull would normally be hidden behind a book. Jack thought it was the coolest thing imaginable when they brought him to visit the house.

"Jack. It's Mom. Are you in here?" Sara asked as she knocked on his door. Not hearing a response, she poked her head in the room. He wasn't there. Seeing the bookcase open, she assumed he was up in the attic playing. The sound of faint crying drew her up the steps. "Jack," she called softly, fearful that she had truly hurt the sensitive little boy's feelings by snapping at him so quickly in the kitchen.

"Jack sweetie, I'm sorry about before. I shouldn't have jumped on you about the mirror. Come on down," she said gently as she walked up the stairs. "Jack?" Sara was completely puzzled when she hit the top of the landing. The room was empty.

The crying sound was gone. She stood there a second, thoroughly bewildered. Could he be hiding? She walked into the cramped space that drew its only light from the tinted window. As she crossed the room, Sara saw what appeared to be the shimmer of liquid on the wide pine planks. The dark crimson color made her gasp and draw back a step. The pool of red disappeared as her body blocked the sunlight.

"Whoa, Sara. Get a grip! It's only the color being cast from the window. Calm down. You have yourself spooked for no good reason," she said out loud. Her uneasiness was heightened by the eerie sound of the winter wind as it whistled through the attic.

Sara crossed her arms in an effort to stay warm, making her consider the fact that the insulation needed to be a heck of a lot better for the tiny room if her son was going to be spending any length of time playing up there. As she was about to head back down, she heard voices coming from outside. It was David and Jack. Peering through the colored glass, she could see them wrestling in the accumulating snow. She smiled, absorbing their simple joy and momentarily forgetting the feelings of confusion and fear. Sara rushed down the stairs and pushed up the window near the little boy's bed. A cold gust of air scattered snow across his pillow.

Sara leaned out over the windowsill and called to the frolicking duo. "Hey, guys! That looks like fun. Can I join you?"

"Mom, come play in the snow with us!" Jack hollered back, full of the innocent excitement that marks childhood.

"I'll be right there," Sara promised, smiling.

As she closed the window, a snowball smashed against it. She looked out and saw Jack, doubled over with laughter. David was pointing at his son, trying to deflect responsibility. Sara grimaced at them and pointed accusingly, but started laughing as she turned away. When she reached the threshold of the room, she abruptly stopped. Drifting down the stairs was a faint sound. Muffled echoes of sobbing popped in her mind. Sara turned to look at the open bookcase door, knowing there was no one up there. Only moments earlier, she had stood alone in the room, looking at her son's old rocking horse and overflowing toy chest. That was it. The consistent rhythm of her breathing was broken as an intangible fear stole the air from her lungs and sent a shiver snaking up the back of her neck. Sara tilted her head but heard nothing. It was gone as fast as it came. She felt her heart pounding very hard against her chest.

"Okay, I'm losing it! I'm imagining that the wind is a person crying," she chastised herself.

With perfect timing, Buster came lumbering down the hall to break the spell. He sank his head under her hand, demanding attention. Jake, the English Springer Spaniel, came right behind him wagging his cropped tail so fast his whole hind end followed the motion. Sara was comforted by their presence.

"Come on, guys," she said, summoning the dogs to follow her out of the room and down the main staircase. She found Madison lying on the carpet in the foyer. "You too, big girl, outside."

Once the dogs had bounded out the front door, Sara went into the kitchen, grabbed her coat, and then walked out to the mudroom to put on boots and a pair of gloves. As she left the protection of the garage, she immediately grabbed a handful of snow to press into a ball, but before she knew it, David and Jack were upon her from behind, pummeling her with artillery made in preparation for her arrival.

"Hey, no fair! Two against one!" she screamed as she ran to take cover behind some shrubs.

"Aw. Poor Mom! Should we show her some mercy?" David sneered evilly while looking down to wink at Jack.

A devilish smile crossed the little boy's angelic face. "No way! Let's get her!"

Snowballs were lobbed back and forth over mountain laurel, holly and junipers. The dogs joined in with attempts to catch the snowballs midair. After a good hour of Sara getting creamed, the family moved on to snowman building. Sara ran into the house and returned with enough vegetables to create a face. There had to be about three or four inches of white powder already on the ground, with large snowflakes falling at near-blizzard pace when they called it quits. Jack's cheeks were as red as apples, his lips the color of plums. He had snow everywhere. Sara's fingers and toes tingled from the cold. She looked at David, who was adding the last touch by transferring his ball cap to the snowman officially named, "Mr. Freeze" by Jack. He turned around, caught her stare and smiled. She smiled back. Jack noticed and immediately centered himself between them. David reached down and scooped him up.

"I think we should call it a day, my man," he said as he repositioned Jack over his shoulder like a sack of potatoes. Jack fell into fits of giggles as David carried him back toward the house.

Carlos, their farm hand, caught their attention as he came around the corner of the garage. He was a decent, hard-working young man. Sara and David offered him the tenant house when they moved to Virginia, but he declined, probably thinking he would never have time off if he stayed on the property. Instead, he found a room to rent in town.

Carlos was huffing and puffing by the time he reached them. "Miss Sara, I brought in all the horses, but it's too early for their evening feed. They all have hay and water. I was wondering if I could leave early since the snow is so bad. I'm not so good at driving in it," he said, rubbing his chapped hands together.

"Carlos, you need gloves. Wait here," she said. She ran into the garage and returned with a pair of men's work gloves. He smiled appreciatively when she tossed them to him.

"*Gracias*," he said.

"Now go home and get warm. If the weather's still bad tomorrow morning, don't come in. I can feed," she insisted.

"*Gracias*," he repeated and turned to head toward his car. Carlos waved from behind the wheel as he slowly passed them.

"Be careful," David yelled after him, and then turned his attention to the status of the farm's second-in-command. "Does Emma get back from England tonight or tomorrow?"

"Tomorrow. Her flight is supposed to land at four o'clock. She should be back sometime in the early evening. Hope she had a good time visiting her folks. Good thing this front is supposed to move out of here by morning," Sara said.

"At least we'll have her for Sunday. I'll do the stalls tomorrow if Carlos doesn't make it," David said. His tone of voice made it clear that he knew what a great guy he was for the offer.

Sara knew too and gratefully grinned at him. She wrapped her arms around his waist and squeezed tightly while simultaneously trying to avoid getting kicked in the head by one of Jack's snowy boots. "Thanks."

"You're welcome. How about we get inside? I'm beginning to get hypothermic."

"Couldn't agree with you more," Sara replied.

"Take off your coat and boots, then run upstairs and put on some dry clothes," David told Jack as he set him down inside the mudroom.

"Okay, Dad. Will you build a fire so we can get warmed up and roast marshmallows?"

"Sure. Now get going," he said, patting him on the behind for encouragement.

Jack ran through the sun porch and vanished around the corner.

"Do you want to hang your mirror before you go to the barn?" David asked Sara, who was busy sloughing off layers of clothing.

"Yeah, I think so. I need to walk through the house. My mom's phone call and playing in the snow distracted me. I want to try to get a feel for where it hung before. Any thoughts?"

He looked squarely at her before answering flatly. "Sara, I don't make those decisions. You make those decisions. I don't decorate. You always ask my opinion, then go ahead and do whatever you want anyway. What's the point of asking? I don't get it."

"Your opinion is very important," she insisted, feigning shock. He looked at her and rolled his eyes. "I do listen to you," Sara continued to protest as she yanked her slushy boot off.

"Sure," David said as he disappeared into the sun porch.

"Okay…put it in the foyer."

"Really…are you sure?"

No answer. He had slipped away. She took off the remaining boot, and then padded through the sun porch in damp socks. The dogs rushed ahead of her, veering off into the family room where David was already shoving some logs into the fireplace.

"I'm going to look around the house and see what I think. I'll yell for you when I'm ready to hang it," she called to his hunched-over torso.

"I told you so, as predictable as the sunrise," he mumbled, barely loud enough for her to hear.

Sara ignored him as she walked out of the kitchen to look around. She thought back to when they first visited the house. The moment she stepped inside the front door she was sold. Light streamed in from every window, making the empty rooms warm and inviting. Through a layer of dust and cobwebs, she was able to envision the splendor and beauty that the house once possessed. Over the course of a month, the estate underwent a gradual meta-morphosis, as if waking from a long sleep.

Now, Sara stood in the foyer, gazing around, satisfied with the transformation that she had so painstakingly crafted. She walked toward the staircase and started to climb. Reaching the second floor, she felt the padding and comfort of the new carpet beneath her feet. The sun usually radiated beautifully through the windows in the late afternoon, but the grayness of the day cast a more melancholy feel. Walking around the balcony, she came to a long expanse of bare wall. Stopping in the center, she reached out to touch the newly painted surface. Static electricity ignited her fingertips, making Sara instinctively pull her hand away. She cocked her head the way a dog might when contemplating something out of the ordinary. Reaching out again, her fingers fell short of the wall. She took a deep breath and snapped them shut against her palm. Just then Jack spoke from behind her. Sara jumped, letting out a frightened squeal. This in turn had the same effect on Jack.

"Jack, you scared me to death!" she yelped.

"You scared me too!" he said with eyes the size of silver dollars.

"I didn't hear you coming. Make some noise like a normal child next time," she joked.

"Sorry, Mom," he said as he looked at the wall. "Is this where you're gonna put your new naked lady mirror?"

Sara looked back at the wall and tilted her head to one side, then the other. "I think so," she said, glancing down at her son.

"It'll look good here," he replied with an air of confidence.

As he turned and walked back toward his room, Sara remembered the strange sounds she heard earlier that afternoon while searching for him. "Jack, wait," she called abruptly halting the boy halfway down the hall. Sara felt somewhat silly for asking, but she felt compelled to do so. "Have you heard any odd noises in your room? Anything up in your secret room?"

"Like what?" he wondered, comically lifting one eyebrow as he spoke.

"I'm not sure. Sorry, it must have been the wind. Go on," she told him.

He walked back around the balcony into his room. At the same time, she saw David coming up the rear hallway.

"Did somebody scream?" he inquired with the air of an accusation.

"Jack caught me by surprise," she answered, somewhat embarrassed.

"Did you find the perfect spot?" David prolonged his teasing by grabbing hold of Sara's waist and tickling her. She giggled and squirmed. He changed the atmosphere by pulling her to him so they were standing groin to groin. He bent down and passionately kissed her. She could feel him hardening against her belly. She became aware of the sudden rush of desire to have her body naked against his. They needed one another now more than ever to shatter the barriers they had recklessly constructed during the past year. David drew back from her lips and moved to her right ear.

"Jack should be really tired from playing so hard. I bet he goes to bed extra early tonight. We need to finish this," he whispered provocatively.

He slid one hand from her waist down between her legs. Sara's face flushed as she instinctively responded to his touch. She would have had him right on the hallway floor if there wasn't a seven-year-old wandering around the house.

"I can't wait. It's a date," she purred back in a low whisper.

David kissed her ravenously before pulling away from their private moment. "Not quite the foyer, but close," he said composing himself. "I'll go get a hammer and some heavy-duty hooks." He retrieved them and returned a few minutes later, carrying the mirror. After several aggravating minutes of Sara adjusting its position, she was finally satisfied. The couple stood back to admire their masterpiece.

"Very good. Now go feed the horses so we can eat dinner and move on to…other things," he said, nudging her with the side of his hip.

"Alright. I'm going. Don't you think it's cool how it reflects the scenery of the front pasture?"

"Yes. Beautiful. Now go!"

CHAPTER THREE

Sara pulled on her coat and gloves, which were still damp from their snowball fight. She thought about running back to her closet to get a different coat but decided it would be too much of a hassle.

"Madison, Jake, Buster. Let's go. Time to feed the horses," she called. Sara opened the back door and waited patiently as the dogs eagerly responded to her command. They scrambled through the house, bouncing into walls and one another to catch up.

The snow was still falling heavily. Six inches of fresh powder covered the ground, with more on the way. The National Weather Service had issued a severe winter storm warning with predictions of up to four more inches by midnight.

The three dogs ran on ahead to the barn, knowing the destination of this outing. Sara stood still. It was quiet. She loved the silence of a snowstorm. The birds had migrated and the few that were left were hushed. She was content. Life was good now. The beauty of the moment cemented her belief that they would find peace on their new farm. Sara thought about her mom's fears and laughed. If she could only see how wonderful everything was, how the scattered pieces of their lives had finally been falling back into place, she would rest easy. The last few years had been so tumultuous, so hard on all of them. They had dealt with her father's illness and subsequent death, the news of her adoption and, most recently, the loss of their baby girl during a long and difficult delivery. Sara had hemorrhaged so severely that the doctors feared she wouldn't make it either. She swore there was a presence by her side protecting her, pulling her back from the hands of death. Sara and David named their lifeless daughter Grace and buried her. At the time, they didn't understand how much of themselves and their marriage had slipped away that day. Sara slid into depression, unable to let go of what should have been, while David became consumed with building his business as a corporate security consultant. Leila threw the couple a life-preserver after David confided in her how strained things had become. She invited them to Virginia for a long weekend. Sara had initially fought the idea of moving, but when the realtor showed them the farm something reached inside her heart and tugged at all her childhood dreams, and in doing so, lifted her out from under a veil of grief. They needed to move. Sara and David were determined to focus on the future and let go of the past.

But now what was going on with Maria? Sara shook the snow from her shoulders and walked toward the barn. That question was plaguing her as she measured out feed for each of her impatient equine companions: a retired old horse she had had since the end of graduate school, two Connemara ponies, and three thorough-breds. Two were imports, one from England and the other from Ireland. They were bigger boned than her American bred horse. She threw each a flake of hay, then topped off a string of water buckets.

Sara tightly closed the barn doors and whistled for the dogs. The Springer came immediately, always eager to please and hoping to get there in time to garner some affection. The two Danes came around the corner, biting at one another in play. They immediately took positions on either side of Sara. As they approached the garage entrance, Madison and Buster caught wind of something. They went rigid and the hair on their back stood up. They were looking out to the front pasture. Sara squinted to try to see what they were focused on. The sky had been darkening, so between the heavy snow and the lack of sunshine she could barely make out the line of trees that sliced the field in half. The two dogs started growling, exposing their large white teeth. The Springer had run around behind them for protection, but was uttering a low rumbling as well.

"What do you see?" she asked them.

Sara had never seen them so agitated. She reached down to steady them, to reassure them that they were okay. Immediately, the large dogs were off with the little one following closely on their heels, flying through the snow out into the darkness. She could hear them barking wildly. Sara could tell from their volume that they were covering ground quickly.

"What the heck?" she said out loud to herself. "Madison! Buster! Come back, Jake. Come on!" Sara continued to call out their names at the top of her lungs and finally resorted to whistling as their barks drew farther and farther out of range. All of her attempts to regain their attention to redirect them were in vain. She figured they had to be close to the far edge of the front field by now. Then nothing. No barking. Just dead silence. She called again and again. Then Sara heard the unmistakable sound of a gunshot echoing through the stillness.

"Shit!" she screamed. Sara charged to the door leading from the garage to the house and yelled frantically for David.

"What the hell's the matter?" he asked, out of breath after sprinting from the living room.

Sara told him what happened while tears started to stream down her panicked face. "Do you think someone shot them? We have to find them!"

"Okay. Okay. Jack, stay in the house. Do not come out under any circumstance!" he bellowed over his shoulder.

"What's happening, Dad?" Jack asked as he poked his head around the corner.

"Stay in the house and lock the doors. You only open it when your mother or I tell you to. Understand?" David said sternly. Jack nodded his head. "Sara, grab the flashlight."

Sara grabbed the lantern from a shelf in the garage and David grabbed his BB gun.

"You're kidding, right?" Sara challenged.

"Don't say a word. This is all we have thanks to your brilliant philosophy of 'No guns on my property!'" he said imitating her. "And I don't have time to run down and put your dad's old shotgun together. Not that we have any shells for it anyway," he added with disgust.

They ran out, following the tracks of the dogs. Eerie howling started to fill the night air as they drew farther away from the light cast by the house. Sara and David made it about halfway across the pasture when they saw them. The three dogs were trotting back, their bodies covered in blood.

"Oh my God!" Sara screamed, running toward them.

"Holy crap! What happened?" David said. He reached them first and just stood there for a second in shock. Sara's legs buckled at the sight and she crumpled in the snow, tears drizzling down her cheeks.

"Are they shot?" she asked while touching one after another, checking every inch of their bodies for wounds.

David put down the gun to help search through their coats, which had been slicked down by the sticky red liquid.

"I can't find anything. Can you?" she asked, looking across at David while praying that he would say the same.

"Nothing," he answered with relief.

The dogs busied themselves by licking their bloodied paws and shoulders.

"Maybe they attacked someone. I better go check. Get them back to the garage," David said as he stood up.

"No! Are you insane? You're not going out there alone. It could be some psychopath."

"Sara, someone could be hurt or worse. I need to go find out," he answered.

Buster shook, sending droplets of blood spraying in a circle around him.

"Please, please, let's go call the police," she desperately sobbed as she hugged Madison tightly around her neck.

"Sara, go back to the house. I'll be all right," he insisted.

"No!" she stood up and grabbed onto his arm with her blood-covered hands. "David, stop! It has to be some nutcase. Who else would run around this time of night shooting things? Or wait… maybe it was a hunter and the dogs got to the kill first. Either way, I don't want you out there."

"I'm going to follow their trail back. If it was a deer or some other animal, I'll find it. If it was a person, well, I'll find him or her. Now get the dogs back to the garage. I'll be back in a few minutes," he said in a tone to try to reassure her, but one that would leave no additional room for negotiation. He pried his arm free from Sara's vice-like grip, leaving her bloody handprint in its place. Taking the lantern and toy gun, he strode off into the darkness.

Sara wiped her cheeks with the backs of her hands. She watched his light move farther and farther away. The dogs were engrossed with their cleanup. Sara was adamant that she was not going to move until he returned. He must have reached the end of the pasture because she was able to make out the rise of the stone wall. David seemed to be turning around and around. She watched him climb over the wall to the other side but was surprised when he came right back. By the time she realized that the light had started back, her heart was beating so hard she wondered whether she was going to vomit. In another few minutes David returned. All the color appeared to have drained out of his face. He was as white as the snow around them.

"I thought I told you to head back," he said, shaken.

"What was it?" Sara asked.

"Nothing. I couldn't find anything. Well, nothing bloody at least. The dogs' footprints went to the base of the big oak tree. The snow was dug up and they had been hitting the ground underneath, but nothing, no animal, no person, and not even any blood. There were no other tracks around the spot. I don't know. I don't get it," he answered. Now he looked like he was the one who was going to vomit.

"What? There had to be with the amount of blood on them. I don't understand," Sara said, clearly confused by his explanation.

"Nothing. There was nothing," David said, turning in frustration and fear. As he started walking back toward the house, he gave the dogs a whistle. They followed alongside, Sara behind, cold, confused, and bloody. David turned around as they reached the garage. "I'll take them down to the wash stall in the barn. Go in and check on Jack. I'm sure he's frightened," he said.

Sara was about to start in on a string of questions about what just happened, but she thought better of it. David was striding away, still clutching the BB gun and the lantern.

Sara knocked on the door. "Jack. It's Mom. Let me in," she called.

"Mom? Is that you?" the little boy asked.

"Yes. Open the door," Sara confirmed.

"You sound funny. If it's really you, tell me my middle name," he asked suspiciously.

"Todd. Your name is Jackson Todd Miller. Now open up."

After hearing the correct answer, he allowed her to enter. He caught sight of her bloody hands and froze. "Gross!" he yelled with a contorted face.

Sara realized she must be an awful sight.

"What happened? Did the dogs kill something? Are they hurt?" he asked, becoming afraid for his pets' safety.

"I'm not sure, baby. Daddy couldn't find anything out there in the dark. He's down at the barn washing the dogs off. They're fine. Just dirty," she answered trying to sound as if nothing unusual just took place. At the same time she knew this was anything but the truth. The fact was that strange things had been happening all day. Some birthday, she thought.

Sara made it to the kitchen sink and flipped on the water with her elbow. The warm water ran over her icy, stained hands. As the sink went red, nausea and dizziness swept over her. Sara was sure she was going to pass out as she started to sweat and get flushed. Blackness crept in from the corners of her field of vision. She thought she may have gotten out Jack's name or even called him "baby" as she went down. It was a dreamlike feeling as her limp body hit the floor. She sensed that it was happening but not happening. Sara saw the blood, all the blood. It was trickling down the stairs. Hands covered in blood. Sobbing in her ears. She felt herself retching, her body convulsing in an attempt to vomit. Pain, stabbing pain across her abdomen. The next thing she knew, David was shaking her and calling her back from somewhere she didn't want to be. He was patting her face with a cold wet towel. She could hear Jack's cries echoing in her mind. Through the darkness, her body struggled for a breath.

"Mommy, don't die. Please, don't die," the terrified child

whimpered as his tears rained down on his mother's cheek.

"Sara, Sara, please, Sara wake up." David looked ashen kneeling over her.

As her eyes fluttered open, she could see Jack perched over her husband's shoulder, his green eyes puffy from crying.

"Mommy, Mommy, are you okay?" he asked through his sobs. "When I heard you fall I ran to the barn and got Dad. Are you okay?"

"Yeah, I think so. What happened?" Sara asked trying to focus, but things were still fuzzy.

"You passed out while you were washing your hands. You're lucky you didn't crack your skull open on the edge of the counter on the way down," David informed her. "Christ, you scared me. Jack came running down to the barn screaming that you were dead."

"Mommy, don't do that again. You scared me too!"

She could see Jack shaking as he desperately tried to hold back his tears. It was no use. Jack climbed over Sara to nestle into the crook of her armpit while she was still sprawled on the floor.

"Oh, sweetie, I'm so sorry, I don't know what happened. The blood must have made me dizzy. It'll be okay. I'm just sore. My head hurts a little, but I'm okay. Come on now," Sara said trying to soothe him. Holding him tight with her left arm, she wiped his tears away with her right hand and by doing so noticed that her skin was clean.

"Well, I guess I washed all the blood off before I went down," she said in a vain attempt to lighten the moment.

"Let me help you up. Jack, Mom's feeling better. Let's get her up," David said as he tried to pry his son off his wife's body.

Jack was clinging to Sara the way he did when he was a baby and a stranger would try to hold him. He was not about to let go.

"Please sit up, pumpkin. I promise, you can sit with me on the couch," she urged, propping herself up on her elbows.

Sara realized that her head hurt like a son-of-a-bitch. Jack stirred, then finally stood up. David reached a hand under each armpit and lifted his dazed wife to her feet. Grabbing her around the waist, he led her into the family room. The fire was still going but had weakened. He lowered her down into an over-sized chair.

Jack climbed in next to her, resuming his infant-like position. David poked at the fire, then disappeared into the kitchen. He returned carrying a glass of water.

"I thought you could use this," he said handing her the water. Bending down, he kissed her gently on the top of her head.

"My hero. Actually, my two heroes," she joked, giving Jack a squeeze. He responded by offering up a weak smile as he nuzzled in closer to her side.

"I have to go get the dogs," David said. "I wasn't done cleaning them off. I'll be back in a few minutes. No more crises, okay? There has been enough excitement for one day in this house." As he started to walk out of the room, he turned around and pointed a finger at Sara. "Don't move!"

"Yes, sir," Sara uttered in complete agreement.

David reappeared about fifteen minutes later with three tired and wet dogs. They simultaneously collapsed around the fire without their usual ceremony of preparing their beds. David veered off into the kitchen and soon reappeared with a tall drink for himself. "Tonight I'm going straight to the bourbon," he joked as he held his glass out for all to see as he slouched back on the couch.

"What just happened?" Sara asked, shaking her head.

David took a long drink, then swooshed the amber liquid around in the glass, making the ice cubes clink together. "Beats the hell out of me," he replied, eyes fixed on the swirling bourbon. He took another drink, paused and looked at Sara. "I don't know. They were digging under that tremendous oak tree. Maybe they found an injured animal and ate it whole, simply tore it to shreds, then swallowed every piece. They've been able to do that to more than one piece of furniture. I couldn't even find a scrap of fur or any blood. That's the weirdest part. I don't understand how they could be covered in blood and there be no trace on the ground. I guess I could have missed it. I'll go out tomorrow morning and look again in the light. The snow has almost stopped so I should be able to see where the tracks lead," he said. He was talking to Sara but clearly trying to come up with an acceptable explanation for himself. She could tell he was chewing the events over in his head by the way the muscle along his jaw would rhythmically clench and release.

"Mom, are we going to eat your birthday dinner?" Jack asked from her side. "Daddy and I made you a cake while you were busy shopping this morning."

Motherly instinct told her that he was returning to normal if he was focused on food. "A cake! Why you little devils," she said.

Sara gave Jack a squeeze, followed by a kiss on the head. "This has been quite a day. If you didn't have that teacher in-service day, you would have missed it all," she teased.

"Uh-huh," Jack added.

"Come on, Jack. We're supposed to be cooking dinner for Mom tonight. Plus, I don't think I trust her in the kitchen yet. She would take one look at that pasta sauce and down she would go again," David kidded. He finished up his drink and winked at her before rising.

"Very funny," she replied sarcastically.

Jack was giggling. He had finally let go of his vise-like grip. He smiled, then kissed her on the cheek. She could see that a sparkle of joy had returned to his eyes.

"I love you, Mom," he whispered.

"I love you too," she whispered back.

David motioned for Jack to come. He followed him into the kitchen. She could hear pots and pans clanging, water running, and the seal of a jar popping. They were going to make ravioli, a dish that was pretty hard to screw up. Sara stood up and finally took her coat off. She walked down to the mudroom and hung it on the hook next to David's. She could see that the arm still had the bloody imprint from her hands. It would have to wait until tomorrow to get washed, for another wave of nausea and dizziness was building momentum. Sara quickly retreated back to her chair near the fire. It was an emotional roller coaster of a day, leaving her tired and looking forward to sleep. She longed for dreamless sleep and reckoned she could achieve that with enough wine. Dinner eased her into a more relaxed state of mind. The food was pretty good, with the exception of the garlic bread. A few minutes too long under the broiler left it sporting a scary shade of black. The cake came with the opening of a second bottle of Chianti.

"Mmm, cake with wine. My favorite!" she joked, her head swimming from the effects of the alcohol.

David set the brilliantly lit cake in front of his wife while Jack belted out "Happy Birthday". Sara took a deep breath and blew out all the candles except one. A second attempt did the trick. "I wish for a calm, quiet, and definitely uneventful life," she exclaimed.

"Mom, you spoiled your wish. You're not supposed to say it out loud or it doesn't come true."

"Oh, great. Now you tell me," she said, teasing him.

"Hey, Jack, it's getting late. Up to bed as soon as you finish your cake," David said, tapping his watch.

A few minutes later Jack was scurrying up the stairs as David started in on clean-up duty. Sara sat sipping her wine while fingering butter cream icing from the sides of the cake. She wasn't thinking about anything other than the taste of the sweet confection against her tongue.

"Ready," Jack yelled down, cuing them to tuck him in.

Sara left her glass and led the way up the stairs. When they opened the door to their son's room, he was already changed into flannel pajamas and sitting up in bed. He was holding up a thin gold chain with a little gold key dangling at the bottom.

"Hey, what do you have there?" David asked as he approached the bed.

"Mom's necklace. I forgot to tell you that I found it," he said, smiling in triumph.

"What? That's not mine. Where did you find it?" she asked, reaching to lift it from his fingers.

"On the steps going to my playroom. I found it this afternoon when we came in from outside. It was sort of in a crack. I thought it was yours because you were in my room. Remember? We threw a snowball at you," Jack explained.

Sara thought back several hours to the incident in the attic playroom. The tiny hairs on the back of her neck stood up as she replayed the disturbing cries in her mind and recalled how she jumped with fright when she thought there was blood on the floor. The same paralyzing fear that had seized her earlier in the day had her again in its grip.

"It must have been from the family that lived here before. It was probably overlooked, especially if it was down some crack. Pretty, though, huh?" David commented. He took the necklace from Sara and held it up to look at it. "I guess it's yours now," he added, handing it back to her.

"I think it unlocks something. Maybe a secret treasure chest," Jack said excitedly.

Sara looked at its tiny gold outline in the palm of her hand. She wasn't happy that she couldn't shake off that creepy feeling.

"Here, let me put it on you," David said, reaching out to take it back. He had opened the clasp and swung it around her neck before Sara could answer. As the miniature key fell to the point just above her breasts, Sara let out a gasp.

"You okay? That wine is probably getting to you. You drank over a bottle yourself," David said, coming back around to face her. "Very nice. Don't you think, Jack?"

"It looks great," he heartily agreed. "Mom, it's perfect."

Sara held the key between her thumb and forefinger, feeling its ornately carved ridges. "I'm ready for bed," she said uncomfortably. Longing to be unconscious, Sara kissed Jack, then started out the door. "Goodnight, sweetie. David, I'll meet you down there."

"I'll finish cleaning up and be right in. Happy birthday, honey," he added with an air kiss in her direction.

Sara forced a smile before leaving the two behind. The clouds had cleared off and the moon was casting an eerie light through the windows. She walked down the hall, passing the gilded edge of the present she had bought herself earlier that morning. Out of the corner of her eye, Sara caught a reflection that pulled her to a sudden stop. Shaking, she slowly backed up to face the image. Staring back at her was her face, her brilliant green eyes, her mouth, but instead of her brown, shoulder length hair, there were long red curls. The sweater Sara had on was gone. In its place was a lacy white bra. The ornate key hung around her neck, nestled provocatively in her bare cleavage. She reached for it, touching it on her chest. The image had her completely transfixed.

"It's pretty, isn't it?" David asked, suddenly right beside her.

Sara screamed and bolted sideways. Her dilated eyes spun to him, to the mirror, and then back to him.

"Mom, are you all right?" came a small voice from down the hall.

"Great, Sara. Freak him out again," David whispered angrily.

At that moment, the only thing that registered for Sara as real was that David had startled her. She could feel herself starting to hyperventilate.

"Mom's fine. I snuck up on her, that's all. Go to sleep," he yelled out to the little boy.

"Okay, goodnight," came a distant reply.

"Sara, what is your problem?" David asked.

"You don't understand. It wasn't me. Well, it was, but it wasn't. Oh, God, didn't you see her?" Sara asked.

"Excuse me? Come again," David said, indicating she needed to explain what she was saying.

"Did you see the reflection?" Sara asked.

"Yeesss," David drawled.

"Then you must have seen her. It wasn't me. The face was, but the hair, the clothes…," Sara said trembling. She stepped forward to look back into the mirror. It was her exact image, her own reflection this time. "David, I swear, it wasn't me! What's happening? Weird stuff has been going on all day. First I hear this crying, but no one is there. I think I see blood and it's just light through the stained glass. Then we have the incident with the dogs, followed up by me passing out as I wash the blood off my hand. And to top the night off, Jack finds this necklace, which apparently someone else is wearing when I look in the mirror! What on earth is going on?" Sara said without taking a breath and with escalating volume that had her on the verge of hysterics.

"Quiet! Sara, I saw you and only you. You're going to scare Jack again. Let's go downstairs," David said, taking her arm to lead her down the arching front staircase.

Once in their bedroom, David turned to face his agitated wife. "You have to calm down. You know you hit your head pretty hard and you drank a fair amount. It's been an emotional day because you're worried about your mom. Everything that has happened can be explained."

"No, it can't!" she insisted.

The commotion roused the three dogs, who ambled in to investigate what was going on. This was the first time they moved since being washed.

"What about them?" she said, pointing to the three weary animals.

"I'll figure it out tomorrow in the light. They had to have killed an animal," David said, trying to soothe her.

"What about the gunshot?" she countered. "And I know what I saw. Remember what Jack said today when he first looked in the mirror? He said he saw a lady. And the man at the antique store said there were rumors about our house."

"Sara, what are you suggesting, that the house is haunted, or just the mirror? We've been here for weeks and nothing like this has happened. It's all blown out of proportion by an apparent head injury and booze. Please relax or you're going to end up fainting again. Come here and sit down," David said, patting the bed next to him.

Sara was pacing the room. She stopped to look in the mirror above her dresser; only her reflection looked back. "Take this damn thing off me," she said, crossing over to her husband to get him to unclasp the necklace. David obliged without comment and handed it back to her. She walked over and put it in her jewelry box.

"Get ready for bed. I'll only be a minute turning off the lights." He walked over to her and hugged her tightly. Sara didn't want to leave the safety of his arms. He finally pulled away and kissed her forehead. "I'll be right back, cross my heart," he said softly before leaving the room.

Sara went into the bathroom and brushed her teeth. She desperately wanted to sleep. As she climbed between the sheets, she prayed that everything would be back to normal in the morning.

CHAPTER FOUR

Sara woke up at eight o'clock the next morning with a miserable headache. Her mouth was coated in what felt like Elmer's glue and she desperately needed to take a pee. The room spun when she sat up.

"Ow, crap. I hope I don't puke," she moaned, pinching the flesh on the bridge of her nose. Sara was grateful for the lack of dreams, or at least ones that didn't linger. She emptied her bladder and then moved to the sink. Looking in the mirror, she spoke to her reflection. "Glad to see you, even if you do look like road-kill."

Sara brushed her teeth and then rifled through the medicine cabinet for something to silence the painful tune being played on the inside of her skull. Shuffling past the bed, she noticed that David was already gone. The only clue that he had slept next to her was the unmistakable concave indentation left in his pillow. Most likely he was out feeding the horses. Sara assumed that Carlos had opted to avoid the slippery trip in from town. After changing into jeans and a sweatshirt, she walked barefoot out to the kitchen to search the refrigerator for a Coke. The two tablets were easily washed down her throat by the rush of cold, sweet liquid. Her dehydrated cells screamed for relief, prompting her to guzzle down the rest of the can. The icy floor pushed finding socks to the top of the day's agenda.

"Good morning, Mom," Jack called from the second floor as she made her way back to the bedroom to attend to the task at hand.

"Good morning, sweetie," Sara answered, painfully swiveling around to focus on her son.

"What are you doing?" he asked with a volume so loud that it made her head swell. The child was perched on his tiptoes and had draped his upper body across the banister.

"Jack, don't hang on the railing like that. I couldn't handle an accident this early in the morning," she cautioned. Vertigo lapped dangerously along the edge of her field of vision, alerting her that she could be teetering on the verge of a full-blown hangover. "I'll be out in a little bit. I have to go put something on my feet."

"Okay. Sorry, Mom."

Sara made it back to bed and collapsed into a ball. The unrelenting rhythm in her head was briefly interrupted by the sound of David's heavy footsteps resonating across the hardwood floors as he walked through the house. His deep voice added another level of pain to the symphony as he exchanged morning pleasantries with their son.

"Hello, sleepyhead. How are you feeling?" David asked as he entered their bedroom.

"Ow," she said, repeating her earlier assessment.

"Ah-ha, I thought that's the way you would feel. I guess you don't want to come out for breakfast. Did you take anything? It might make you feel better, but then again, your liver will probably quit on you," he commented smugly.

She looked at him through bloodshot eyes and grimaced. "Your sage advice is too late. I popped those babies first thing. Liver failure, here I come," she answered.

"Carlos made it in while I was out feeding. He's only turning the ponies out since they don't have shoes," David said.

Sara envisioned the horses precariously pivoting on snowball stilts compacted into their horseshoes. She was relieved that Carlos had used good judgment. It was a pain having to use a hammer to break up the snow packed into their hooves as they slid their way back to the barn.

"Do you want anyone else out today?" David asked.

"No. They can get hand walked on the plowed driveway for 15 minutes each. I need to call a blacksmith to either get the shoes pulled or have snow pads put on the four big guys. They can probably go out the beginning of the week. Tell Carlos to give them extra timothy hay throughout the day and a flake of the alfalfa at lunch," she answered with her forehead in her hands.

"You gonna make it?"

"I'm too old to drink that much."

"Honestly, you never could drink that much. Plus, you may have a bit of a concussion from your trip to the kitchen floor. In hindsight, you probably shouldn't have been drinking at all, although it certainly let you sleep. You were out in minutes. I wasn't quite so lucky."

"Listen, I'm going to lie down for 20 more minutes until the drugs kick in," Sara said, closing her eyes as she reclined on the bed, her throbbing head cushioned by the soft pillows.

"Maybe I should join you. I have a great way to get natural endorphins to clear up that hangover," he said, half-joking as he leered down at her.

"Are you nuts? Men! You guys would hump a dead woman. Get out of here," she said, cracking one eyelid to look at him.

"Gee, the thanks I get for taking care of all your animals. No respect. I'll shut the door on the way out," David said as he left the room.

The pain was rising to a white-hot crescendo, making her wish that she had asked him for a cold washcloth to put across her forehead. Sara drifted back to sleep within minutes. This time she did not experience the benefits of sedation. Through the warped lens of a dream, she was cast into another place in time, a place rife with turmoil and sorrow. Sara wanted to escape. She needed to escape. Unable to breathe, she opened her mouth and sucked in air but still she couldn't find the light. Where was the light? In an instant it was gone and she was jolted awake. Sara found herself sitting up, her hair matted with sweat, her mouth agape, and heart racing so hard she thought it might burst. The two Danes were on high alert at the end of the bed, their eyes riveted on her. She could see the hair on their backs standing up. Heavy footsteps came running across the foyer. David's unchecked speed caused him to come crashing into the room, sending the doorknob straight through the dry wall.

"I heard you scream," he said as he skidded to a stop by her side.

Sara's breathing was slowing but her mouth was still open. It didn't register in her mind that she had yelled out. Her eyes moved in their sockets, acknowledging his presence while the rest of her body remained motionless. When David extended his hand to touch her, she winced, as if expecting to be struck.

"Sara. It's okay. It's me, David," he softly reassured her. "It was a bad dream. You're safe."

"What time is it? How long have I been sleeping?" she asked.

"About 40 minutes. I thought it would be good for your headache, so I didn't come back in," he explained. David sat down on the bed facing her. He touched her cheek in silence. "What frightened you?" he asked.

"David, I saw her again," Sara said in a voice barely above a whisper. "The woman from last night. The red-haired woman in the mirror, only she wasn't in the mirror. She was kneeling on the ground, sobbing. And she was wearing the key that Jack found. I could see it dangling around her neck. She wasn't alone. There were others. Two men, but one was older, maybe by 20 or 30 years. I could see them arguing and could tell they were furious with her. They were pointing, accusing the cowering woman of something. Then the older man raised his hand and threatened to backhand her. I don't recall what they were saying, the reason they were so angry, but it was very…real."

Sara paused and closed her eyes in an attempt to recapture the fleeting snapshots. She shivered. The emotional intensity of the dream pierced through the threshold of consciousness, ensnaring Sara in its delicate web.

"I think the red-haired woman was trying to get the younger man to help her. I could see her reaching out, begging him not to leave, but he turned and walked off into blackness. I don't know exactly what happened next or where I went. I think I must have drifted to another place. There was a lapse. The dream jumped and I couldn't follow what was happening," she said with a sigh of frustration. "Can you get me a towel?"

David silently obliged. He watched her strip out of her damp clothes and towel off. Sara slid her naked body into her terry cloth robe, pulling the belt snugly around her waist. Looking down at the jewelry box, she flipped open the top and took out the miniature gold key.

"I saw this a second time, but it was in someone's hand," she said as she turned to face David. "And there were sounds echoing in the background. Different voices. There was crying. There was this tiny cry, like when Jack was a little baby. Do you remember that? And blood again," she added as the images began to overwhelm her. "So much blood. I could see it on the floor, red liquid making its way across the boards like a stream. I watched as it trickled down old wooden steps, one after another. And then the water, it was red. I could see a white porcelain sink turn crimson as someone washed the blood off their stained hands. I had to get out of there. It wasn't safe. I had to get out."

"Honey, it doesn't surprise me that you dreamt of strange things. Your mind is trying to make sense of what happened last night," he said sympathetically.

She shuddered as she felt the tiny key between her fingers. "Maybe, but what if this place really is haunted? It's creepy. The house was empty for years. Why didn't anyone else buy it? We know nothing about the people who lived here other than it was some Mc-family whose daughters took off," Sara said, convinced that her dream meant more than David was suggesting. She looked into her palm. She wanted…no, needed to find out what this key opened, what secret it held locked away.

"Sara, the farm is not haunted. We've been here weeks with no sightings of ghosts. You had a bad dream because there were a bunch of coincidences yesterday," David explained rationally. "Come on. Your mom has you all wigged out. You were on edge most of the day. Why don't you shower? I think it would make you feel a whole lot better. Time to put all these crazy notions out of that cracked skull of yours. Jack is busy occupying himself in the family room. He's been watching cartoons. Lucky for us he didn't hear you. Plus, Leila will be here in a couple of hours."

Sara rolled her eyes. She put the necklace down on the marble top of the dresser and went in to start the jets of water.

"Do you want me to wait?" David said, sticking his head through the door.

"No, I'm fine," she answered curtly. She didn't agree with his appraisal of the situation.

David took the opportunity to vanish as she stepped into a cloud of steam. The warm spray immediately encased her body in a liquid blanket. Tense muscles released their hold. When she turned the water off, her headache was gone.

"At least that's good," Sara commented to herself while stepping out of the shower. She was redressed and ready for the day in half an hour. As she hung up her robe, her stomach started emitting loud rumbling sounds. The next stop would definitely need to be the kitchen.

Sara poked around in the cabinets, deciding on whether to go with a late breakfast or early lunch. She decided on the former after smelling some freshly baked muffins that David must have whipped up from a mix. The destruction left in the wake of his cooking attempt lay all around the kitchen. She satisfied herself with a cup of tea and a warm blueberry muffin. Jack had retreated up to his bedroom to play after giving his mother a peck on the cheek. David was getting ready to go outside when she flipped on the television.

"I'll wash our coats later. Grab a different one," she called out to him.

"Already did. I'm taking a hike out front to see if I can find the carcass," he replied.

"Have fun," she mumbled as she stretched out on the couch.

Sara pulled a throw blanket over her legs. Nothing seemed to hold her attention as she fingered the remote control. She was uncomfortably distracted, her mind unable to free itself from the events of the past 24 hours. She looked out the window, but the overgrown hedges were too high to see David or much of anything else. The only view seemed to be the sky, which had assumed a brilliant crystal blue color, a gift from the high-pressure system, which settled in after the storm. If she was going to watch David, the best place to do this was from the second floor. Sara went up the back stairs and into Jack's room. He was sitting on the floor playing with Lego blocks.

"Hi, Mom. Want to play?" he asked.

"Not right now. I'm spying on Dad," she answered.

"Cool! Can I do that too? We can be secret agents," he said, jumping to his feet.

She smiled as she raised his blinds. Unfortunately, they couldn't see David due to the branches of a large maple obstructing the view.

"Drat! I don't see him," the little boy protested.

"Let's go to the staircase windows," Sara said.

As they left his room, she realized that they would have to pass the mirror. The memory of last night swept over Sara, making her instinctively freeze.

"Mom, come on," Jack said, several feet ahead of her.

"This is silly," she said to herself. Sara walked up to the mirror with trepidation and looked in. She smiled and sighed, just her, looking better than first thing that morning.

From their perch at the top of the steps, they could see David inspecting the perimeter of the far stone wall. Large old oaks ran adjacent to the neatly stacked stones, making it look like a picture out of a "Welcome to Virginia" brochure. One tree was particularly huge, dating back several hundred years. Its hulking skeleton dwarfed the man climbing back and forth from one side of the wall to the other, repeating the path he took the night before. When he returned to the spot under the largest oak, they could make out that he had crouched down.

"Maybe he found something, Mom," Jack said.

"We'll see."

Finally, after several minutes, they saw David rise and walk back to the house.

"Speaking of finding something, can you show me where you discovered that necklace?" she asked, looking down into Jack's big green eyes. Sara was so glad they looked like hers. They were dark green around the edge of the iris, which then lightened to a brilliant Kelly green, which faded into yellow near the pupil. Exactly the same as hers, a genetic stamp for sure. People commented on the resemblance all the time.

"Sure, follow me," he yelled as he ran off around the balcony to his room.

Sara obeyed, only pausing briefly to catch her image on the way back.

"In here, Mom," he called from the hidden staircase.

She walked through the bookcase and found him kneeling on the first step.

"It was in this crack, right here," he said, pointing to a crevice in the wood. "I saw the chain and pulled at it and out popped the key." He was obviously still delighted with his find.

Sara bent down to touch the step. "You really are quite the detective," she said. Sara wondered how long it had been lost down there. She felt sure the key had belonged to the red-haired woman. "Thanks a bunch, sweetie. You've been a first rate private eye. I'll be up later to play."

Jack beamed from the compliment.

Sara stood up to walk out but then hesitated. She looked up the stairs. "Hey, let's go see your playroom a minute," she said.

"Okay. You want to play with something up there?" he asked, scurrying up the steps on all fours like one of their dogs.

"No, not really," she answered.

When they made the top step, she looked down at the floor. They had it refinished with the rest of the hardwoods. Sara walked in and picked up a small area rug. She saw nothing unusual as she scanned the floor from corner to corner. Jack was obviously confused by his mother's search. "What are you looking for, Mom?" he asked.

"Just checking to see how beautiful a job the refinishers did on these old boards. Jack, are you sure you've never heard anything weird up here?" Sara was hoping he had overlooked something.

Jack pulled his lips from one side to the other as he mulled over her question.

"Umm, I've only heard the wind whistling or my music play-ing," he said, pointing to the little radio sitting on a pine stool in the far corner. "Why? You asked me that yesterday."

"Oh, nothing. It was really windy yesterday and it just sounded funny, that's all. Let's go find your dad. Gosh, it's freezing up here. We definitely need to bring up a heater if you're going to be playing in here all winter."

Sara and Jack made their way to the kitchen, where they found David pouring himself a tall glass of milk. He looked up when they entered the room.

"Hi, Dad. Did you find anything?" Jack asked.

"Nope. Nothing. Why don't you go in the other room and watch a DVD? I'll be in to hang out with you in a minute," he suggested as a way to hustle the little boy out of the room.

"Sure!" Jack answered, darting off.

"Well?" Sara asked, picking up where her son left off.

"Still nothing. I'll be damned. Whatever the dogs got they must have finished off. The only explanation I can come up with is that they covered over any bloody snow when they started digging under that tree. I don't know. Maybe they ate the snow. Anyway, I saw no footprints other than my own. If someone fired a gun it was from far away. It was barely dark when you heard the shot. Someone could have been hunting at dusk. Whoever it was lost their game to our dogs," he said, shrugging his shoulders before finishing half the glass in one gulp.

"Need more milk." He showed her the empty container.

"What do they hunt this time of year? I thought hunting season is reserved for the fall," she asked, ignoring his last comment.

David looked at her and shrugged. "You're talking to the wrong guy. I'm a fisherman, not a hunter. The deadliest piece of equipment I have is a fly rod," he explained.

"We need to post some 'no hunting' signs. I don't want our dogs or horses accidentally shot. This place has been empty for so long that people may not realize that a family with large animals lives here now. It wouldn't be a bad idea to pay a visit to all our neighbors. We may even be lucky enough to uncover some details about the family that lived here before," Sara said.

"Good idea. That can be your new project. Let me know how it goes," he said with a slap on her back before leaving to join Jack.

CHAPTER FIVE

The dogs in the living room sprang to life. The three of them ran back and forth from the side window to the back door while barking wildly. Sara looked over at the digital clock on the microwave oven, which read eleven-thirty. Surprisingly, Leila was a bit early. They didn't expect her until after twelve o'clock.

"Now, that is amazing," Sara mumbled to herself.

A few minutes later Leila came through the door, fighting her way through a thick wall of excited canines.

"Can you call off the hounds?" she begged.

Sara whistled and yelled for them to come lie down, which resulted in three dogs backing up about two steps, enough for Leila to close the door behind her.

"Hey, girl, happy birthday!" she said, thrusting a colorfully wrapped box toward Sara.

"Thanks," Sara said, taking it out of her hands.

"Got some goodies for my little man too. Where is he?" Leila asked while trying to squeeze her way through Madison and Buster, who were now panting heavily.

"Upstairs. I'm sure he heard the announcement of your arrival. He should be barreling down the steps momentarily."

"So, how was your birthday?" Leila asked as she pulled a couple of bottles of Cabernet out of the bag and set them on the counter. "I saw the snowman in the yard. He is styling with that cap. Looks like you had some fun."

"Oh, my favorite non-sister-in-law bearing gifts of fine wine," David said, entering the room.

"Hello, non-brother-in-law. Did you treat your wife like the princess she is on her birthday?" Leila joked, throwing an arm around Sara's neck and kissing her cheek.

"Well, let's just say it was, ah…memorable. A day we won't soon forget," Sara said, casting a glance in David's direction.

"Yes, the princess can fill you in on the gory details," David said, moving over to take Leila's coat and gloves. "In the meantime, let me take these for you. I'm going to run to town to pick up the steaks. The roads are clear, aren't they?"

"Oh, they're fine. Why do you think that I've graced you with my presence so early? I thought I would have a hell of a time getting out here, so I gave myself extra time, but look, here I am. It was a breeze. You should have no trouble."

Leila had a head of thick brown hair that fell in soft curls down to the middle of her back. In fact, it was so dark that it was almost black. She swished her mane around after peeling off her outer layer and handing it to David.

"I'll drop your things in the hall closet on the way out," David said, making a hasty retreat. "I'm out of here. See you two later."

"Okay, spill it. What did all that mean?" Leila asked, curiosity flashing in her cool blue eyes as she pressed for answers. "Did Maria call you back? Did she tell you what the deal is? Come on, cough up all the dirty details."

Sara shifted her focus from the box still in her hands to Leila. She thought how pretty her friend was when she was excited. Fiery, really. Everything about her was. Leila was still single, but never alone. She gravitated toward older men with loads of money who had the propensity to spend it on her. She had the strict rule of never staying with one man longer than six months for fear that they would attach themselves to her permanently. A long string of rich old men happily flew her here and there. Leila enjoyed many warm, tropical beaches and fine four-star restaurants on their dime while squirreling away the money she made from her interior decorating business in stocks and bonds. She had seen her parents go through an ugly, violent divorce and she swore she would never put herself in that position. The only security and consistency through the years was her friendship with Sara and subsequently, David and Jack.

"Come on, come on, I can't stand it. What happened?" Leila asked practically jumping up and down with anticipation.

"I don't know if I want to get into that now. Let's just open my present," Sara said, smiling wickedly. She knew prolonging the tale would make Leila crazy.

"You little witch. Now tell me," Leila squealed, grabbing the present out of her hands so fast Sara saw the box move before she felt it.

"Okay, okay. Keep your panties on. Honestly, you are not going to believe it."

"She's getting remarried, right? That's it. I've been thinking about it since you told me yesterday. I could barely sleep last night trying to guess who she has been dating."

"No," Sara said, shaking her head with her eyebrows scrunched up in a, 'Have you just been released from an insane asylum?' expression. "No. It has nothing to do with my mom. We still don't know what's up with her. And I can guarantee that she isn't preparing to spring a secret engagement on me. My birthday was memorable only because it ranked up there in the 'Welcome to Sara's Wacky World' way of life. David seems to think it's all coincidence and concussion-induced, but I don't." Sara used a tone of voice that signified that Leila would understand what David could not, due to his more practical and rational nature.

"What concussion?" Leila asked, immediately switching to concern. "Did you ride yesterday and fall?"

"No, no. Let me start at the beginning," Sara said. "I told you about the great mirror that I purchased that had originally been part of this estate."

"Yeah," Leila answered, sliding onto a stool at the breakfast counter.

Sara went on to recount the whole tale up until the events that took place a few short hours before her friend's arrival.

"So, now I've come to the conclusion that I'm either psychotic or we're living in a haunted house," Sara explained, finishing up with a deep breath.

Leila had been leaning forward on the counter, silent throughout Sara's rambling story. She sat up straight and offered up her heartfelt diagnosis. "That's really messed up!"

"Thank you. That's my opinion too!" Sara said feeling vindicated. "So what do you think? Do you think it's haunted?"

"It must be. Although, I've always suspected that you had one or two screws loose up there in that head of yours. There is only one way to know for sure. Show me this mirror." Leila jumped off the stool with enthusiasm.

"It's upstairs," Sara said, pulling Leila by the hand.

Leila followed her excited friend up the back stairs. When they reached the top, they heard Jack's voice. He was reciting something that sounded like gibberish. He was going through a phase where he insisted that he was really a wizard and could do magic if only he could get the wording of the spell "just right". Sara took comfort in the fact that he was not alone in this obsession. There were a few million other children around the globe suffering from this magical craze brought on by series of books about a group of young wizards and witches.

"Hey, Jack, Auntie Leila is here," Sara called.

"Auntie Leila, yeah!" he said, running out to greet her in the hall, still wearing his black cape, wizard's hat, and fake round glasses.

"Let's take a good look at you, little man," Leila said, fawning over him. "Jack, I must say, you take my breath away! What do you say you grab your broomstick and we fly away together?"

"Okay!" he answered definitively. "Did you bring me presents?"

"Of course. It is Auntie Leila's job to spoil you so no one will ever be good enough for you."

"Can I have them now?" Jack pleaded.

"In a minute. Your mom wants to show me her cool new mirror," Leila answered with a wink.

"Let me show you," he said, racing to be the first one down the hallway. "Here it is! It has naked ladies on it!"

"I see. Mommy likes pornographic mirrors," Leila drawled, teasing Sara with a nudge.

"What's pornographic mean?" Jack asked on cue.

"It means beautiful, of course," Leila said, in an attempt to back pedal after catching the dirty look that Sara had shot her way.

"I'll explain it later, sweetie. Auntie Leila is not too bright and clearly mixes up the meaning of words."

"What a cool mirror," Leila purred, ignoring Sara's sarcastic comment. Reaching out, she ran her finger along the figures, examining the craftsmanship. "He looks like the devil to me," Leila said, pointing to the face. "Do you think he is supposed to reflect the sins of the flesh?"

"Mom, what does that mean?" Jack asked.

"Sweetie, do me a favor. This is way too boring and complicated for a kid. You know, interior design talk. Why don't you go down to the kitchen and get a cookie before opening your presents?" Sara suggested, trying to avoid another distorted attempt at an explanation.

Jack howled with joy and ran back down the hall. When the child disappeared from sight, Sara glared at Leila, who meekly shrugged her shoulders.

"You have no sense. I can't believe I ever leave him with you," Sara lectured.

"Sorry," Leila said, rolling her eyes before quickly shifting her attention back to the wall. "So don't you think I'm right? I mean, here you have the devil overlooking and reigning over naked and voluptuous women. It's perfect. I can only guess how old it is. I'd have to really examine it to be certain. I'm sure it weighs a ton. Did you notice any markings on the back before you hung it?"

"No," Sara answered.

"I bet it was the craftsman's intent to convey that message," Leila said as she spun around to face her friend. She was clearly pleased by her analysis. "Ghost or no ghost, if you ever want to get rid of it, I'll take it."

"It's yours if it keeps creeping me out," Sara said.

"I don't see anything but us."

"I know. It was like that earlier."

"It's a great spot you picked for it. It will draw your eyes up as you enter the house. And it reflects a pretty view from the window as you come around to it. See how it picks up your front pasture with those big trees. You need to keep some horses out there. Or better yet, some people 'doing it', you know, getting back to nature," Leila said smartly.

"Gee, I'm sure the neighbors would love that," Sara remarked. "Someday, you are going to burn in hell, girl."

"Where is this key?" Leila said, changing the subject.

"Downstairs in my bedroom."

They took the stairs closest to them to the main floor. Sara led the way over to her dresser. She picked up the chain, allowing the key to delicately dangle at the end.

"Pretty. I wonder if it actually locks anything or if it is just an ornate little piece of jewelry," Leila contemplated aloud.

"No idea," Sara said.

Jack entered the room after them and was gearing up for a full throttle whine. "Mom, Auntie Leila, come on. It's time for presents," he moaned miserably.

"Alright," Sara said in an effort to avoid the imminent meltdown.

"Mom, wear your necklace, pleeease," Jack begged, drawing out his plea. "Did she tell you that I found it on her birthday? So it's hers."

"I don't think so," Sara answered.

"Please, please. Don't you like it?" he insisted.

"Come on, you big chicken," Leila said, daring her to don the little gold key. "Let's see what happens. Where is the girl who bravely jumps over enormous logs that don't fall down? Who jumps down banks that should have ski lifts running up and down them?"

"You know it's not fair, both of you ganging up on me," Sara said while opening the clasp. She slipped the chain around her neck, sighing with resignation as she glanced at herself in the dresser mirror.

"Let's go get presents!" Leila said, picking Jack up to carry him into the kitchen.

Once in the other room, Leila deposited the child on a stool. She located her oversized shopping bag and pulled out two multicolored gift bags. After ceremoniously handing them to Jack, the beaming woman stood back to enjoy the little boy's excitement. Tissue paper flew around the kitchen as he dug for the prize.

"Cool! Mom, look! A book—*The Official Guide to Becoming a Wizard*, and…," he said, pausing as he searched bag number two, "a new wand!"

"It's a special wand. It's supposed to have unicorn hair in it," Leila explained.

"Oh, thanks, Auntie Leila. Thank you so, so much!" he said, giving her a hug. "I'm going upstairs to practice spells with my new wand. See ya." Jack grabbed his loot and was gone.

"You know, when my son grows up, he's going to be in therapy saying, 'I was raised in a Satanic cult. All I remember from my childhood is witches and wizards.' He's so obsessed with magic that I'm surprised we haven't had a visit by the school counselor," Sara said with a laugh.

"Your turn," Leila said pointing to Sara's box.

Sara smiled with anticipation and tore the paper off. She slid the top of the box onto the counter and found a beautiful little oil painting of her first pony.

"Leila, this is wonderful!" Sara said as tears welled up in her eyes.

"I found some old pictures and had an artist in Middleburg do it," Leila said.

"Thank you. I love it. I can't believe how thoughtful that was. I can't wait to show David," Sara said, wiping the moisture from her cheeks before changing the subject in an attempt to control her bubbling emotions. "You want a drink or maybe some lunch?"

"Are we going to ride?" Leila asked. "Because if we aren't, I'll have some wine. If we are, then I'll wait. I'm not really hungry yet."

"I don't know. Frankly, it's such a pain when it snows, and the horses have shoes on."

"I can ride one of the ponies. Aren't they barefoot?" Leila asked.

Sara nodded and said, "I guess I could ride Trevor. He only has front shoes, but I haven't been on him in months." Sara bought Trevor right out of college. Nearing 25, the old guy had earned himself a carefree retirement and was seldom ridden.

"Come on, Sara. We won't be out long. Remember how much fun we had as kids riding bareback in the snow? Let's ride bareback," Leila said with excitement.

Sara looked at her and pictured them as children riding through the snow on very fat and very hairy ponies. They would be giggling as they slid back and forth on the ponies' slick backs.

"Alright, we can go. But we have to wait for David to get back to stay with Jack. Why don't you bring in your travel bag while I run down to tell Carlos to start grooming the horses for us? He'll need to go catch one of the ponies anyway."

"Excellent. I knew I could twist your arm," Leila said.

David pulled in the driveway a short while later as Sara was zipping up her well-worn chaps. The dogs went through their usual house-rattling repertoire as he walked in.

"I'm impressed. You two are a lot braver than I thought. Be sure to wear your helmet. All you need is another crack to your head," he said as he shoved the steaks into the refrigerator.

"Yes, sir!" she answered, smartly saluting him. "We'll take the dogs. It'll be good for them to run around a bit. Hey, look at the painting Leila got me. I love it. It's my first pony, Confetti."

"Very nice," David said as he examined it.

Leila joined them a few seconds later, wearing a pair of dark brown, fringed chaps over a pair of faded jeans. She had pulled her coat on over a turtleneck sweater. Sara grabbed her own jacket and zipped it up. "See you later," they called in unison as they made their way to the back door.

Carlos had plowed the driveway that morning, which left a firmly compressed path for them to step out onto as they trekked to the barn. It was still quite cold. The snow was not even close to melting. Sara had set up a rule years ago that she wouldn't ride if the temperature dipped down into the twenties. As she has gotten older, the level of that cut-off kept inching higher.

Through the open barn doors, Sara saw that Carlos had Trevor and Sassafras ready to go. "*Gracias*, Carlos," she called.

"No problem, Miss Sara," he answered before heading off to attend to other chores.

Imprisoned by the snow, the other horses methodically chewed on their hay in consolation. One large, dappled gray horse lifted his head and whinnied when he heard Sara's voice.

"He is so gorgeous!" Leila said, pointing to the attentive horse.

"Gale Force? Sure is," Sara agreed. "He is the ultimate Irish sport-horse, can do just about anything, and is as brave as they come. He even came with a solid, unflappable brain. I swear it would take a freight train to rattle him."

Sara took Trevor's reins and led him to the end of the aisle. She climbed onto a tack box, grabbed his mane, jumped, and swung her leg over his back. He turned his head to look at her foot, rather annoyed that he was being asked to go to work.

Leila in the meantime had brought Sassy outside and had vaulted onto her back. The pony raised her head in protest and backed up as Leila swung her right leg down over her side.

"Just like old times," Leila said. "Next the pony will buck me off like that ancient appaloosa used to."

"No, she'll rear and dump you backwards if anything. Be sure to pull sideways if she goes up," Sara cautioned.

Sara applied a little pressure from her heels to Trevor's sides, and he stepped forward. Leila joined her at the barn entrance. The riders made their way down the paved drive, then cut off into some fresh powder. They followed the edge of the front yard, traversing the site of the snowball fight, where they spotted Mr. Freeze.

"There's an opening down here that we can get through," Sara said. She could feel the radiating warmth of Trevor's body on the inside of her thighs, which stood in sharp contrast to the cold that gripped her everywhere else.

"So we haven't talked about your mom," Leila said.

"Who knows? Maybe her weird feeling was right. I mean, look at all the bizarre stuff that happened yesterday," Sara replied. "Can we just enjoy the ride? I don't want to think about it."

Leila rode on quietly for about five minutes, but she finally caved in and broke the silence. "You know, maybe it's just Maria's guilty conscience preying on her about lying to you your whole life about being adopted. That's why she's been having nightmares leading up to your birthday. That's a much more likely explanation. She has a hard time grasping the real world, let alone having any inclination about what would be going on with some ghostly phenomenon here in Virginia," Leila suggested.

Sara looked at her with a blank stare for several seconds before responding. "I knew you couldn't let it go," she stated.

"Sara, think about it. Wasn't it around this time last year that she developed panic attacks? The year before she sent you those odd little gifts because she thought you were mad at her for something or other. I think it's all a pattern. She has a nervous breakdown each time your birthday rolls around. Not that she doesn't deserve to, but still, don't go using your mother's issues as evidence for your theory about this place. It's a great farm. No, actually, it's an awesome farm!"

"You're starting to sound like David. Watch it. I need someone on my side."

"Give me a break. I'm always on your side. I just don't think you need to go running up to New York to confirm that your mother is a wack job. We know that already," Leila said with an air of authority on the subject.

Sara was silent for a few moments as she mulled over what Leila had been saying. "Maybe you're right. Last night just gave me the 'heebie-jeebies'. Now can we drop it?" Sara pleaded.

"Okay," Leila said while urging the pony to keep up with Trevor. "Can I ask you about David? How are things going between you two?"

"I think we're on the right track," Sara answered, showing Leila her crossed fingers. "He's trying. I'm trying. There's a glimmer of hope that we'll be back the way we were. Happy."

"That's great! The best thing you guys ever did was get the heck out of Pennsylvania, away from all those bad memories."

"They weren't all bad," Sara said defensively. "We lived there for over 10 years."

"You know what I mean. Grace's death made a mess out of

both of you. It was time to put it in the past where it belongs—behind you. And now look. It's almost like having the old Sara and David back. What would Jack have done if his parents threw in the towel? Hell, come to think of it, what would I have done?"

Sara smiled. "God only knows. It's a good thing I have no intention of finding out."

The horses were leaving a shuffled trail in the snow while the dogs were zigzagging through the drifts beside them. Buster had put his whole head under the snow at one point and came up covered. Both women caught sight of him and laughed.

When they reached the stone wall bordering the far edge of the field, they turned right. Sara knew they were coming up on the site where the dogs had run to the night before. She was surprised that the dogs didn't seem to take notice and kept up their playful antics.

"Yikes! Look at that. Did the dogs dig all this up?" Leila asked as they approached the spot under the big oak.

"I suppose. But see, not a trace of blood," Sara replied pointing to the uncovered ground as the horses veered off to either side. "Ouch! Damn, that hurts. I have the sharpest pain in my chest. It's burning like crazy right between my boobs." Sara grimaced with pain.

"I suspect you may have a little reflux churning away from all the red wine you consumed last night, my dear," Leila teased with a dismissive little laugh.

"Yeah, guess it could be that. Let's keep going. We can get into the other field a little farther down," Sara said as they kicked their horses on.

The conversation drifted from decorating tips to Leila's latest lover. They were out for about 45 minutes when Sara realized that her face and fingers were frozen. "I don't think I can get much colder. How about we call it a day?" she suggested.

"Considering that frostbite has taken hold of my hands and feet, I would say you have expressed my feelings exactly," Leila agreed. "By the way, how's the gut feeling?"

"It was my chest. And the pain is gone. We started chatting away and it seemed to pass. How about that? You're usually the one causing the indigestion, not curing it."

"Funny, so funny."

The women headed back, cutting through a small pass that led out into the driveway. The chugging rhythm of a salt truck on the main road seemed to perfectly match the cadence of the horses' hooves. Carlos was alerted to Sara and Leila's return by the dogs speeding along in front of them. He met them outside the barn door and held Sassafras for Leila to dismount.

"I'll take care of her, Miss Leila," he said, leading the pony back to her stall.

"Thanks, Carlos," she replied.

Wary of hurting her toes, Sara dismounted slowly, and then led Trevor back to his stall. She took off his bridle and handed it to Leila, who promptly deposited it on a hook in the tack room. Sara found Trevor's blanket and swung it over his back, then fastened it securely under his belly. On their way out, the women stuck their heads into the tack room. "*Adios*, Carlos," Leila said.

"*Gracias*, we really appreciated all your help," Sara added.

"*Si, de nada*," he replied, blushing slightly from the attention.

"He is such a nice guy and very cute, silent and sort of brooding," Leila said in a purring tone on their way up to the house.

"Leila, if you seduce him, I'll kill you," Sara sternly said. "Good, loyal help is impossible to find and harder to keep. Plus, the 'silent and brooding' you are referring to is actually a lack of sufficient English vocabulary combined with the good sense to be afraid of you."

"I was only commenting. He's not rich or old enough for me."

"If you weren't my best friend my entire life, and God only knows why that is, I would kick your slutty, self-absorbed, shallow ass and suggest you get a life," Sara said, shaking her head before pausing to add, "…and definitely some therapy."

Leila smiled wickedly as she reached over and hugged Sara around the neck, causing them to knock heads. "Oh, I'm touched. You really do love me."

Sara rolled her eyes, shook her head, and sighed.

CHAPTER SIX

David and Jack looked up when they heard the back door open. A roaring fire crackled and popped in the background, and classical music filled the air. They were sitting on the floor in the living room playing Clue. Sara and Leila, half frozen, took up positions near the fireplace after carefully stepping over the two opponents.

"Hello, ladies," David said with a nod in their direction.

"Hi, Mom. Hi, Auntie Leila," Jack added.

"Hey, guys. Have you figured out who murdered who, where, and with what?" Sara inquired.

"Not yet," Jack answered.

"Do you two crazy broads want something to drink after your cold ride? Maybe some coffee or you can start in on one of the bottles of Cabernet," David suggested.

"Mr. Miller, I knew there was a reason I liked you so much. Always so focused on the needs of others. A prince. See? One more reason I can't get married. You have the only man worth settling down for," Leila kidded.

"You know he has a single brother," Sara offered.

"Oh yeah. I can see that now. A match made in heaven," David laughed, almost choking on his words. "The two of you are oil and water."

"You know, everyone said that about the two of you!" Leila loudly protested. "Miss 'Wild Hippie Chick' and Mr. 'Straight Laced Jock.' It's scary how you have grown more alike."

"That's true," Sara agreed. She stood up and walked into the kitchen. "I'm going to open the wine. It's too much of a hassle to make the coffee."

"Sounds good," Leila answered.

Sara uncorked the least expensive of the bottles and poured two glasses of the deep red liquid. "David, do you want any wine?" Sara asked.

"No, thank you. Jack would surely take advantage of me with alcohol coursing through my veins. I'll have something after we're done with the game," he answered politely.

"Suit yourself," Sara called as she stuffed a decorative crystal stopper in the top of the bottle.

"Did you ask Carlos about working tomorrow and taking off another day next week? I don't want to be left short-handed if Emma can't get back," Sara asked as she returned to the living room and handed a glass of cabernet to Leila.

David looked up from moving his game piece into the library and shook his head in exaggerated disgust. "Yes, dear. I did. He said it would be fine. I told you that this morning while you were in a mind-numbing daze."

"Oh, sorry. Thanks," she replied a little sheepishly.

He returned his attention to the game only momentarily before asking her about his coat. "Have you had a chance to wash my coat yet? I would like to be able to wear it without having blood all over the thing."

"Oh, shoot! I can't believe I forgot. I'll do it now. Be right back." Sara excused herself to attend to this chore.

The coats were still hanging up in the mudroom. She grabbed them without a glance and set off for the laundry room. While bending over to open the lid of the washer, she realized that the key was still around her neck. It had swung out from her sweater, catching her eye. Sara fiddled with it for a second as she tucked it back inside her top layer. After punching in the cycle for the washer, she searched behind the detergent for a bottle of spot remover. After more than 20 hours, the blood would have absorbed into the fabric's fibers and dried, making it tough to get clean. Sara didn't think David would be very happy if she told him that he had permanent red handprints on his coat. She shook the bottle of stain-treater while searching over the coat's left arm. Surprisingly, there were no marks. Puzzled, she examined the tan canvas again, certain that she had grabbed her husband's left arm in the chaos. Still finding no trace of the previous evening's bloodbath, she switched to the right sleeve. Sara closed her eyes. No blood. No handprint. Nothing.

"Shit," she muttered in a low voice. Sara opened her eyes, hoping that she was mistaken, that reality had maybe skipped a beat. She combed over the rest of the coat. "It has to be here! Where is it?" she repeated under her breath.

Sara dropped the coat on the floor, backed up and sat down on the hamper. It couldn't be. Her hands had been covered in blood. They both saw the imprint of her palm and fingers. Blood didn't just disappear. As conflicting thoughts flooded her mind, she noticed her own coat crumpled up on the dryer. The whole front of it should have been stained with blood from hugging Madison. Even before inspecting it, she knew what she would find. Nothing. Her head was dizzy. Hyperventilating, Sara pressed her hand to her chest, her fingers passing over the key's jagged outline. Flashing back to the sharp pain that seared through her sternum while riding, she realized that it had hit directly below the key.

"Why is this happening?" she said to herself while looking up at the ceiling of the small room.

Sara was shaking from a combination of anger and fear. She had almost let herself forget about the odd events from the night before. It seemed like days ago with Leila at the house, distracting her. She stood up, picked up the coats and shoved them into the washing machine. They were getting washed, blood or no blood.

After composing herself, she returned to the living room as if nothing unusual had taken place. By then, David was winning the game.

"Miss Scarlet, in the library, with the candlestick," David shouted out as she sat down next to the fire again.

"No fair! No fair! I want a rematch," Jack whined.

"Don't be such a sore loser. People don't like to play with someone who can't lose gracefully," David warned.

"Humph!" Jack exclaimed, folding his arms over his chest.

"I know exactly who he takes after. That child is his mother's son," Leila exclaimed.

David and Jack looked at Sara for a reaction, but none came. She was a million miles away.

"You okay there, honey?" David asked.

"What? I'm sorry. Were you talking to me?" she answered.

"Yeah. You seem distracted. Are you feeling all right? You didn't respond to Leila's frontal assault. Very unlike you."

"My head must have been someplace else," Sara responded.

"I'd say," Leila added.

"Don't worry. I'll get her back when she least expects it." Sara nudged her friend with her elbow, making them both smile.

"Auntie Leila, how about you play with me?" Jack asked. "Dad doesn't let me win like you do. I like playing with you the most."

"When you put it that way, sure," Leila answered.

As the focus of attention shifted from her to other topics, Sara took a long sip of wine from her glass. She realized that she felt cold, very cold, even with her back close to the fireplace.

That night, David cooked steaks on the grill out in the snow. When Jack went to bed, the three adults stayed up talking while finishing off the remaining wine that Leila had so generously supplied. They noticed the lights of Emma's car pulling past the window at the precise moment when the grandfather clock started to chime ten o'clock. The car slowly made its way back toward the tenant house.

"I'm glad she made it back tonight. Carlos will be especially happy," Sara commented.

"Ladies, if you'll excuse me, it's getting late and I'm tired. I'm going to bed. Are you two going to stay up?" David asked.

"I think I'll join you," Sara said, extending her hand toward her husband, prompting him to yank her onto her feet.

"Party poopers. It's no fun to stay up by myself," Leila teased as she made her way up to the second floor. "I'll be sure to check your mirror for ghosts."

Sara had prepared the guest bedroom closest to the main staircase for Leila's stay. She would have to pass directly in front of the mirror to reach her room. As the couple crossed the foyer, their inebriated and flamboyant friend could be heard fawning over her reflection.

"Sorry. No ghosts tonight. I only see myself and I must say, I am one gorgeous image to behold. Goodnight," Leila called before blowing an air kiss down to them.

"So humble," David mumbled.

"See you in the morning," Sara replied as her husband's arm closed around her waist.

"Come, my dear. Carnal pleasures await you," he growled seductively in her ear. "You've held me at bay long enough. You are mine."

Surprisingly, the wine didn't have the same sedating power on Sara as it had the night before, suggesting that the combination of the excitement and the crack on her head had exaggerated the alcohol's effect. Her mind wandered back to yesterday afternoon when she and David were hanging the new mirror. She vividly recalled their hallway encounter, how her body had instinctively ached for him when his hands teasingly brushed over her. As they climbed between the sheets, their naked bodies intertwined like an intricate Chinese puzzle. They kissed passionately, desire building as they coaxed each other to let go of any inhibitions. They connected, body and soul. Tremors of ecstasy overwhelmed them, leaving them breathless and satiated. Leaning over his wife, David brushed the hair from her face to kiss her lips lightly. She smiled with her eyes closed.

"I love you," he cooed.

"I love you too," she replied in a barely audible whisper.

Framing her face with his index finger, David followed the curve of her neck down to the key nestled between her naked breasts. Teetering on the brink of sleep, Sara had forgotten to take it off. Conforming his body to her curves, he pulled the covers up, encasing them in a down cocoon. From a semi-conscious state, she heard him utter his pledge.

"Don't worry. I won't let anything happen to you," he promised before surrendering to his own inner world.

The dreams made their way back to Sara like an old movie playing in a lonely cinema. She watched the command performance as the sole member of the audience.

A familiar woman stood partially naked in a bedroom lit by a single flickering candle. Heavy locks of hair obscured her facial features as she looked down. A tall, dark haired man emerged from the shadows. Moving around behind her, he pulled the hair away from her neck as he fastened a gold chain around her throat. The woman's skin was so white it almost possessed its own luminescence, as if she had never seen the sun. He kissed her neck then turned her, taking her face in his hands. Kissing her mouth deeply, he slid his arms around her. The woman moaned and pushed at his shoulders, but he held her tighter.

She whimpered. "No, please, you know we can't."

"You will be mine, only mine, forever," he answered, stopping only long enough to make his undeniable intentions clear as he stripped away her remaining clothes.

The man picked her up like a child and carried her to a bed. Triumphantly he stood over her as she recoiled under his gaze. Undeterred, he climbed in next to his female prize, kissing her while exploring her nakedness. Instinct led the way as she relented and kissed him back. Protests gave way to passion as her legs snaked around his, pulling his naked groin to hers. The woman's face turned from under his rigid torso. She bit her lip in rapturous agony. The contours of the man's back were defined by flexing muscles.

A half-hearted plea escaped from the woman's lips. "Please, we must stop. It's wrong, a mistake," she vainly tried to protest, but it was too late.

"Yes," he uttered in a long, low groan as he pushed up from her in convulsions of pleasure. A gold key and a cross were cradled between the heaving white breasts of the pinned woman. A tear slid down her cheek.

"Oh God. Oh God," she yelled out, not in ecstasy, but for forgiveness.

Sara shook herself awake. It was dark. David was lying asleep next to her. The only sound in the room was the consistent rhythm of his breathing. Again, a stabbing sensation ripped through her abdomen. She slid out from the warmth of the sheets and walked into the bathroom. The cold night air made the tiles against her feet feel freezing. Within seconds the rest of her turned to ice. Goosebumps had spread across Sara's bare skin, making her wish she had grabbed her robe, since she seemed unable to rub them away. As she reached the bathroom sink, she doubled over, feeling ill. Turning on the faucet, she cupped her hands and splashed cool water on her face. Looking up at the wet reflection in the mirror, she saw something glint as it caught the light of the moon, which streamed like sharpened daggers through the window. Sara stared at this twin trapped in the glass before her, the gold key swinging around her neck. Images swarmed across her mind, passing glimpses into her dream that vanished as quickly as they came. Was she the woman from the dream? She couldn't be certain. Looking at her own face, the difference seeped through into her awareness. She touched her hair. Red hair. The woman she saw in these images had red hair. She shivered as her eyes took in her own naked form.

The pain was gone and all she wanted was to be back in bed with David. Sara hurried back to find him turned toward the far wall. She immediately pulled herself flush against his body, wrapping her right arm around his waist and burying her face between his shoulder blades. Visions of the dark-haired man's back as he arched in orgasm collided with the haunted expression painted across the red-haired woman's eyes. Sara pushed these back, trying to think of something else, anything else.

Having finally fallen back asleep, Sara was unpleasantly surprised when the alarm clock's buzzer went off.

"Five more minutes," David mumbled as he turned to hit the snooze button.

"Why did you set the alarm?" Sara asked, irritated by the unnecessary early awakening.

Through the purplish black haze of a winter's morning, the clock's red digital readout flashed seven o'clock. David didn't answer; he had either fallen back asleep or decided to ignore her. After considering the possibility of slipping into another bizarre dream, Sara decided that being awake was safer.

CHAPTER SEVEN

Sara found the dogs waiting for her in the kitchen. She scooped out dry kibble for them before starting the coffee maker. As she waited for the dark liquid to fill the pot, Sara scooped two teaspoons of sugar into a silver travel mug. Looking out the window, she noticed the lights switch on at the barn. Emma was already up and feeding the horses. This prompted Sara to pull another mug from the cabinet for the young Brit. In the meantime, the dogs finished their meal and were waiting for her to join them at the back door. Unfortunately, they were clogging the exit and there wasn't a free hand available to help maneuver through them.

"Move! You're too damn big," she said as she tried to sandwich herself between Madison and Buster while pushing the Springer Spaniel ahead of her with a tap from her foot.

The three dogs looked at her as if completely offended by her raised tone. Balancing both mugs in one hand, she eventually opened the door. The rush of frigid air made Sara consider going back inside as the dogs raced around her, spinning her body like a top.

"Idiots! Run over me, why don't ya? I swear, nothing but a damn bunch of rotten animals," she cursed as they sped away. "I can't wait until winter is over. I hate the cold."

As she got closer to the barn, the unmistakable rhythm of a Latin beat was playing on the radio, signaling that Carlos was already on the premises.

"Emma, welcome back," Sara yelled as she reached the crack in the barn door.

In her early twenties, Emma was a top-notch exercise rider and groom. She poked her bleached blonde head out of a stall at the end of the barn. "Thanks. It's good to be back. The trip home was a bitch. Being there was great, but traveling in winter is no fun at all. Between the normal delays and the extra security measures to deter terrorists, it's a downright pain in the bum," she answered without emerging.

Sara reached the voice and found Emma in the midst of switching Gale Force's stable blanket to a turnout rug. "Oops, I'm sorry. We aren't turning these four out in the snow. Only hand walking today. Change of clothing for nothing. I have a blacksmith coming out tomorrow. The folks at the feed store recommended him. They said he's old as dirt, been around shoeing in the area since Virginia was a colony. I think his name is John or James Sullivan. I wrote it down on a notepad in the kitchen. I'll let you know later."

"Very good. I take it that the horses aren't going to the Florida circuit after all. Are you sure you don't want to send them? I'm more than happy to go along to take care of them, and I can even show them if you want," Emma said, feigning concern.

"I know what a sacrifice that would be for you, Emma. I could never ask that of you. Nice try, though," Sara said sarcastically, making her English friend's smile sink into a frown. She held the warm travel mug out for Emma. "Your consolation prize."

"Your generosity is overwhelming," Emma said, reaching for the mug. "I'll take him out and walk him in this first, then I'll change him back. Less to do in this miserable weather."

"Good enough," Sara replied.

"How have things been here?" Emma asked.

"Strange. It's a long story. Take a break and I'll fill you in."

Emma followed Sara into the tack room, the warmest place in the barn. The thermometer on the wall read a balmy 25 degrees Fahrenheit. The two women talked for about a half an hour, catching up on events from both sides of the Atlantic. Emma was certainly more intrigued by the odd happenings at the farm than Sara was by the gossip about people she had never met.

"I'll let you know if anything creepy happens at my place. So far no ghosts, only me and the mouse who moved into the cupboard while I was away. I think I need to get a cat," Emma declared with a shrug of her shoulders.

"If you want, I'll get David to run out to the hardware store to get a mousetrap," Sara offered.

"As long as it's a quiet one. Now that you've given me the willies, all I need is to hear the thing squealing after getting wholloped in the middle of the night. You'll hear me screaming all the way up at the main house!"

"Good point. Maybe a cat would be a good option."

The two walked toward the front of the barn as they finished their conversation. A muffled sound caught the women's attention. Turning toward the entrance, they heard it again, David's barely audible voice. Sara was surprised that she could hear anything at all with the barn doors tightly closed and the music blaring.

"Honey, breakfast is ready," drifted through the air.

"I wonder how long he has been calling for me? Time to go. See you in a little while," Sara said, waving to Emma as she trotted away.

The cold air tightened the skin on her face. Sara pulled her scarf up to cover her nose and mouth. Glancing back, she recognized Carlos' huddled figure fighting the wind as he made his way back from turning the ponies out. It was gusting so hard that it was picking up snow particles and sandblasting everything in its path. Sara waved to no avail. He didn't see her. This was the type of morning that sent you back inside as soon as possible. She thought of Emma's offer to go to Florida. She had to admit that being someplace warm and tropical sounded pretty darn good at the moment.

When Sara pushed open the back door, she was met with the mixed aromas of coffee, bacon, and eggs. In the kitchen, David and Jack were engaged in an animated conversation. She was surprised when she heard Leila's voice chime in the discussion. If anyone had taken bets on the estimated time of her friend's awakening, Sara would have laid 100 dollars on the table that Leila wouldn't have crawled out of bed until noon. Yet there she was, chatting away with the boys, ultimately proving her wrong.

"What are you doing up?" Sara asked as she joined them.

Leila looked over at her with a mouthful of food. She attempted to answer but only succeeded in mumbling something completely incoherent.

"Really?" Sara joked.

David kissed his chilled wife on the cheek as he offered her a plate with a bacon, egg, and cheese burrito. "Thanks," she said taking up the stool next to Jack.

By this time, Leila had finished swallowing what was left of her food and offered a more understandable answer. "Your evil husband enlisted your son in getting my butt out of bed for some breakfast. I have to admit that I was a bit displeased with him at first, but these are actually pretty darn good."

David smiled and bowed dramatically in recognition of the compliment. "What can I say? Sara is just the luckiest woman in the world. I am a true gem," he added, waving his spatula in circles through the air.

This sent Jack into a fit of laughter that resulted in half chewed eggs being sprayed in several directions at once.

"Gross!" Leila squealed, her nose wrinkled up in disgust.

"Quit it, Jack!" Sara said leaning away from him. "See what you started!" she told David. "Since you're such a gem, you can clean it up too."

David turned his back on them to hide his smile. "Really, the thanks I get! I'm totally unappreciated. Here I am, getting up early to slave away to make you breakfast and all I get is criticism," he said with exaggerated flair.

"I say you dump the old nag and come home with me," Leila teased him. "I'll let you be my private chef."

"Speaking of going home, when are you?" Sara asked.

"Why? Are you sick of me already?"

"No. I wanted to know if you wanted to go shopping with me today. It's way too cold and windy to ride. I thought we could go and check out some of the shops and antique stores in the area. What do you think? We could take two cars and you can head home from there. Of course, only if that's acceptable to the chef here."

"What do you think, Jack? One more 'guy' day of kicking back, watching TV, and eating chips on the sofa. You think we can manage without them?" David asked.

"Yeah!" Jack whooped. "How soon can you leave?"

"Now who is unappreciated?" Sara said.

"It sounds like a plan to me. I'll go get ready and we can head out in about an hour," Leila said, vanishing up the stairs within seconds.

David offered a friendly warning to Sara as she was sliding her plate into the sink. "This time, avoid anything that came from this house. We don't need you bringing back anymore little treasures that freak you out."

"Gee, thanks for the advice," she smartly replied.

David came up from behind, grabbing her around the waist. He kissed her neck and whispered low enough so Jack could not hear. "You sure thought that last night. If I remember correctly you didn't protest when I had my way with you," he teased.

Sara froze for a second as the veil of a memory shifted in a way that was chilling. Last night's dream had surfaced with his touch. She shook her head, pushing through David's arms. He looked at her, surprised and hurt. She turned, walking out of the room without an explanation. How could she attempt to describe what she herself couldn't wrap her head around?

It wasn't long before Sara was showered, dressed, and back in the kitchen, waiting on Leila. David was behind the sink, cleaning up, when she walked in. He looked at her suspiciously. "Are you mad at me? Did I do something wrong? I'm confused." He was clearly still stinging from her earlier abruptness.

"No. I'm not mad at you at all. I'm sorry. I can't really tell you why I reacted the way I did. It's just…it's just that I had this weird feeling when you said that to me before. Last night I had another strange dream. It's all foggy. I can't really remember the details, but that struck a nerve with me. It was like having a déjà vú moment. I'm sorry. You didn't do anything wrong," she struggled to explain.

"Sara, I love you. What can I do to help? Don't shut me out

again," he said, wrapping his arms around her while kissing her on the forehead.

"I love you too. I don't think you can do anything other than what you're doing right now. Just keep me focused on the moment, here and now with you, in your arms, safe and loved," Sara said in a hushed voice, laying her cheek against his chest and closing her eyes.

The atmosphere was abruptly interrupted as a loud bang-bang-bang echoed through the kitchen followed by a "Son of a you-know-what!" Alarmed, Sara and David spun around to look at the rear stairs. Leila's overnight bag had tumbled to the bottom.

"Would you mind taking that to the car for our guest?" Sara asked David.

"No problem," he answered.

"Thanks," Leila said to him when she caught up with her bag.

"Just don't forget to tip the bellman on your way out," he added.

"Quite an entrance you made," Sara teased. "Do you always come in a room that way?"

Jack emerged from upstairs before Leila could answer. He had heard the commotion coming from the kitchen. "Auntie Leila, are you hurt?"

"No, I'm fine, but aren't you the sweetest thing!" she answered.

"Are you leaving now?" he asked. "I'm gonna miss you."

"I'll miss you too, but I think you're better off having me visit. I can spoil you better that way." Leila's eyes softened as she looked at him.

"You're all set," David said returning to the kitchen free of luggage. "You two behave today. No cocktails if you go to lunch. The roads are still slick."

"Yes, Daddy," Leila snickered.

"I mean it. I don't want to have to peel you off a tree or bail you out of jail," he emphasized.

"Yes, we heard you the first time. Sometimes your dad thinks we have no common sense," Leila explained to the child hugging her midsection.

David rolled his eyes.

"Don't worry. I'll be good," Sara promised.

Sara and Leila pulled out of the driveway in their own cars. They spent the morning roaming from one shop to the next. Sara bought a pair of antique porcelain figurines shaped like foxhounds and some small oil paintings for the living room and library.

Strolling along the sidewalk, they spotted an old second hand bookstore set behind some overgrown holly bushes. The tiny brick building was tucked into a side street. With such a large library, Sara thought it might be a good idea to locate some old books to use as filler for the rows and rows of empty shelves. Places such as this would frequently get in books when people either moved or died.

"I want to stop in here," Sara said, tugging on Leila's arm so she would follow her inside. Once in the musty store, she told the shopgirl that she was looking for some bargain books to add to her home library. "Do you have anything available that wouldn't set me back too much? I'm not picky," Sara explained.

"We only bother to shelve books if they're recent bestsellers, look unusually interesting, or are of any real value," the young woman said. "The others get boxed up for people to purchase in bulk. You'll find what we have against the far wall. They run ten dollars each."

"Ten dollars a book?" Leila gasped.

"A box," the woman clarified, looking over her glasses at Sara and Leila.

"That's a high price for a bunch of out-of-print garbage," Leila snickered under her breath.

Apparently Sara was not the only one trying to look well-read. At ten dollars a box, she thought the books were a bargain. At the very least, David would be excited. There might actually be something interesting enough for him to read. She picked through the boxes looking at the titles and dates. Leila grew increasingly bored. The majority of the items were from the fifties and sixties. Others were more recent, while a scant few were published earlier.

Sara was picking her way through the last box when she found an old, thick, leather-bound book. Its spine listed no title. When she pulled it from the box and turned it over, she was surprised to discover a tarnished lock. It looked as if the book had been sealed shut for a long time.

"I'll be darned," Sara mumbled.

"What did you say?" Leila asked.

"Oh, nothing. Talking to myself," Sara answered.

"Listen, I have to get going. I have a date tonight with Richard. Remember him, the big litigation lawyer who went after the tobacco and asbestos companies? Are you almost ready?" Leila asked, checking her watch.

Sara stood up with the book still in her hand. "No. You go ahead. I'm not quite done here. Thanks so much for coming out. We had a great time."

Leila gave Sara a hug. "Bye. We'll talk later this week," she said with a wave from the door.

"Drive safely," Sara called, looking back down at the book in her hand. She pushed on the little button in an attempt to trigger the release. It didn't move. Only the person who possessed the key could unlock its secrets.

"Hmm, we'll see about getting you opened later," she said to herself. Sara dropped it on top of one of the boxes.

"I'll take all six of these," she informed the storekeeper. Pleased with her bounty, she was grateful that David would be home to help her carry them in.

It was nearing dusk when Sara turned into the gravel drive. The lights illuminated the barn, allowing her to spot Emma walking down the aisle, carrying the horses' evening feed. Sara waved at the busy girl whose hands were too full to wave back. The Brit nodded a reply in the direction of the car. Upon opening the back hatch, Sara lifted one of the heavy boxes. Straining to carry it into the house, she decided to leave the rest for David to retrieve. He was doing exactly what he had predicted that morning: sprawling out on the couch watching television. The dialogue drifting out of the living room sounded like an old spy movie.

"Hi. Find anything worthwhile?" floated David's familiar voice from behind the high cushions of the couch.

"Some trinkets for the house and a ton of old books to fill up the shelves in the library. Can you help me carry them in?" Sara pleaded in the sweetest tone she could muster. She leaned the box against the kitchen counter to rest her arms.

On the television, the tone of the male voice switched from giving orders to lines of seduction. She stretched backward so she could see who it was. A buxom actress she didn't recognize was scantily clad in a bikini on some exotic beach. The movie looked to be from the early 1960s.

"Definitely a different measure of beauty back then. Now the women are thinner and muscular. They can seriously kick some ass," David said, more to himself than to Sara.

"Honey, did you hear me? I have lots of heavy stuff out in the car for you to bring in," she emphasized, the sweetness meter dropping a little.

"Yes, yes. Leave it until later. I'm in the middle of a movie," David answered.

"Fine," she grudgingly answered, shaking her head in defeat.

Sara tightened her grip around the box in her arms and maneuvered her way out of the kitchen. She walked through the foyer to a hallway that opened up to a lofty semi-circular library. The curved areas of the exterior wall were original glass that provided a spectacular view of the front property. The interior walls were lined with bookshelves that reached 14 feet high. About a third of the shelves were filled with old novels and college textbooks.

She set her load down on the large antique desk positioned in front of the windows. Peering outside, she could see six deer off in the distance and a lone cardinal perched on a branch of a bare maple. She inhaled deeply and thought how fortunate they were to have found this farm, haunted or not. She couldn't imagine the heirs of the estate choosing to get rid of it.

"We'll have to learn to live with each other. Their loss," she said out loud.

"Whose?" Jack said, causing his mother to jump and spin around.

"Jack, you have to stop sneaking up on me like that! Seriously, you are going to give me a heart attack," she said sharply.

"Mom, you are not going to have a heart attack. It's only me," he replied dismissively.

Sara shook her head in frustration.

"What's this?" he asked trying to peek into the box. He climbed onto the desk chair to answer his riddle. "Oh. Just some old books. Yuck. They smell funny."

"That sometimes happens when paper gets old. I have a bunch more in the car. I'm going to get another box. Maybe it will motivate your dad to get off the couch. I'll be right back," she explained, leaving him rifling through the box.

"Doubt it," he said.

"Careful not to fall," she called out to him as she walked down the hall. Sara returned to find Jack sitting on the desk, looking at the leather journal. He was pawing at the lock, just as she had in the shop. She dropped the second box next to the first.

"Look, Mom. I found a diary," he said, pushing the book out for her to see. "Why would someone sell their diary?"

"Not sure," Sara answered. "Could be that the person didn't know it was in the pile of books that were sold."

"It seems like you would always know where your diary is. Don't you think?" he asked.

"I would think so, but things sometimes happen. Maybe the owner died, and when family members cleared everything out, they didn't bother to look at what they were shipping off."

Sara walked around the desk, slid open the top drawer, and felt around. Jack's dangling legs accidentally pushed the drawer shut, almost catching her hand as she withdrew a pair of scissors.

"Jack, get down! You are going to hurt one of us," she said, lifting his firm body off the grandiose desk.

With a dejected look, he sulked over to one of the two large, leather chairs that faced the desk. He catapulted his body into the one on the right with a thump. The journal in his hand quickly recaptured his attention. Sara looked over at him. Jack was dwarfed by the size of the chair. David had painstakingly picked the pair out himself. They perfectly fit her husband's large stature, but seeing Jack sitting on the oversized chair was an image that appeared to be plucked straight out of a cartoon. Jack looked up from the book to see his mother gazing across the room at him. The scissors in her hand piqued his curiosity. "What are you going to do with those?" he asked.

"I'm going to cut open that journal. Maybe we can find out whose it is," she answered, moving around the desk toward him.

"No! No, you can't," Jack yelled jumping up from his seat.

Sara was taken aback. "Why the heck not?" Frustration spiked her tone.

"You told me that you are never, ever supposed to read some-one else's diary. You said that it's a special safe place for someone to write down their secret thoughts. You can't read it! It wouldn't be right, Mom," he insisted.

She hated being caught by her own words. "Yes, sweetheart, but the person who owned this diary gave it away, or as I said before, he or she may even be dead," she explained, still intent on cutting it open.

"Mom, no! What if it was given away by accident? Even if the person is dead, they didn't give you permission to read it. It would be like stealing," he said, making a case that she found hard to argue with.

"Fine. You win. I won't open it," she said, exasperated.

Sara replaced the scissors in the drawer. Jack smiled, thoroughly pleased with his victory.

"Hey, Mom. Let's go play. You can let Dad bring in whatever is left. Please," he begged.

Melting like an ice cube in warm tea, she gave in to his smil-ing face and enthusiasm. They left the journal lying on the chair. She would finish this task another day.

CHAPTER EIGHT

Sara hated Monday mornings, and this Monday was no exception. David had a business meeting in Richmond, leaving Sara alone at the house for the first time. He had been working from home since they moved in a little more than a month ago.

"Come on, Jack. If you finish your breakfast in 10 seconds I'll drive you to the bus," David said. "I can't be late."

Jack nodded and shoved the rest of his toast in his mouth.

"I won't be home until about seven o'clock tonight," David reminded Sara. "And don't forget that I have that trip to California coming up next week. It's going to be pretty hectic."

Sara rolled her eyes and moaned. "I think I remember. You've only told me, like what, a dozen times? Just don't forget that we promised my mom that we would do a quick trip up to New York this weekend."

"Maybe she'll calm down by then and we won't have to go," David added. He gave Sara a kiss good-bye as he pushed Jack out the door in front of him.

"Wishful thinking."

Sara watched David's car pull down the drive and disappear. After finishing her coffee, she went through a mental checklist of the day's chores. Sara wanted to have them finished before heading out to the barn. The new blacksmith was arriving later that morning, which translated into at least three hours spent supervising his work.

First stop on the list was Jack's room. Sara needed to collect his dirty laundry, which was supposed to be piled in a basket in his closet. In reality, most of the clothes were near that vicinity but few actually found their way into the target. She was leaning over to pick up a discarded pair of socks when the miniature gold key swung out from under her blouse. Having forgotten that she had been wearing it, she stood straight up to listen for any eerie or unusual sounds. Silence. She stuck her head out of the closet door to listen more closely. Still nothing. Letting out a sigh of relief, Sara carried the now full basket to the next stop, the guest bedroom where Leila had stayed. She collected the sheets and towels, adding them to the heavy load of soiled clothes.

When Sara made it to the laundry room with her load, she realized that she had forgotten about their coats. They were still in the washer from the other day, a semi-dry, wrinkled mess. As she reset the controls to rinse, goose bumps exploded up her arm, triggering memories that seeped back from a time and place long ago, memories that were not her own. Sara held onto the side of the washer as her head started to spin.

An infant's distinctive cry echoed in the small space. The cocoon of darkness, pierced only by a single light, created a pale blue aura around the woman's outstretched arms. The swaddled baby found temporary comfort at her heaving bosom as the scarlet river carried her away. There was no turning back.

"No, no, no. Stop it! This is not real," Sara insisted. She covered her ears with her hands until the world was silent again. When she removed them, the sound of a truck rumbling toward the barn signaled that the spell was broken. The milky images faded away, leaving Sara shaken but back in the present. Trying to recover, she looked around the room to get her bearings. Her watch read eight forty-five.

"Okay. It was nothing. I'm fine," she assured herself. "Only the blacksmith. And he's early. We may have to hang onto this one."

Thankful for the immediate distraction, Sara whistled for the dogs to join her. Outside, she saw an older man climb out of his pickup truck. The rear bed of the vehicle had been converted into a traveling workshop. Approaching the barn, she could see a man who looked too old to still be doing this kind of backbreaking work. He smiled when he saw Sara with the massive dogs trotting by her side.

As Sara came within a few feet of him, he held out his hand to offer a polite greeting. She noticed that his hands were thickly callused, with knuckles that were cracked from the combination of dry skin, cold weather, and manual labor. Deep crevices lined his face, and a full head of gray hair capped him. The only features that still looked young were his deep blue eyes.

"Hello there, ma'am. I believe we spoke on the telephone the other day. I'm James Sullivan," he cheerfully announced.

"So glad to meet you. I'm Sara, and this is Emma, my groom. The large dogs are Buster and Madison, and that little ball of fur is Jake." While Sara was speaking, she became aware that the black-smith was staring at her with the oddest expression. "What?"

"Oddest thing. You look familiar to me. Have I done any shoe-ing for you before? I usually don't forget folks I've worked for in the past."

"No, this is the first time. I guess I have one of those com-mon faces found in equestrian circles…weathered," she kidded.

"Well, I would hardly call you weathered. I guess I could be mixing you up with someone else, but I've always been pretty good about keeping people straight. There's definitely something famil-iar about you. I'll have to think on it. I know I've met you some-where. Most likely while I was covering a show, just not sure where."

Sara let it drop as they walked through the barn.

"What do you recommend for winter shoeing?" Sara asked. "Should I add snow pads, pull shoes, or follow their regular shoe-ing protocol? I didn't face this problem in Pennsylvania because we had an indoor ring at our place. Not so lucky here. We may need to build one."

"I would recommend sticking with what you have on those show horses, ma'am," James said. "In my experience, it's always better to avoid pads whenever possible. You can do plenty of hack-ing on the plowed dirt roads running adjacent to your property. That will keep your mounts in fine condition. They really don't require fancy shoeing for this surface. I would recommend screw-ing in your small road studs for traction. Plus, I put faith in the predictions made in *The Farmer's Almanac*, and this year it's calling for an early spring."

The sage old man made a convincing enough case for both Sara and Emma. They nodded their heads in agreement. Sara stayed to watch his work. Gale Force was the first horse led out. James took one look at the enormous steed and patted his muscular neck.

"Sure is a big fella, isn't he? Do you hunt him?" he asked as he bent over and lifted his front left hoof.

"He came over from Ireland not too long ago. He was hunted a few times over there. Honestly, I think all the horses and ponies over there start out that way. Personally, I haven't taken to it. He's strictly going to be a show horse here in the States. No need to risk ending up with an unnecessary injury," Sara answered.

"Ain't that the truth. But still, he looks built for it," he said, looking up at her from under the gray horse's belly. "Used to be that the hunt rode right through this property. They haven't in many years though. Not since Patrick shot himself. They couldn't bring themselves to ride here anymore." He returned to his task, not realizing that he had just dropped a bomb.

"What?" Sara said, startled.

Nobody had mentioned anything about someone committing suicide out here. The two women were stunned by what the old man had revealed.

"What happened?" Emma asked as she sat down on the trunk closest to the action.

"Old Pat had gone a bit mad near the end," he said as he attended to pulling off the old shoe and trimming the horse's sole with a curved blade.

Buster darted back and forth, stealing the cast-off hoof slices. Sara expected to find them in a regurgitated mess later. She was too distracted to yell for him to go away.

"I'm not sure about everything that happened out here. True, I was his blacksmith for a long time, but I only came by every seven to eight weeks. He wasn't one for talking much either. Lester, the old farm manager, knows a lot more, but he's been off living in the Blue Valley nursing home for years. I'm not even sure he's still alive," he said, straightening up to stretch his back. The old man switched to the other side of the horse to pick up the right front hoof as he continued talking. "Lester lived out in the tenant house for decades. I'm real surprised that you didn't know about the suicide, but I reckon they wouldn't put that in a sales brochure. I think that's why the place stayed empty for so long. None of the locals around here wanted it with its history of bad luck and all."

"You mean the suicide?" Emma chimed in before Sara could spit out the same sentence.

"Well, that and little Michael dying. Years earlier, their son, Michael, was out riding with his older sister, Katy. They were racing and there was a terrible accident. He went flying off his pony and hit his head on the stone wall. No helmet. The boy never regained consciousness. Died a few days later. Katy was devastated. He was only about eight or nine and she was just a few years older. She blamed herself, and the worst part was that old Patrick, their dad, blamed her too. It was the beginning of the end for the family. Maureen, their mother, was never the same. She had been a real feisty redhead, a good match for her tough husband. Lester told me the little boy's death shattered her spirit. She was nothing but a shell afterward. The poor broken-hearted momma would bring flowers out to the wall every year on her baby boy's birthday and sing him a lullaby. She had the most beautiful voice, like an angel. I remember stopping my truck on the lane one time. She was out there all alone, kneeling down. I wanted to make sure she was all right. She just kept singing. Didn't even acknowledge my presence. Nearly ripped my heart clear out of my chest."

He stood up and leaned on Gale Force, making him shift his weight, before returning to his story. The two women sat motionless, their mouths open in a speechless stupor.

"After that I think Patrick terrorized them all with his temper. He shot the poor pony in a rage the night after his son died. He drank more and more. The hunt had to ask him to step down as Master because he had become too dangerous to ride with. Eventually the older girls moved away. I heard some say to New York or somewhere up in New England. I was here once when one of the girls came back. I wasn't sure if it was Grace or Eileen. They were real lookers those two, had dark hair and blue eyes. I was kind of sad he ran them off. I wouldn't have minded dating either one of them. Their little sister Katy, well, she couldn't forgive herself. She became a nun. I guess she felt she needed to serve God afterward."

Mr. Sullivan stopped long enough to move his small, wheeled box of tools back to Gale Force's hind leg. He bent down to resume his work and his story.

"I used to ask Patrick about the girls. Sometimes he would tell me a little, other times he would just get angry, so I would drop it. I think the two older girls got married and had a whole slew of kids. One time he mentioned that Eileen was having another child, like her ninth or tenth. Can you imagine? Nine or 10 kids, now that'd be sure ta drive you bonkers. But then again, they were good Catholic girls."

"I can't imagine at all!" Sara said. Emma nodded in animated agreement.

"Whatever happened to Maureen?" Emma asked.

"She passed away pretty young, way before Patrick did. Honestly, I think it was from a broken heart. She sort of withered away from sadness over the loss of her son. The girls got as far away from this place as possible and never looked back. You can't blame them. Patrick had become a real tyrant. One episode stuck in my head. I remember getting here really early one morning. I had made plans to go to visit my sister, but Lester had called the night before saying one of the horses had thrown a shoe. He wanted a favor. He asked me to stop on my way out of town to stick a shoe on some mare. So I get here first thing and I see one of the girls with a baby. It was after they had moved away. I guess she had brought a grandbaby back to show her parents. Anyway, Patrick was swearing and yelling at her to leave and never come back. I could see Maureen at an upstairs window, looking down at them. I'm not sure what the heck took place, but believe me when I say it was ugly. I could tell he was really scaring that poor girl. I yelled up to them because I thought he was going to haul off and hit her right there in front of me. But she took off, got the hell outta here. It was one morning I wish I had been late. He stormed back in the house, and to be frank, I was thankful for that. The last thing I needed was for him to come after me. He was a big man and could have beaten the tar right out of me. Ugly. Just ugly. I never saw any of the girls after that. Lester told me that was the last straw. It was only Patrick and Maureen from that point on," he said, still focused on his task.

"I'll be damned," was all Sara could think to say. She was reeling from the shock.

Emma sat shaking her head. They were silent while James finished the last hoof. He walked to the back of his truck and selected shoes for Gale Force. After heating them in a small gas furnace, he took a few minutes to pound out each curved piece of steel. Plumes of awful-smelling smoke rose up around him, as he moved from leg to leg, pressing the red-hot shoes to the bottom of each hoof. This gave Sara some time to chew on everything she had heard.

"You know, the last few days we've had some strange things happen out here. My husband and I are starting to think the place is haunted," Sara said, as the old man plunged the hot shoes into a bucket of cold water to cool them before the final nailing.

"Wouldn't surprise me if Patrick refused to leave," he declared matter-of-factly. "Stubborn old S.O.B. that he was."

Sara's mind was whirling through the details of his story. She wanted to run up to the house to call David right now, but he was probably already in his meeting. She tried to imagine how she would go on if anything ever happened to Jack. She knew the heartache of losing a child at birth. You grieve for what could have been and the sparse time with a barely known life. To lose your child after watching him grow, sharing his life with all its joys, sorrows, little hurts and large triumphs would be unbearable.

Sara felt sorry for the family that had lived there before. What torture the little girl must have gone through, blaming herself for her brother's accident and then the disintegration of her family. She wondered if it was the guilt that had driven her to become a nun. Did she give her life to God as a way to even the payment of her brother's lost life, or could God have been her only salvation in the months and years after? It would have made sense that, in a household with a father drinking himself into madness, a mother who became vacant, and sisters who fled as soon as possible, she turned to God as a means of survival. Sara suspected that Katy had repaid the Lord by devoting her life to his cause.

"I wonder if they're still alive?" Sara asked under her breath.

"Pardon?" Emma asked, indicating that she didn't hear the question.

"Oh, sorry. I said I wondered if they were still alive, the three daughters," she clarified.

"I think they probably are. Someone told the bank to liquidate everything and sell it all off. The trustees would know where they are. I bet it took a good while for them to track those girls down," the old man shared as he finished up hammering a shoe on a hind hoof. "Lester may know. That is, if he's still coherent or alive. He lived here as long as they did. I bet 60 years."

"Explains the condition of my place," Emma said sarcastically.

Sara nodded in agreement.

"He couldn't stay here alone once Patrick died. In the later years, his primary role must have been to keep old Pat company. Lester was part of the farm after all that time, a permanent fixture. They let the place go. No more horses or hounds. He couldn't keep up with the chores. They stopped mowing and caring for the grounds. Hell, I bet they didn't do anything to the house in twenty years. I think Patrick was just waiting for the time to pass so he could join Maureen. I guess he couldn't wait any longer. It's sad. A real tragedy," he said with genuine sympathy.

"Well, he isn't going to scare Sara and her family off. We only believe in good things happening. Right, Sara?" Emma emphasized.

"Absolutely. I'm pretty tough and stubborn myself. This is my home now and nobody, alive or dead, is going to drive me out of here. So he can move on along to his final destination, because I am home!" she said with solid determination.

The old man looked over at her. A broad grin swept across his face, making the creases around his mouth and eyes deepen. "I like that in a lady. No nonsense here. I guess Patrick has met his match. Good luck with the place. I'm glad to see fresh life in here. Look at all you have done already. I haven't seen it looking this good in decades. And I must add, you two are an improvement over Pat and Lester in both looks and attitude," he said, giving the ladies a wink.

Sara's attention was drawn away to Buster, who she could see out beyond the truck. He was hunched over, vomiting up the discarded pieces of hoof that he had been greedily gorging on the entire morning. The grisly sight made her grimace in disgust.

"Very attractive," Emma said, nodding in the direction of the sick dog.

"I better put the dogs in after he finishes puking or this will go on all day," Sara said. She stood up and walked past the truck.

All three dogs perked up, sensing her departure.

"Thanks, Mr. Sullivan. I'll be down in a little bit with a check," she said. "Come on, you revolting beasts. Up to the house."

CHAPTER NINE

When Sara made it back to the house, she remembered the coats in the wash. She hung them up to dry and stuffed another load in the washer. She could hear the beeping of the answering machine in the other room. She followed the sound and saw that she had four messages. The three dogs darted around her, making it nearly impossible to reach the flashing button. Finally managing to secure a clear path to the insistent machine, she hit play. The first recorded voice was David's.

"Hi. I was getting bored driving down here so I thought I would check to see how your day is going. I'll call when I get a break. Hope you get to ride. Love you."

Message two was from a mortgage company seeing if they wanted to refinance. Message three was from the mother of a little boy in Jack's class whose son was having a birthday party. She was calling to see if Jack could attend. The last phone call came from her Aunt Donna. The tremor in her voice spoke more than her words. She wanted her niece to call her immediately.

Frozen by the last message, Sara stared at the answering machine. She hit the play button again, this time skipping over the first three. Listening to her aunt's wavering tone, she sensed that something bad had happened, something very bad. As she picked up the phone, tears silently started rolling down her cheeks. In her heart, she knew it had to do with her mother without having to confirm it. Sara dialed and waited for her aunt to answer, but was surprised when she didn't pick up. Instead it was her old neighbor, Mrs. Shilling.

"Oh, Sara. I'm so sorry. Your aunt, well, your aunt isn't in any condition to talk right now." The voice at the other end faltered for a moment. "Sara...I'm so sorry. Your mother passed away last night. I'm not clear on all the details. I came over when I saw the ambulance arrive. The EMTs have sedated your aunt and are trying to get the specifics on what happened to your mom. I'm not certain, but it sounds like it may have been a heart attack or a stroke."

Sara felt weak, as if someone had removed the bones from her legs. Buster seemed to instinctually gravitate to her side like a magnet. She sunk down to her knees and clutched the big dog's neck. She wasn't sure if she could breathe. It seemed like all the air had suddenly been sucked out of the room. Frantically her mind argued that this couldn't be real, it couldn't be true.

"Oh, God," was all she could get out.

"Sara, I'm so sorry. Is there someone I can call to come stay with your aunt? Do you have other family close by?" asked the voice on the other end.

Sara was having a hard time focusing. She heard herself speaking from a distant place. It was as if she had stepped outside of her own skin. The shock was buffering her senses. "Yes, I'll come as soon as I can get there. David is down in Richmond. I'll have to call him to come home. We'll try to get there tonight."

"Please, do you have someone to call for your aunt? I can stay, but I'm sure she would prefer family," Mrs. Shilling said delicately.

"Of course. I'm sorry. Um, I guess my cousin, Laura. She's in Connecticut...Stamford. She's Donna's daughter. She should be able to get to you within the hour. I'll call her now."

"Really, I don't mind. I imagine that you have other calls to make as well as travel plans. Why don't you let me call your cousin? The name was Laura, right?"

"Yes, that's correct. I appreciate all you're doing. Hold on for a moment and I'll get you her number." She reached over Buster's neck and felt for the address book sitting next to the base of the phone. She found it and read off the number.

"I'm so, so sorry, Sara. I know this must be awful. If I can do anything else, please let me know," urged the familiar person from her childhood.

"Mrs. Shilling, I'm so grateful that you're there. I'm sure my aunt is a basket case. She shouldn't be alone. If you don't mind, would you please ask the EMTs what they are going to do with my mother? Where are they going to take her?" Sara asked, while wiping her cheeks with her shirtsleeve. She was left hanging as the distraught neighbor inquired.

A hand cupping the receiver muffled the mixture of voices on the other end of the line. "They said to go ahead and contact the funeral parlor you wish to use. Someone from the home will pick her up from the hospital morgue. Of course, that's assuming that you don't want an autopsy. The ambulance worker said there are telltale signs of a massive heart attack."

"No, no. There's no need for an autopsy. Please tell my aunt that we will be getting in very late tonight. I'll call the funeral home from here to alert them to the situation and confirm that I'll see them in person sometime tomorrow. Thanks so much, again. Bye."

"Good-bye, dear."

Sara hung up, sat on the floor, and sobbed. The distance that had allowed her to move through the conversation had collapsed, sending her careening into a wall of ugly and unwanted emotions. Long buried fears of abandonment surfaced along with feelings of intense vulnerability. Sara's entire body was racked with rhythmic spasms as her defenses were cruelly torn away from her. Buster, who was sprawled out in front of her, swung his head up, resting his jaw on her thigh. She wrapped her arms around the large animal and held on tightly. She used him as an anchor to the present as wave upon wave of bittersweet memories washed over her, threatening to drown her in unspeakable despair. It must have been 30 minutes or more before her mind surfaced from the unyielding onslaught of anguished feelings that had essentially crippled her. The brief respite was long enough to call David. The clock on the wall showed that lunchtime was approaching, giving her hope that he would answer his cell phone. It rang but immediately flipped over into his voicemail.

"David, it's me. You need to come home right away. My mother died. The paramedics think she had a massive heart attack.

I need you. God, I need you. Please call me," she sobbed.

Drying her face, she spoke to the enormous dog next to her. "Buster, how could this happen? I don't understand. I'm going to be sick. I don't think I can make it. How do I go on without my mom? How could she leave me like that?"

He looked up with droopy eyes, giving her the impression that he understood her sadness.

"Okay. I need to focus. I need to get organized. I don't have time to fall apart. God, there's so much to do. I need to make the final arrangements, pick up Jack, pack our things, tell Emma and Carlos…and Leila. I have to call Leila," she said to her furry companion.

Sara decided to attack the list in reverse. She had just hung up with her best friend when David called. He listened quietly as she repeated the information she had left on his voicemail.

"Don't worry, honey. We should be ready to leave in a matter of hours. I've already explained the situation to my clients, and I'm on my way to get Jack. Right now, the last thing I want is for you to get behind the wheel of a car. Your only job is to have everything ready when we arrive," he explained. "Sara, I can't tell you how sorry I am. You'll get through this. We'll do it together. I love you and Jack does too. Remember, you still have us. I promise, I'm not going anywhere. You are not alone."

"Thanks, hon. I know that. I'll see you in a bit. I love you too," she replied.

Sara dreaded returning to the barn to tell Emma, but it had to be done. As she approached the younger woman, Sara knew that her red eyes revealed her inner devastation.

"My Lord. Are you all right? What's happened?" Emma asked, causing the old blacksmith, who was nailing a front shoe on Trevor, to pause in mid-swing.

Sara sighed deeply before speaking. "I received a call from New York. My mother died. It looks like she had a heart attack. David is on his way home as we speak. We'll be leaving as soon as he pulls in. I need you and Carlos to take care of the farm while we're gone. I suspect that we'll be away for at least a week."

"No. I can't believe it. I'm so sorry. Don't concern yourself with the farm for an instant," Emma assured her. "I'll ring Carlos to see if he'll consider staying with me during your absence. He can sleep in the house with the dogs. Truth is…I'm not brave enough to be the only one here after listening to Mr. Sullivan's account of the estate's tawdry history."

"Asking Carlos to stay here is a good idea. It's safer, ghost or no ghost. Here's a signed check. Fill it out for Mr. Sullivan when he finishes with the shoeing," Sara said, handing it to her.

"You're taking the news quite well. I swear I would be nothing more than a blasted puddle."

"Ha. Looks are deceiving. Buster bore the brunt of the storm. He may not dry out for days. Unfortunately, a major drawback to being an only child is having the responsibility of managing all the details. Planning the funeral falls squarely on my shoulders. Come to think of it, I'm not sure if that's good or bad. I don't have time to wallow in my grief."

"I didn't consider that. Not an enviable position," Emma concluded.

"Sorry, ma'am. It's a terrible thing to lose your mama," the old man said before she left.

"Thank you. I appreciate your kind words. Hopefully your next visit will be uneventful," Sara replied, forcing a weak smile.

He nodded in agreement as she walked away.

Sara spent the next hour packing for her family. There were two small suitcases and one garment bag near the back door when the garage door opened. She could tell that Jack had been crying on the way home. The little boy was unable to hold back his tears when he saw her. He wrapped his arms around her waist and cried.

"It's not fair, Mom! Daddy told me Grandma went to heaven and I'm never going to see her again. It's not fair! She never told us she was going away! How could she leave? Didn't she love us? I want her to come back," he repeated over and over.

"I know, Jack. I agree. Life is sometimes terribly unfair. And this is one of those times. But I promise you that she loved us and wouldn't want us to be so upset," Sara softly said, trying to soothe the child's pain and conceal her own.

David silently took both of them in his embrace.

Over the next few days, grieving friends and relatives replayed the experience she had with her son like a skipping record. The chorus sang out in melancholy harmony how unjust and untimely her mother's passing had been. Sara drifted through a cocooned fog of condolences during the wake and funeral, but the tenuous emotional barrier cracked when her mother's coffin was lowered down next to her father's. At that moment, her entire world shifted. Feelings of isolation strangled her, making it hard to breathe. Even with David, Jack, and Leila by her side, not to mention the throng of near and distant relatives that materialized to show their respect, these feelings were still there. They bubbled up from a place deep in her soul, where the instinctual thread that tells an infant to rely on the profound love and protection only a parent can provide dwells. All that was left was an innate, unsettling fear. Sara recognized that her delicate connection to feeling whole and secure was broken, lost to the inevitability of death. She was on her own. Sara shivered when she felt Jack touch her hand. Looking down she saw tears lining his red cheeks. She pulled him closer to her and kissed the top of his head. She was determined that he would always feel safe, no, be safe.

It had started to sleet by the time they had turned to walk back to the waiting limo. David had made an executive decision that they should stay at a hotel versus Sara's childhood home. Climbing into the long black car, a wave of apprehension came over her at the thought of walking into her parents' house, knowing they were gone. Sara's cousins had managed to take care of her aunt as well as prepare the post funeral reception at the house. She had switched into business mode after learning the news, refusing to let herself cry since that first morning in Virginia, but now, she wasn't sure if she could maintain that composure. David sensed this and held her hand tightly on the 15-minute drive from the cemetery. He eventually broke the silence by bringing up something the funeral director had shared with him.

"Sara. I've been meaning to give this to you," he said, pulling a blue Waterman pen out of his coat pocket. He handed it to his wife. "Apparently, the medical examiner had passed it along to Mr. Volpe at the funeral parlor after prying it out of Maria's hand."

Sara recognized it as a birthday present she had given her mother a few years back. She remembered she had wrapped it up along with some pretty writing paper engraved with her mother's initials. The idea that her mother was holding the long, sleek instrument when she died pierced cleanly through Sara's heart making her wince. She tried to hang onto the stoic demeanor she had so desperately constructed, but this was too much to ask. Tears spilled down her cheeks as tremors ignited every muscle. David silently laid her head against his shoulder as she abandoned any hope of remaining detached.

"It's all right. I'm here. I know your dirty little secret: You're not nearly as tough as you want people to believe. I probably understand you better than you do yourself, Sara Miller. You are not alone. I have you and I'm never going to let you go," he promised.

David smoothed her hair and kissed her forehead. Sara was about to ask something when the limo pulled to a stop. She closed her eyes for a minute, not wanting to think about having to make small talk for the next couple of hours. When she opened them, the driver had the door open and David was encouraging her to step out. She rolled the pen between her sweaty palms and slid it into her purse. After wiping the salty streams from her face and blowing her nose, she followed Jack out into the cold. The enormous willow tree that once held her tree fort looked sad, dripping in what was fast becoming an icy coating. It appeared that it too was mourning. She felt David's arm come around her waist, coaxing her up the path that led to the front door. She could see her cousin, Isabella, through the bay window, alerting everyone to her arrival. The smell of lasagna and other Italian dishes filled the air in the living room as they entered. Sara's stomach turned at the thought of food. As she greeted the few guests who were already in the house, she could hear car doors closing, marking the arrival of additional grievers. It wouldn't be long before the room was crammed so tightly that you couldn't see the opposite wall.

"Here. Let me take those damp things," Isabella said, giving them each a peck on the cheek before grabbing their coats and speeding off to attend to the newly arriving guests.

Sara saw Leila walk through the door, only to be whisked away by another one of her cousins. They waved to one another from across the room, but that was as close as they could get.

Claustrophobia engulfed Sara as a constant barrage of people filed by, wanting to know how she was "holding up." She would have fled outside, but the weather was getting worse. She finally tugged on David's arm, alerting him to her escape.

"I need a minute to myself. I'm going to start screaming my head off if one more person asks how I'm doing. Can you block anyone from coming after me?" Sara whispered.

"You got it. Send up a smoke signal if you need me. I'll come running with a fire extinguisher," he said, trying to elicit a smile.

Sara kissed him on the cheek, a reward for his gallant attempt at making her feel better. As she sneaked down the hallway, memories from her childhood played in her mind. She inched the door open to her old bedroom and stepped back in time. It was the same color, but most of the trappings from her childhood had been removed. On the dresser sat a lone music box. She turned it over and wound the key, releasing the notes to a tune she had not heard in years. An angel with a chipped wing turned in time to the music. Sara walked over to the window that framed the backyard. Looking through the frosted glass, she reminisced about her neighborhood friends and the time they had spent playing silly games. The children had all grown up and moved away. The last note of the music box signaled for Sara to move on.

She closed her bedroom door before turning toward her parents' room. Sara took a deep breath, not certain of whether she could find air once inside its walls. The idea of having to sort through her deceased parents' belongings made her feel queasy.

After her father's death, her mother had been unable to part with most of his personal possessions. Now the responsibility fell on their only child. But it would not be today, for today was for remembering how things were while they were alive. Whereas Sara's room evolved, her parents' room had stood still. It was exactly as it had been when she was a child. It even smelled the same. Ironically, this both comforted and ravaged her senses. The happiness that filled her early years cut too deeply as she measured what had been stripped from her life.

Sara sat down on the bed facing her mother's dresser. The depth of her loss seemed to take hold as she inhaled the memories of this room. Tears flowed in spite of her efforts to push back her emotions. She suddenly felt very alone and frightened.

Some time had passed before she realized that Jack had materialized next to her. He was able to bridge the gap from what used to be to the present moment. He took her hand in his and reached up with his other to gently caress her cheek. Through his innocent wisdom and uncomplicated love he touched her heart, lifting her out of a dark place.

"Mom, don't be so sad. Grandma and Grandpa are in heaven and they are happy to be together again. They must have missed each other a lot. Now we will have lots of angels looking over us. You still have Daddy and me and we love you more than anything," he said in a soft and comforting whisper.

She took him in her arms and hugged him, the present saving her from the past. David appeared at the bedroom door.

"Is everything all right in here?" he asked.

Sara looked up from the embrace. "It will be," she said, snuggling back into the crook of the little boy's neck.

David extended his hand, encouraging Sara and Jack to return to the reception.

Jack stood beside his father waiting for his mother to join them.

Sara glanced around wiping the tears off her face. "It's not going to be fun going through all this stuff," she said without looking at David.

"I know. Worry about that tomorrow. Just get through today," he answered.

"You're right," she said turning to him, turning toward her future.

The next couple of hours were spent listening to relatives express their ongoing shock over Maria's sudden death. She recognized that David was steering the subject toward other topics, as she became more and more mentally depleted. She was not alone in needing a protective shield. Sara's Aunt Donna spent the afternoon sitting on the sofa in a tranquilizer-induced haze. Due to Donna's fragile state, everyone avoided questioning her about the circumstances surrounding her sister's death. Sara was curious about what was behind her mother's urgent desire to see her, but it seemed cruel to try to get answers so soon.

By three o'clock, the weather turned foul with sleet firing down from the gray sky. All those who had congregated gave their final farewells and set out to brave the elements.

Leila retreated. "I'll see you guys at the hotel. I'm out of here before I get stranded."

Laura and Isabella had cleaned up and were getting their mother into Laura's sedan when Sara noticed one of her cousins running back toward the house.

"What's wrong?"

Laura reached the front landing and pulled her coat tighter around her neck before speaking. "Listen, my mom is insisting that I tell you about your mother's notepad. I guess she had been writing something down that she wanted to show you. My mom said you were supposed to come up this weekend to talk to her about some nightmares she had been having. Anyway, she's all worked up because we forgot to let you know where it is. Mom discovered it on the floor when she found your mother. Apparently, she stuffed it in one of the nightstand drawers. I haven't looked, so I can't tell you which one or what the tablet contains. She's agitated about it and adamant that you read the thing. I guess the drugs are wearing off."

"Thanks for telling me and for everything else you did today.

Assure your mom I'll go read it right now," Sara said with a tired smile. "Please be careful driving home. It's turning to snow, which means the roads are going to be a real mess. We don't want to go to any more funerals."

Laura nodded in agreement, waved, and ran back to the car. Sara stood at the door watching as they drove down the street. David had overheard their conversation and retrieved the pad even before Sara had closed the front door.

"You want to do this now or back at the hotel?" he asked, handing it to her.

"I'm not sure. I have to wonder if her medical condition contributed to those nightmares and anxiety," Sara commented.

"I don't know if it works that way, honey. I guess it could even be the other way around. Ultimately, it doesn't really matter. Trying to figure out cause and effect would be a waste of your energy," David suggested.

Sara looked at the notepad in her hand. It was a small spiral notebook with a red plastic cover. She sat down in her father's favorite armchair as pictures of a young version of her parents proudly holding her as a baby gathered dust on a nearby side-table. David took a seat across from her on the couch. She could hear Jack humming a tune down the hall. To Sara's relief, he was busy entertaining himself.

"Go ahead if you are going to read it. Otherwise we need to get moving with this weather," David prodded.

Sara opened it and started to read the disjointed sentence to her husband. "An old man yelling at a young woman. I don't remember what he was saying. She is afraid of him. There was a lot of blood. I don't know where I am. I think I'm in a small room with no windows. I saw a woman crying. She is older than the woman from the other night. She is different, but I see the same man. He appears over her shoulder. He tells her to be quiet. That no one will ever know. It was taken care of. I don't know what it means."

Sara turned the page and continued reading. "The man was back tonight. He was angry, really angry. He was in darkness and I could barely make him out. He was saying that she came back.

She was never supposed to come back."

Sara shook her head in frustration and flipped through the written pages. It looked like there might be about a dozen or more pages, each with a few lines written on them. About halfway through, something caught her eye. She turned back a couple of sheets.

"What?" David asked. "The color is draining from your face."

"It can't be. Oh, my God. I'm going to puke," she said bending at the waist to put her head between her knees.

David crossed the room and took the pad out of her hand. "It's a key. It kind of looks like the one Jack found," he said. "The writing below it says…Save my baby! Save her. Get her out of the house. He will kill her if he has the chance. Go! Go now! The key will give her the answers. I have to tell Sara. She has to get out of there."

Sara lifted her head from between her legs. She and David looked at each other and for a moment both were speechless.

"David, how can this be?" she asked, taking the notebook back from him. She was visibly shaking. "It's not possible."

"Go to the last page that she wrote," David suggested.

"Still there. The key will save her, set her free. Tell Sara. Tell Sara, or it's…." Sara said. "She didn't finish. It ends in mid-sentence. Maybe she had the heart attack while writing." She didn't want to think about the implications that this held for all of them. She remembered what David had told her in the car.

"The pen, remember the pen?" she asked. "You told me it was still in her hand. Whatever's happening at our house killed her. I really think I'm going to be sick." David put his hand on his wife's shoulder. She looked up at him and handed the book to him. "Take it. I can't read anymore," she said as her eyes welled with tears.

He read through the rest silently. "Basically, the entries include a couple of women and an older man. She describes a lot of crying and blood but doesn't say where the blood is coming from. And she mentions a key and needing to warn you. The same stuff seems to be repeated over and over again," he summarized.

Sara watched him flip back the pages from the last entry.

"What are you doing?" she asked out of curiosity.

He held up a finger, signaling for her to wait a moment until he finished whatever it was that he was doing. "Sara, the one entry with the drawing of a key…." David paused before completing his sentence. "Honey, it landed on your birthday. That was the day she called wanting you to drive up here and the night that Jack found the miniature key in his room. See? She dated it."

Sara closed her eyes and put her head against the back of the chair. She wanted to flee from this craziness, but somehow she understood that she was entrenched beyond escape. She felt David's hands on her knees. He was squatting in front of her when she opened her eyes.

"I don't know what to say. It's nuts," he said, making her realize that he was clearly as perplexed as she was.

"What should we do?"

David shook his head. "About what?"

"What do you mean, about what? Are we in danger? What the hell is going to happen next?"

"Take a breath and calm down. Honestly, I don't have a clue. I can't comprehend how your mother could have been dreaming about these things. How she could know what that key looks like? I don't know why it's happening or what we do about it. Probably nothing. It has to be some sort of freaky coincidence," he said with a sigh.

"Yeah! I would definitely say it's a coincidence. But is it more than that?"

They sat without speaking for a few moments. The only sound was Jack's humming coming from Sara's old bedroom.

"Do you want to move? We could put the house on the market. Hell, we've done a ton of improvements. Its value has skyrocketed," David suggested.

"No, damn it! It's my house. So whoever or whatever is trying to drive us away isn't going to win. When we get back, I'm going to find a church and get a priest to bless the house. They can do an exorcism or whatever they do when someone has a ghost prowling around."

David was taken back. Her mood had switched from disbelief and fear to anger. Amazingly, her feisty, stubborn nature was pushing through the grief.

"I'm not so certain that we aren't becoming puppets in someone else's tragedy," she added. "And frankly, I don't like it one bit. But I sure as hell am not going to give up without a fight."

"Let me get this straight. Your plan is to go home, guns blazing, with a battalion of preachers shooting holy water out of their cannons," he joked sarcastically.

"Basically. What should we do about Jack? Do you think he should go to your parents until we sort all this out?"

"The jury is in; you've lost your mind. You want to keep him out of school to de-ghost our house? When I spoke to Emma, she said there hasn't been anything out of the ordinary. For Pete's sake, Sara, really! A ghost flying up here from Virginia didn't kill your mother. She's had high cholesterol and blood pressure for years. Freaking out over these dreams may have killed her, but that's more a reflection of her anxiety-riddled personality than anything else," David argued.

"I don't know. I guess you're right. But it's just so bizarre, since she hadn't even seen the house yet," Sara replied.

David pushed a lock of hair away from her brow. "I'm sure I'm right. Come on. We'll go home next week and live happily ever after. Just like we're supposed to. You're letting your imagination run wild, but if you would feel better getting the religious 'all's clear'—well, that's fine with me. I love you, you crazy woman."

Sara leaned forward and took her husband's face in her hands. "I know, and I love you for that. You and Jack are my world. I don't want to move again. I know we're supposed to be there. That's the point. We're the ones that are supposed to figure it out."

"Assuming there is anything to figure out," he stressed.

"Let's get out of here. It's been a very long day, and I am ready for a stiff drink," Sara said.

David stood up, pulling his wife out of the chair as he did. He put his arm around her shoulder and squeezed. He briefly left her side to round up Jack. They headed out to the car while Sara closed up the house. She turned the key in the lock and heard it click. The sound made her shudder. The rooms were dark and quiet. She realized that soon it would be some other family's home. Full of life again, the way a house should be. The sound of the engine starting behind her signaled that it was time to leave. She inhaled the painfully crisp air deeply into her lungs as she started toward the car. The snow seemed to part around her feet as she followed the nearly-covered path left by her friends and relatives.

CHAPTER TEN

The drive home for Sara, David, and Jack was long and uneventful. Boxes filled with china, photo albums, and Maria's jewelry were jammed into the back of the SUV. Sara carried the items from her mother's safety deposit box in a manila envelope on her lap. She hadn't had time to go through all the contents. They had located a copy of her mother's will for the attorney and then stuffed everything else away for further inspection later. The three of them were overjoyed when they finally pulled into their driveway late in the afternoon on Wednesday. They had been gone for nine days.

Virginia had experienced a warm front while they were in New York. Sara was surprised to see that almost all of the snow had melted. When she opened the car door, it smelled like spring, a welcome change from the consistently miserable weather they had endured for the past week. Sara was hoping this marked the turn of seasons, an early spring, the chance for life to renew itself. She needed this now more than ever.

The dogs were barking wildly in the house, adamantly demanding their release. The two frenzied Great Danes were standing on their hind legs with their front paws pressed against the windows. The Springer Spaniel was bouncing up and down underneath them.

"We better get up there before those idiots crash right through the glass," David warned.

"Get down," Sara yelled up toward the dogs, which only made them more agitated.

David and Jack were already bounding up the stone steps when Sara spotted her two employees strolling up from the barn. "Honey,

I'm going to talk to Carlos and Emma for a minute. I'll be right in."

David waved an acknowledgement without looking back. She walked toward the barn, meeting her help halfway.

"Hi, Sara. It's good to have you back. We are so sorry for your loss," Emma said glancing over at Carlos, who nodded in agreement.

The two women briefly hugged as the young man kicked at the dirt underfoot.

"I can't tell you how much I've appreciated the two of you taking care of the farm. And I wanted to thank you for the beautiful flower arrangement that you sent for the funeral," Sara said.

"You're very welcome," Emma replied, eliciting another nod of agreement from Carlos.

"How have all the non-human residents fared in our absence?"

"The horses were fine, but those bloody hounds were another story," Emma said.

"I'm sorry, Miss Sara. The dogs, they didn't like that you were gone. They howled and wouldn't eat. I think they must have lost 10, maybe even 15 pounds each," Carlos explained, looking down. "I tried everything, but they wouldn't eat. Buster was the worst. He was either pacing in the house or taking off down the field."

"Thanks for the effort, Carlos. It's not your fault. These big dogs are more sensitive than you could ever imagine. They'll gain the weight back in no time," she said, aware that he felt as if he let her down. She didn't want him to feel badly. It was an unavoidable situation and Sara was just happy to have people she could trust.

"Wait till you see the huge hole Buster dug," Emma added.

"Where?" Sara asked.

"Out front. That's why they're inside now. I haven't had time to fill it in," Carlos explained.

"Don't worry about it. Maybe we'll make it into a ditch or water jump."

"*Si*, Miss Sara. Whatever you want."

"I'm exhausted and I have a ton of unpacking to do. I'll see the two of you later."

"Give a shout if you need us," Emma added.

David had let the dogs out as Sara turned toward the house. The three came leaping across the lawn, joyously barking and yipping. They didn't seem capable of stopping in time to avoid a collision. As she braced herself for the tackle, they amazingly splintered off and ran around her. Sara spent time petting them, allowing them to welcome her home. She agreed with Carlos that they had lost a good bit of weight. Sara was as happy to see them as they were to see her. She was thrilled to be back and ready to leave all the pain behind her.

Sara could hear the television when she opened the back door. Jack was belly-laughing about something as she passed the living room. She longed to return to the regular rhythm of family life, cartoons and all. Unfortunately, in the back of her mind, she did not expect it to happen soon. As she made her way to the bedroom, she was distracted by David's voice resonating from the library. She could tell from his tone that he was on a business call. The timing of her mother's death could not have been worse for him. She listened outside the door to try and hear what he was saying.

"Yes, ma'am. The time of that flight into San Diego will work. And for the return, are there any direct flights that are earlier? Wonderful…yes. I have the flight numbers," he said.

He was apparently rescheduling the trip he had to cancel. Sara knew this trip was vitally important for her husband's business, but she dreaded the thought of him leaving.

"Very well then. I'll expect the confirmation via e-mail. Thanks for your assistance."

When Sara heard David hang up, she walked down the hall to talk to him.

"Hi. How are Carlos and Emma?" he asked when he saw her in the doorway.

"They're fine. Overworked and underpaid for sure. Carlos felt badly that the dogs lost a few pounds. I told him it wasn't his fault, but I'm not sure if he believed me," she said moving through the room to take a seat facing David. As Sara went to collapse into the chair, she noticed that the old locked diary was still lying across the cushion. She moved the leather journal out of her way, tossing it onto her husband's desk.

"I guess I never finished putting these away," she said pointing at one of the boxes filled with old books.

"A forgivable oversight," David replied.

"Yeah, but one more thing to unpack," she sighed. "Can you bring the stuff in from the car?"

"I think I can manage that," he said.

"Good, because I'm wiped out. I think I could use a long hot shower."

"Unfortunately, I have some other news that you're not going to like. The company I'm consulting with wants me out in California first thing Monday morning. I tried to push it back, but it was either go or lose the job altogether. I'm sorry. I didn't want to leave you so soon."

"I understand. You have to go. We'll be fine. I'll be fine. What day are you flying out?"

"First thing Sunday morning. I think I would feel better if Leila came out and stayed with you. What do you think?" David asked.

"I think Leila has missed enough of her own life over the past week. She took off all last week for the wake and funeral. The last thing she needs is to lose her business. She doesn't have to come out here to babysit me. I have Emma and Carlos around if I need them."

"Sara, you've been through hell. And I know you're still dwelling on your mother's dreams. Coming back to the house has you a little rattled. I don't like leaving you and Jack here alone."

"Then tell me, what exactly would Leila do? She isn't some psychic that can tell the 'ghosts' to go away. I told you that I'm going to handle this and I will. I want to talk to the old guy who used to work here. Apparently he's in a nursing home close by. Who knows? Maybe he can tell me something useful. Plus, like I said, I plan on getting a priest to come out to douse the entire place in holy water," she said adamantly.

He sat silently, observing her for a minute. "You win this round. But if anything, and I mean anything, weird starts happening and you get scared, grab Jack and go stay at Leila's. Promise me," David demanded.

"We'll see. I don't scare very easily," she answered. "But if anything spooky starts happening, I'll be sure to take Jack over to Leila's. However, I'm staying put. You want me to up and leave Emma here all by herself? That's just plain ridiculous. Sorry."

"Honest to God, you're impossible. Fine. Have it your way," he said, completely exasperated by their sparring.

"Fine. I'm going to shower now. Please bring the luggage inside so I can unpack when I get out," she said, rising to leave.

"Sara," David called as she stepped out of the library.

"Yes," she answered glancing over her shoulder.

"I love you."

"I know," she said with a smile.

It was nearing dusk by the time Sara stepped out of the shower. She wound one towel around her wet hair and rubbed another along her body until her skin was sufficiently dry. Looking into the partially fogged over mirror, she grabbed her toothbrush, applied a thin line of pale blue toothpaste to the bristles and scrubbed her teeth. After rinsing the foam from her mouth, she straightened up to unwrap her damp hair. She had just finished pulling the towel from her head when she caught a reflection of the shower door in the mirror. Standing perfectly still, Sara could feel the blood pounding violently in her neck. The name of her dead daughter, Grace, was spelled out in the mist that clung to the glass. Sara turned to face the shower, but the letters were gone. She looked back into the mirror, which confirmed that the name had vanished as quickly as it appeared. Sara walked over to the shower door. She ran her hand all over the interior of the door, brushing away the condensation. There was nothing inside but the soap and shampoo.

"You leave my daughter out of this. Do you hear me? What the hell do you want with us?" she said, pissed off that Grace was somehow being used to taunt her.

She heard David open the door to their bedroom and rattle

through with some luggage. The next thing she knew he had stuck his head in the bathroom. "Did you say something?" he asked.

"Jesus, David. I was just talking to myself. Let it go," she snapped. The last thing Sara wanted to do was tell him what happened after their go round in the library.

"Okay then," he grumbled under his breath, instinctively backing off from a situation that could easily escalate. He dropped the luggage on the bed and left to make another trip to the car. When he returned, he carried the manila envelope containing the items retrieved from Maria's safety deposit box. He tossed it onto the dresser. Sara came out of the bathroom and stood next to him. She wore no makeup, but had finished drying her hair. The towel wrapped around her body started to unravel as she searched through drawers for a sweater and jeans. It took only a minor movement to send it falling to the floor, leaving Sara completely exposed.

David backed up several steps and cocked his head. Sara caught him staring and flashed him a disgusted glance.

"What? I can't admire my beautiful wife?" he said.

"Please. I know you better. If you thought I would rise to the occasion, you would as well," she said as she picked up the towel and threw it across the room at him.

"I take great offense at that. I'm always a gentleman and you know it. Plus, I'm smart enough to realize that you are still terribly vulnerable, not to mention volatile. Not a safe combination under any circumstances," he added as he made a timely escape into the foyer.

"Go ahead. Run away before I can hurl something else at you!" she called after him as she slipped into a worn pair of jeans with ease. Normally she would need to suck in her belly to squeeze into this particular pair of pants. The stress from her mother's death had melted the pounds away. While admiring her sleeker figure in the dresser's mirror, Sara noticed the oversized envelope. As she reached for it, she heard a knock on the door.

"Mom? Are you in there?" asked Jack.

"One minute. I have to put my shirt on," Sara answered. She pulled a beige sweater over her head. "Okay. Come on in."

The boy climbed onto the bed, pouting. "Mom, do I have to go to school tomorrow?"

"Absolutely. Why?"

"I don't want to go. I want to stay here with you."

"Jack, you have to go to school. You've missed a week already. I know it must feel kind of awkward going back after being gone for so long, but you'll see, after 10 minutes, it will be like you never left. Your friends will be really glad to see you," she said, trying to reassure him that everything would be fine.

"That's not it. I don't care about my friends. I just don't want to leave you. What if something happens while I'm at school? I'm scared. What if you die like Grandma? If I'm home, I can protect you," Jack said, tearing up as he gazed at his mother.

This caught Sara off guard. She cradled her son in her arms, tightly hugging him. Clearly, she wasn't the only one shaken up by how suddenly her mother was taken. Sara hadn't anticipated that Jack would jump to the conclusion that she could leave him.

"I'm so sorry you're frightened. I promise you that nothing is going to happen to me or to your father. You need to go to school. How about if I wait with you for the school bus tomorrow? Dad has been hogging you every morning since we moved here. That will give us some extra time in the morning. What do you think?" she asked.

"Okay, Mom," he said with an uneasy smile.

"It's settled then. Why don't you go see if your dad needs any help bringing in the rest of the things from the car?" she suggested, hoping to get his mind off his worries.

Jack nodded in agreement and gave her one last neck-cracking hug before trotting to the door. "I love you, Mom."

"I love you, too. More than anything in the whole world, pumpkin," she said amazed at what a wonderful gift he was.

Sara sat on the bed for a few minutes, analyzing the situation. She had been so absorbed with her own grief that she had lost sight of Jack's reaction. Angry for not being more attentive to his need for psychological security, she swore to herself that she would be better at making sure he felt safe. The motherly need to protect one's child had shifted Sara's thoughts back to Grace's name appearing on the shower door. Was Grace trying to tell her something? She sifted through the bits and pieces of the last couple of weeks, unsure how they connected. Sara was left feeling both desperate and frustrated.

Picking up the towel that she had thrown at David, she realized that Jack had distracted her from looking through the envelope. She hung the towel on a hook in the bathroom, took another glance at the clear shower door, then returned to the bed to sort through the important items from her mother's safety deposit box. Sara unclasped the little metal rabbit ears that held the manila envelope closed and dumped the papers out onto the bed. She started at the top, looking over trust documents that her parents had set up more than a decade ago. She found their 1959 marriage certificate and her father's death certificate. Both of her parent's birth certificates were there, as well as her mother's baptismal record.

Sara set them aside and reached for the last item. She thought it odd that this envelope was sealed shut. Concerned about ripping whatever was inside, she retrieved a metal nail file from her bathroom drawer. She pushed the tip under one corner of the top flap and slid it along the edge, creating a clean slit. Sara sat on the edge of the bed frozen: In her hand were the documents detailing her adoption. Sara pulled out the old pieces of paper and looked at them. Sara's adoption had been handled privately, something unusual for the 1970s. Apparently, Maria's doctor had an associate in his practice whose patient wanted to give up a baby. The two doctors arranged for the transfer, with an attorney finalizing the paperwork. There were receipts from the various transactions, totaling about $500. Sara paused when she came across an agreement that her adoptive parents signed, promising that she would be raised Catholic.

Sara read over this and shook her head. She found this particular detail to be truly ironic, since she had refused to attend church from the time she was a teenager. Maria and Joe had done just about everything to push, demand, coax and outright bribe her to go, yet Sara's stubbornness withstood it all, and eventually her parents relented. She couldn't stomach the hypocrisy she saw on a weekly basis. Flawed, if not evil, people would confess their abhorrent behavior, assured of absolution for another week. Then on Sunday mornings, they would sit one after another in the church pews, feeling no responsibility toward the numerous victims they left in their wake. It made her so disillusioned that she chose to purge it from her own life.

Sara wondered what it would feel like, stepping back inside a church to ask for help after turning her back on religion so many years ago. She had visions of bursting into flames as she walked through a pair of heavily carved doors. This shook her into the present, causing her to set down the paper she still held in her hand. Sara picked up and unfolded the last item, a one-page legal document. It was the Surrogate Court Order finalizing her adoption. It listed her adoptive mother and father as being the petitioners to the court. Under that, the name of her birth mother, Grace Anne McCarthy, was typed. No biological father was identified. As her eyes scanned the old sheet of paper, she found the name she was given at birth. What an odd thing, she thought, to have a whole other identity. She never realized that babies were named before they were given up. Sara said it out loud, "Kathleen Teresa McCarthy." She didn't understand why her mother hadn't given her these documents when she told her about the adoption. Maybe Maria had been afraid that, with a name, Sara would search for her birth mother.

All sorts of scenarios were jumping through her mind when David walked into the room. Sara looked up at him from where she was sitting and thrust the paper out to him without a word.

"What's this?" he asked, taking it from her.

"Read it," Sara said. She followed David's eyes as they scanned down the page.

"Wow. You okay, Kathleen?"

"Very funny," she answered as she stood up. "Weird though, isn't it? I had another life. This other woman created me, named me, and then gave me up to strangers. I guess I have a hard time imagining how someone could do that. They would have to kill me first to take Jack away."

"We're not privy to this woman Grace's story. Who knows? Maybe she was some kind of drug addict or prostitute. She did you a favor. The bottom line is that your parents loved you," David said, in an effort to console her. "However, I do find it strange that we named our daughter Grace. That's a little creepy. Downright odd coincidence going on there."

"Christ! That's a little too bizarre for me." Sara felt as if she had been kicked in the stomach. It was too much of a coincidence that her birth mother and her dead daughter were both named Grace. And the writing on the shower door? She was sure it was all tied together. But how?

"Listen, I think it has been a miserably long day for all of us. This is the icing on the cake after one hell of a week. I think you need to come out and spend some quality time with your family. Get away from this muck. If you don't, it's going to suck you in like quicksand. It can wait," he said, folding up the paper and tossing it on the bed with the other things.

David wrapped an arm around Sara's shoulder and led her toward the bedroom door. As they went to leave, she glanced back toward the bed. Instinctively, she knew that David's assessment was chillingly correct. It would be waiting, waiting to reveal the multiple layers of its puzzle.

CHAPTER ELEVEN

When Sara awoke the next morning, a thick fog blanketed the fields. The weatherman on the radio was forecasting that it would rain on and off all day. Moisture clung to the barren branches of the tree that stood outside her bedroom window. She had planned to walk Jack out to the end of the driveway to meet the bus, but the nasty conditions made her re-evaluate her plan. They would take the car instead.

Jack was ready to leave in about 45 minutes. "Please, Mom. I really don't want to go to school. I think it's better if I stay with you. I can go to school anytime," he begged, repeating his reservations before climbing into the passenger seat. Jack was allowed to sit in the front for the short trip down the lane.

Sara's answer was the same as the previous day. "Jack, you have to go. I'll be fine. Nothing is going to happen to me or anyone else. Understand? Now relax. End of discussion."

As they backed out of the garage, Sara could barely make out Carlos' car through the mist. She was thankful that he made it to the farm safely.

Jack was uneasy and fidgeted nervously in his seat. "I bet I've missed a bunch of stuff at school. Do you think I'll have to make it all up? I hate that. You shouldn't have to do what you missed because then you have to do twice as much work as everyone else. It's not fair."

Sara was about say something to him when she slammed on the brakes. The force sent his wizard-themed lunchbox hurtling to the floor. A herd of deer seemed to magically emerge from the right. The nimble animals danced one at a time across the driveway, just a few feet in front of the stunned occupants. Sara couldn't believe her reflexes stopped the car before flattening "Bambi" right there in front of Jack. In what seemed like an instant, the lot of them disappeared, shrouded by the unyielding fog.

"Sorry, buddy. We don't want to have an accident in our own driveway." She retrieved the lunchbox from under her right leg and placed it back on the seat next to Jack.

"Thanks, Mom. Hope my sandwich didn't get too smooshed."

"Hope not. It didn't fall that far. I'm sure it will be edible."

At the end of the driveway, Sara turned the car off. They listened to the world news update for a few minutes before the flashing lights of his ride to school materialized. When the large yellow bus rolled to a stop, the driver pulled a lever to open the door. Jack leaned over and gave his mother a kiss on the cheek.

"Love you, Mom. I'll see you this afternoon," he said as he took hold of the door handle.

"I love you, too. Have a great day," Sara called after him.

She watched as he climbed up the steps of the bus and took a seat halfway back. He waved from the window as they pulled away.

Normally, Sara would have backed the whole way up to the house, but the fog was making it impossible to navigate in reverse. She decided that the best thing was to turn around. As the rear tires left the hard packed gravel, the sound of rubber spinning in mud was unmistakable, the high-pitched squeal of ceaseless grinding drowned out the radio. "Oh, shit!" Sara said as she repeatedly tried reverse, then drive. She could tell that the back tires were getting no traction at all.

"I knew we should have gotten four-wheel drive!" she yelled to no one but herself. Sara opened the door and stepped out to get a first-hand look at her predicament. The mud had engulfed her tires up to the rim.

"Crap, crap, crap!" she screamed, kicking the side of the car.

Sara knew she was going to have to hike back to get Carlos. They would need to bring the tractor down to pull her car out. As she started walking up the drive, it started to drizzle. Thankfully, she had thrown her coat on before leaving the house. She flipped the canvas hood up over her head in an attempt to limit how drenched she was becoming. It was remarkably quiet, not even a bird chirping. Visibility was only about 10 to 15 feet, making her wonder whether she would be trampled by a stray deer on the way back to the barn. The trees, stone walls and fences were completely enveloped, giving her no clear markers to judge her progress.

Out of the silence, Sara thought she could hear singing. She stopped walking to listen. It was low, but it sounded like a woman singing a lullaby. It had that soft, gentle sound used to soothe a child. She pulled off her hood, straining to make out the words. The rain quickly plastered her hair to her head. It was impossible to tell from which direction the voice was coming, for the haunting music seemed suspended in the air all around her.

Sara turned around several times. Cupping her hands to amplify her voice, she bellowed "Hello!" but the singing continued without any change in rhythm or tempo.

Sara tried again. "Hello. Is someone there?"

Still the lullaby floated delicately through the air, teasing her senses. It took her a minute to realize that she no longer knew which direction led up to the house and which led back to the car.

"Fantastic! This is starting the morning off just great," she mumbled to herself, not sure what to do next. "Hello. Can you hear me?" She hoped that either the singer or Carlos would respond, but neither did.

The soft lyrics grew slightly louder.

"Where are you?" she asked. Looking down at her feet, she wished she thought to put on her green "Wellies," but unfortunately she had slipped on leather loafers. By now she was completely drenched and pissed off. "Well, I'm not going to ruin these by chasing you out in that wet field."

Sara chose a direction and started walking with the hope that she was headed the right way. The melody drifted farther away and then finally stopped. She was relieved when the house came into sight. She stopped in the garage to change into her boots and then went to the barn to get Carlos. He was going to meet her down at the end of the driveway with the tractor and some chains. Sara's anger was fueling her need to find the source of the disturbing tune.

She walked back down the gravel lane, prepared to follow it out to whoever was singing. She could hear the tractor rattling down the driveway behind her. She stepped off into the grass to let Carlos chug past her. She waited for the sound of the tractor to fade in order to pick up the direction of the lullaby, but it was too late. It was gone. By the time she reached her car, Carlos was done hooking up the chains to the undercarriage.

"I'm ready for you to start the engine. Put the gear in drive and I'll pull you forward," the young Mexican explained.

Sara followed his directions closely, which allowed the car to break free of its muddy entombment within seconds. They both came to a stop once the vehicle was firmly back on the driveway. Carlos took the chains off and came around to Sara's window.

"Emma wanted me to let you know that Murphy's eye is swollen this morning. She was in his stall taking a look when you walked in the barn. She thinks he may need to see a vet," he told her, referring to Sara's big chestnut gelding.

"Perfect! The day is getting better and better. I'll come right up. And Carlos, thanks for pulling me out," she said. Sara raised the window and then crept along behind the tractor, afraid to pull around for fear of getting stuck again.

The fog was starting to thin out a little by this time, improving visibility slightly. For the second time that morning, Sara slammed on the brakes. Carlos didn't notice her stop. Sara put the engine into park and stepped out. Walking around the back of the car, she focused on the ground about 40 feet off to the right of the driveway. As she stepped off the gravel, onto the wet grass, it was as if Sara crossed over to another time. Lying on a large boulder rising out of the wet earth was a bouquet of flowers. She bent down and picked it up—irises, daisies, hyacinths, and tulips freshly cut and tied with a blue silk ribbon.

Sara's mind raced back to the day her mother died. James Sullivan had been at the farm that morning. She shuddered as she recalled the blacksmith's story about the death of the little boy who had lived at the farm. He recounted to Sara and Emma how the deceased boy's mother would carry flowers into the field and sing to him. She tried to remember the woman's name. She recalled that the boy's father was named Patrick.

"Damn it," she mumbled. She couldn't remember. "Emma may know."

Sara turned toward the barn. Carlos had disappeared and she could no longer hear the hum of the tractor. Grasping the flowers in one hand, she jogged back to the waiting car with her loose fitting boots threatening to fall off each time she lifted a foot. Sara tripped as she made it to the driveway, which catapulted her onto the jagged gravel chin first. She could feel the skin tear open on her palms. The flowers flew forward, rolling to a stop under the vehicle.

"Son of a bitch!" Sara cried and crawled over to the bottom of the still running car.

Exhaust fumes filled her lungs. Sara stretched her arm out, reaching for the bouquet, but she found herself swiping at nothing but air. It was too far from the edge to retrieve. She pushed herself back and stood up. Racing around to the driver's side, she got in and moved the gearshift into drive. After pulling forward about 10 feet, she returned the car to "park." Sara climbed out, ready to pick up her extraordinary find, but startlingly, it wasn't there. She checked under the car, assuming that the bundle of flowers were still covered, but they were nowhere in sight. The bouquet had vanished.

"No, no, no!" she screamed. "I saw them. I touched them. Damn you!" She got back in the car and sped the rest of the way up to the barn.

Carlos was returning from parking the tractor in a nearby shed when she screeched to a halt. "What happened?" he asked. "You were right behind me."

"You won't believe it if I tell you. Where's Emma?"

"She should be inside the barn. You're bleeding," he said with worry etched on his face.

Sara didn't respond to him but walked directly in the barn. "Emma, where are you?"

"In here," she called out from the tack room.

When Sara appeared in the doorway, she could tell from the telephone conversation that Emma was talking with a vet.

"Very good then. We will expect you within the hour. Goodbye."

"Emma, I need your help," Sara said with urgency.

Emma turned around. Shock flooded her face as she looked at Sara's chin. "Bloody 'ell! What happened to you?" she asked.

Sara realized she wasn't going to get much farther without providing an explanation for her ragged condition.

"I saw something out in the field, and when I went to take a look, I tripped. Emma, listen. This is very important. Remember the day my mother died? Mr. Sullivan was out here shoeing horses. He told us about the family who lived here, the McHughs. Do you recall their names? The father who killed himself was Patrick, and I think the boy's name was Michael. I don't remember the wife's name or the names of the girls. Do you?" Sara asked.

"You fell? You need to wash up. You're a mess. You have blood dripping down your neck," the young woman said, distracted by the immediate need of the wound. "Let me get you something to clean up with."

"Damn it, Emma. Forget about my face for a minute. I need to know those names," Sara snapped out of frustration.

"Calm down. Let me think. I believe that Patrick's wife's name was Eileen, no wait a minute. That's the name of one of the daughters. Maureen, that was it. Then they had two more girls. The little one that caused her brother's death was Patty. No, that's not right. I'm mixing that up with the father's name. Katy. Wasn't that it?"

"Katy, yes. I think that was what he said."

"Then the last girl's name is easy. I can't believe you don't remember it." She paused for a second to stare at her boss. "It was Grace, just like your daughter."

"How could I have been so blind? How could I have missed this? That's the connection," Sara said, covering her face with her hands.

"What connection?" Emma asked.

When Sara removed her hands to answer, she saw Emma pull a clean towel from a cabinet and wet it in the utility sink.

"Here, your face is streaked with blood. I really think you need to go up to the house. We should get David," Emma said, shaking her head. "Carlos, go fetch him."

"No, we don't need David," Sara said, turning to catch Carlos' attention before he left. She turned back to Emma. "Do you remember the old farm manager's name? James said he was in a nursing home. Blue Valley, I think."

"Lester. We talked more about him after you went up to the house. Last name was Brown. I don't remember if it was Blue Valley or Shenandoah Valley Nursing Home. Why do you need to know all this?" Emma inquired.

"Because I do."

While rinsing off the blood from the towel in the tack room's sink, Sara explained. "I think Grace is the key to all the weird things that have been happening here. I want to go see this Lester to try and find out more about her. Maybe he can lead us to her, or at the very least give us a clue as to what is going on. I'm going up to the house to finish cleaning up. Can you call these nursing homes? Find out which one he is in and get me directions. I'll be back in 10 minutes." She put her hand on Carlos' shoulder as she left. She didn't want them to worry about her. In her gut, she knew she was right.

As Sara was leaving the barn, she heard Emma say, "Brilliant, she has gone mad. She's now going to hunt down some poor old bastard in a nursing home."

"Heard that!" Sara called over her shoulder.

"You better do what the boss lady wants or she'll be putting you in one of those homes," Carlos replied.

About half an hour later, Emma met Sara at the entrance to the barn with the information she wanted. Looking cleaned up, bandaged, and determined, Sara took the directions from Emma's hands. "You are going to have to wait," the Englishwoman said. "Apparently the man just came out of the hospital. The woman I spoke with said he is restricted from having visitors for several more days."

"We will see about that. They're not going to stop me from seeing him," Sara said as she opened the car door.

"This is a bad idea. Please wait. They said it would only be a few days," Emma urged.

Sara slammed the door and started the car.

It took 20 minutes to make it to the nursing home's parking lot. She pulled into one of the numerous open spaces. As she walked toward the building, she was struck by how bleak and ugly the facade was. It wouldn't have surprised her if visitors were few and far between. The grim atmosphere made her feel as if death were an ever-present patron.

Upon opening the door, Sara was met by the distinctive smell of poorly bathed elderly, mingled with urine and feces. She guessed that most of its residents were there on the government's dime, with minimal concern from their families, if they had any. Emma's note said Lester was in room 315. Sara found the elevator and pressed the up arrow. The woman manning the reception desk didn't even bother to look up as Sara passed; the so-called gatekeeper was too engrossed in applying a coat of red nail polish to her fake nails. When the elevator doors opened on the third floor, Sara glanced at the black plastic plaque directing visitors in the direction of their desired room. Turning right, she followed the hallway to the last room on the left. Luckily, this direction avoided the nurse's station.

The door to room 315 was wide open. Sara stepped inside to see two old black men lying in beds. Privacy was an unheard of luxury, since the two were separated by nothing more than a tattered curtain. The first man had the head of his bed elevated and was staring at the television. A game show was capturing his attention. He didn't bother to change his focus, most likely assuming she was another nurse. Since Lester had just returned from eye surgery, she ruled this man out as her target. She made her way across the room and took a seat next to the man whose eyes were covered by bandages. Sara couldn't tell if he was awake or asleep.

"Excuse me, Mr. Brown, is that you?" Sara asked awkwardly. She received no answer. She repeated herself, this time louder. The old man's head turned toward her voice.

"Who's there?" a thin, weak voice answered.

"Mr. Brown, I'm so sorry to disturb you. My name is Sara Miller. I live at the farm that you worked at for many years. I'm here because I would like to talk to you about the family who employed you," Sara said, reaching out to touch the old man's dry and shriveled hand.

"Who is that? Who are you? Have you finally come for me?" he asked with agitation.

"Mr. Brown, my name is…" Sara started to say again, but was interrupted by an obese and angry nurse wearing a disapproving scowl.

"Who are you and what are you doing here? This man isn't supposed to have any visitors for the next few days. He only came out of the hospital last night. I'm calling security," the woman sternly said, the fatty folds of her neck rippling as she spoke.

Sara envisioned the receptionist running in and scratching her with those red painted talons.

"I'm sorry. I really needed to speak with Mr. Brown. It's terribly important. Please, I only need a few minutes," Sara pleaded, rising to follow the woman out into the hall.

"You need to leave. Now!" the nurse said, spinning around to face Sara faster than she would have thought possible for a woman that size. "I'm giving you three minutes to get off this floor before I call security to escort you out. This poor man has gone years without a visitor, and then you show up to bother him after he returns from surgery. Out! Whatever is so urgent can wait a few more days."

Sara looked back at the door, then again at the red-faced woman standing before her. She had no doubt that this woman meant business, yet she was so close. Sara took a step back toward Lester's room. The woman caught her wrist and yanked.

"Don't make me hurt you, lady. If you ever want to step foot in this facility again, you will leave now," the nurse insisted.

Sara, recognizing that she was temporarily beaten, realized that she would have to wait to get her answers until next week. She followed the nurse to the elevator, where the woman stood guard as the doors slid shut. Disappointed, she walked slowly back to her car. When she turned to look up at the building, she could see the same nurse glaring down at her from Lester's window.

"I'll be back. You can bet on that," Sara promised as she climbed behind the wheel.

Following the winding country roads back to the farm, Sara made the decision to keep her adventure to herself. David had an important business trip to focus on. The last thing he needed was to be distracted by the events of the past 24 hours. She decided to postpone telling him about what transpired until he returned from California.

CHAPTER TWELVE

David's flight to San Diego was scheduled to depart at ten-thirty on Sunday morning. He loaded his briefcase, laptop computer, and luggage into the trunk of the car around seven o'clock. Still dressed in pajamas, Sara watched from the doorway of the garage.

"Looks like I'm ready. I'll call you as soon as I get settled into the hotel. I'm so sorry I have to go. The timing couldn't have been worse," he said, walking over to her.

She handed him a travel mug filled with coffee. "I'm just happy you didn't have to postpone the trip. I know how important this account is for you. We're going to be fine. Get your mind off this place and all the craziness we've been through the last couple of weeks. California will be good for you. I'm jealous," Sara said.

David was about to say something when Jack squeezed under his mother's elbow.

"Bye, Dad," he said, rushing to give his father a hug.

"Mornin', big guy," David said lifting the boy up in his arms. "I'm sure going to miss you. You take care of your mom. Keep her in line." He squeezed the small body against his chest.

"I will. I'm gonna miss you so, so, so much! Promise me you'll send me a postcard," he said pressing back against David's strong arms so he could look him in the eye.

"You got it," he replied, sliding Jack to the floor. He looked at his watch. "I better get out of here. You never know how delayed traffic is around DC."

Sara nodded in agreement. David bent down and kissed his son's head before turning his attention to his wife. He pulled Sara into his arms and kissed her on the lips. Sara lingered, not wanting to leave his embrace. Time finally forced them apart.

"One week," she said, as she watched him get in the car. "That's all it is, one week."

"I'll be back before you know it," David added, "I love you."

As he backed out of the garage, Sara and Jack waved and blew air kisses.

"Just a week," Sara said to herself as she turned to go back inside.

After a quick breakfast, Sara and Jack joined Emma in the barn. Carlos had the day off, leaving his co-worker alone to tackle the daily chores. They were surprised to find all the horses out and the majority of the work done.

"Wow! Aren't you efficient? Here I was feeling sorry for you, and lo and behold, you're already finishing up the last stall. When did you get out here, three o'clock this morning?" Sara asked as she leaned against the stall's wooden frame.

"Close. Five," Emma answered as she tossed manure into the wheelbarrow. "Vickie and I are going to drive to Leesburg today to do some shopping. I guess I should have asked you first, what with David leaving and the two of you being here alone. Did you need me to hang about? I can cancel if you need me to."

"Somehow I think we will manage. Right, Jack?"

He nodded in agreement.

"I should be back by four," Emma added.

"Can I help?" the little boy asked, pointing to the hose. "I can fill buckets."

"I think that's a brilliant idea. You can start at the far end and work your way down the aisle," Emma directed.

Sara knew this was his favorite task. He usually ended up drenched by the time he finished. She mouthed a silent "thank you" to Emma.

By ten o'clock, all the stalls were cleaned, fresh hay had been dropped into each hayrack, and all the water buckets were filled to the brim. Emma swept the aisle and hurried off to take a shower. Jack looked out the back doors of the barn at the horses in the paddocks.

"Mom, can we go riding today? It's really nice out. I haven't ridden Gremlin in a long time," he asked.

The sun was warming the air, pushing the thermometer to 50 degrees. She had to admit that the day couldn't be any more inviting and she rarely turned down a chance to ride with Jack. "I think that's a great idea. You haven't ridden at all since we moved here. The weather is finally cooperating, huh?" she said, pulling her son to her side to give him a squeeze.

"Yeah. It was way too yucky before. I like spring better," he added.

"Well, let's not waste this gorgeous day, get moving," Sara said. "We need to change into riding clothes. First one done and back here wins."

Twenty minutes later Sara returned, dressed in tan breeches with slender black boots. Jack had won the challenge and was in the barn waiting for her, decked out in his tan jodhpurs with ankle length, dark brown jodhpur boots, customary for a child. Both wore fleece vests with long-sleeved shirts underneath.

Sara had decided to ride Gale Force. Unfortunately, he was in the farthest pasture from them. They hiked down the grass-covered lane that cut through fenced fields. The ground was still soft from the rain that had fallen a few days earlier. Small pockets of puddles were scattered about as they trudged along. They decided to retrieve Gale Force first. Sara took the halter from the fence-post where Emma had hung it that morning.

"Gale Force," she called across the field but the large gray horse didn't move a muscle. Sara unlatched the gate and turned to her son. "Jack, wait for me here."

"Okey-dokey," he replied, looking at the muddy pups at his side. "I'll stay with the dogs."

Sara was about half-way up the hill, when a red fox emerged from a den wedged between some boulders and a crooked tree. He took one look at her and scurried back for cover. She wondered if Jack had seen it, certain that he would be thrilled by the prospect of seeing such a beautiful animal. Nearing Gale Force, she pulled a carrot from her pocket to use as a bribe to coax the big horse to slip his nose through the halter. Just before pulling it over his ears, something spooked the animal, sending him off at a gallop. The halter and lead were pulled from her hands, landing about ten feet away. Sara stood there, stunned for a moment as she watched the graceful dappled beast trot around, wildly snorting, his tail propped up like a long silver flag. Frustrated, she walked over and picked up the discarded halter. While pulling another carrot from her vest pocket, the unmistakable sound of hounds baying and thundering hooves shattered the morning quiet. Taken off guard, Sara looked around but couldn't spot the hunt. Clearly this was the source of Gale Force's sudden excitement. Hearing the pack of hounds draw closer and closer suggested that they had caught the red fox's scent. The riders could easily have access to her land by jumping over the pasture's bordering stone wall. Worried that they would gallop through, Sara made a dash for the split rail fence to avoid being run down. The sprint left her barely able to catch her breath. She turned around, expecting to see horses leaping over the wall at the top of the hill. Gale Force was staring in the same direction, look- ing like a statue carved from marble. Sara felt a frigid gust of wind. A chill swept over her. The sounds and vibrations of hooves and hounds exploded in front of her, but they were not to be seen. Shaking her head as if trying to brush away cobwebs, Sara looked back to the top of the hill. Nothing. The gray horse's eyes and ears followed the sound down the hill. Then just as quickly as it came, it was gone. The agitated horse went trotting down toward the waiting boy.

Sara was completely befuddled by the phenomenon. Jack climbed onto the metal gate to pet the horse between his eyes. Nei- ther he nor the dogs acted as if they had noticed what happened. Sara looked with concern at the horses in the other pasture. They were undisturbed, still munching on the tender shoots of early grass. Reaching the gate, Sara offered Gale Force the carrot in her hand. He greedily took it from her, ready to head back to the barn. She recognized that he was still wild-eyed from the phantom hunt, leading her to seriously wonder whether they should keep to their plan to hack out into the countryside.

"I can't wait to ride. Hurry up, Mom! We need to get my pony," Jack exclaimed, clapping his hands with excitement.

How could she explain to him what just occurred? She couldn't even explain it to herself. One look into the horse's large almond eyes told her it wasn't only in her head.

"Jack, did you see the fox out near that cluster of trees?" she asked, pointing.

"Sure did. That was so cool. He was real pretty. Do you think it was a boy or girl fox? I think it was a boy. I'm gonna call him Slick. What do you think?" Jack said, all in one breath.

"Did you notice anything else or hear anything?" she asked, trying to act casual as they started to walk toward Gremlin's paddock.

"Not really. I heard you call for Gale Force and I saw him spook and run away, but I thought it was just because of the big wind," he answered with a perplexed look across his face. "Did you hear anything funny?"

"No. I only heard the wind," she said distractedly.

Gremlin was always up for a bribe and came trotting over as soon as he heard the rattle of the gate. The old pony's winter coat made him appear twice the width he really was. Autumn brought an explosion of hair growth that lasted until early May. Jack easily captured his mount. As they walked back to the barn, Gremlin, ever impatient, occasionally would nudge the child on his back, each time eliciting a reprimand from the little boy.

"Quit it! Bad pony," he repeated over and over.

Once inside, Sara and Jack hooked their equines to cross ties. Normally Emma or Carlos would groom and saddle the horses, but today, they were on their own. Jack insisted on trying to tighten the girth of the saddle himself. "Mom, can I do it myself? I know how."

"That's fine. I know you're a big guy now and can do things yourself. But I need to check it before you get on or we don't go. Understand?"

"Yes," he replied with a scowl.

Sara was impressed by his confidence and determination, but

there was no way she was going to let him mount without doing a final inspection. She envisioned Jack and the saddle slipping, with both ending up under the pony's fat belly. As they were finishing their preparations, they heard the double beep of Emma's car horn, her signal that she was leaving for the day. Sara watched as she drove away. Gremlin barely noticed the abrupt sound, but Sara noticed that Gale Force fidgeted nervously under his tack, depositing several piles of manure onto the floor. He only got worse as she approached him with a bridle. Sara was struggling to slip the bit into his mouth when Jack started walking outside with his pony.

"Wait for me to come out before you get on. I need to check your girth."

Sara didn't hear a response. She slid the bridle over the large gray ears, tightened the noseband, and fastened the throatlatch. Taking the reins, Sara led the horse to the tack room entrance to grab her helmet from its hook. Apparently, Jack had left without taking his. She shook her head, prepared to give him a warning about safety. She tucked his hat under her left arm as she slipped hers on, securing the chinstrap. Mild irritation turned to anger when she caught Jack lowering himself onto Gremlin's back.

"You're in trouble, mister! I explicitly told you not to get on. Plus, you aren't wearing your helmet. What are you thinking?" Sara said, annoyed with his outright disregard of her instructions. After burying one child, Jack's safety was not something she took lightly.

"Oops. I forgot. I'm sorry. Did you tell me not to get on? I didn't hear you tell me that. Can't you can check my girth while I'm in the saddle?"

Sara could tell he was trying to dodge a firm scolding. She wasn't about to let him off the hook that easily. There was about a 25 foot gap between them. As she stormed over to Jack, she heard the sound of the hunt. A huge gust of cold wind swept down upon them, sending Gale Force and Gremlin into a frenzy.

"Mom, help!" the boy screamed.

"Jack, get off! Get off!" she yelled, but it was too late.

Gremlin took off at breakneck speed. Jack's frantic pleas for help sent Sara into a state of sheer panic. She didn't think she had ever seen the pony gallop that fast. In the meantime, Gale Force was rearing, pulling her down the driveway. She fought for control, praying she could quickly mount to go after her son. It was a losing battle. The 1200 pound horse won the tug of war, taking off after Gremlin as if breaking from a starting gate. From out of nowhere, the two Danes sped by her, their long legs eating up the ground in pursuit of the endangered child. Sara sprinted down the drive, yelling for Jack to pull back on the reins. She was filled with terror every second she watched them get farther and farther away.

Then, as if Sara stepped through an invisible membrane, a surreal vision flooded her mind. *Ahead of her, she saw a boy galloping on a pony, followed closely by a young girl, long red hair whipping in the wind, astride a beautiful gray horse. Sara could hear a soft voice calling over and over again for the boy to stop.*

"Michael! Michael, stop! Papa said you aren't allowed to take your new pony hunting. Michael, stop! You aren't even supposed to be riding him. You are going too fast! You are going to fall. Michael, No!"

Sara watched in horror as the two horses veered abruptly off the gravel driveway. The animals now raced side by side across the front pasture.

Sara's steps seemed to gain no ground. She slowed to a jog as the past stormed violently into the present. She seriously questioned her sanity as she witnessed the ethereal image of a girl in Gale Force's saddle reach down to take hold of Gremlin's reins. The pony shifted his weight to his hind end and planted his front legs in a number of jolting attempts to slow his forward momentum. Jack flew forward. Losing his balance from the sudden change in rhythm, his small body went crashing to the ground. The red-haired girl's leg floated over the back of the horse like a wisp of smoke. She landed on her feet on the far side of the winded animal.

"Jack! Jack! Oh God, No! Jack," Sara screamed as she cut across the field, carving a direct line toward them.

Gremlin and Gale Force trotted off a short distance as Sara approached, leaving her son motionless and in full view. The girl had vanished, simply disappeared. The dogs reached the fallen child first. They raced around him, barking wildly. The boy was sprawled on his side, his right arm bent in an unnatural position. Sara knelt down and gently said his name. "Jack. Jack. Sweetie, can you hear me? Jack."

There was no response. Luckily, he had landed on the fresh dirt that Carlos used to refill Buster's hole. This had buffered his landing somewhat. Miraculously, he avoided a platter-sized rock just a few feet away. Growing very calm, Sara reached for his neck to feel for a pulse. Relief rained down on her as her index finger picked up his heartbeat. She leaned over his open mouth to listen for sounds telling her he was breathing. Each exhale of Jack's breath warmed her left cheek. Concerned about his injuries, she didn't want to move him. Sara called out to him again.

"Jack. Jack. Please. Can you hear me? Wake up, sweetheart. I need you to open your eyes. Can you hear me? You fell off Gremlin. You're going to be fine. Jack, please, pumpkin. Give me a sign that you can hear me."

The child remained unresponsive. Sara checked her vest pockets for her cell phone. Thankfully she had thought to take it in case David tried to reach her. She stood up and moved about, trying to locate a signal. She punched in 911 and hit send. The call finally connected after several stressful attempts. Relief and hope swept over her when she heard the operator on the other end.

"Hello. 911. Do you have an emergency?"

"Yes. I need help. My son was in a riding accident. He fell off his pony. He was not wearing a helmet. He's unconscious and has a badly broken arm. Please hurry," Sara begged.

"Have you moved him at all?" the operator asked.

"No. I'm afraid that I could paralyze him if he has a spinal injury. God, please hurry!"

"What's your location?"

"36 Standish Lane. We're west of Upperville."

"We have an ambulance and trauma helicopter on the way. They should be there in about 15 to 20 minutes."

Sara ran back to her son's battered body.

"Jack, help is on the way," she said, weeping. "You have to fight. You have to hold on. Oh Jack, please wake up. I can't lose you."

The sound of a vehicle on the gravel driveway caught her attention. It didn't make sense. Why didn't the ambulance have its siren on? Wiping the tears from her cheeks, Sara stood up to wave them down, only to realize that it wasn't the ambulance. It was Emma. The sight of the blonde British girl caused Sara drop to her knees to give thanks and pray.

"God, thank you for small miracles. Now I need a big one. Please don't take him. You've already taken Grace. Please, don't take Jack from me too. If you are trying to punish me for my sins, please, take me instead."

"Sara, what the devil happened?" Emma asked.

Sara looked up to see a reflection of the fear and panic she knew she wore on her face.

"My God! Is he dead?" Emma asked, a hand drawn against her mouth in shock.

"No, but he's hurt very badly," Sara explained, crawling across the grass to return to her son's side. "An ambulance and helicopter are on the way. Can you get Gale Force and Gremlin back to the barn? I'm sure they'll take off again if they hear sirens. At this point, I'm not sure where they would end up."

"No problem. I'll get them straight away. But Sara, how did this happen?" Emma asked.

Sara, terrified, shook her head and cried. It took her a minute to form the words. "Jack mounted before putting on his helmet. The horses spooked and bolted. I can't even begin to explain what happened next. Round them up and I'll tell you more later," Sara said, concerned that another accident was imminent if the horses weren't quickly caught and contained.

Emma executed her orders without saying anything else. Sara was relieved to see the two equines clearing the barn entrance as the sound of the approaching ambulance launched a flock of birds into the sky. *Another small miracle,* she thought. Within minutes, paramedics were running across the field carrying a stretcher. They worked quickly, taking Jack's pulse, looking in his eyes, and asking questions about the accident. Sara left out her vision of the red-haired young girl, certain it would prompt the medics to haul her off to a locked psychiatric ward.

Emma and the Life Flight chopper arrived simultaneously. The airborne medical unit landed about a hundred feet away. The wind from its whirling blades blasted those on the ground. The paramedics treating Jack positioned their bodies so as to buffer the injured boy from the sudden assault of wind. Sara looked down at her watch. The operator was accurate about the time; 20 minutes had passed since her 911 call. She watched as a brace was fastened around Jack's neck. Emma put her arm around Sara for support as they saw the little body being rolled onto the stiff board. The straps were tightly fastened around him to prevent any movement during transport to the trauma center. The boy's twisted arm stuck out at an awkward angle, making the scene even more grotesque and disturbing.

"I'm sorry, ma'am, but you'll need to travel separately to the ER. There's only enough room in the helicopter for the medical staff," one of the paramedics explained.

"No! I want to go with my son. Please. He can't be alone," Sara protested.

"I'm sorry. We have to go. Time is essential here," the man insisted.

"Please, can't you make an exception?" Sara begged as the helicopter took to the air behind her. "No! Wait! Crap! Emma, can you drive me to the hospital? I don't think I can do it."

"Absolutely," Emma replied. "David would have my head if I let you drive. We'd be scraping you off some innocent tree."

As Sara ran to the house to get their insurance cards, the paramedics loaded their equipment into the back of the ambulance. She was trotting back toward Emma when James Sullivan drove in with his blacksmith truck. The old man stopped to talk to the paramedics. Even from a fair distance, she could see the color drain from his face as he was told about the accident.

"History repeating itself," he said shaking his head when Sara and Emma joined him. "You're some nice folks. It's been nothing but one tragedy after another, just like the McHugh family before ya'll. You need to get out of here, save yourselves, before the madness sets in."

"Rubbish, the pony spooked. This isn't some grand plan directed by some dead lunatic. You better be on your way. Sara's devastated enough, and she doesn't need to hear this kind of nonsense," Emma said, protective of her boss and friend.

Standing off to the side of this exchange, Sara was speechless. Haunting images of the night the dogs came back covered in blood, the nightmares she and her mother shared, the mysterious gold key, and the ghostly events that marked the day swirled in her mind. She had a sense that something ominous was stalking them. The past was seeping into the present, and they were all in danger now.

"I'll say a prayer for your son. The Lord tortured the McHugh family something terrible. It took poor Michael almost a week to pass from this world to the next, in a coma the whole time. It was unbearable for the family. I sure hope your son wakes up. I'll add one for you too, that you find the guidance you'll need to break the curse in time," the wrinkled old man said as he turned back toward his truck.

"Crazy bugger!" Emma looked for agreement from Sara and the two men getting ready to climb back in their ambulance. "Sara, don't you worry. Jack is going to be better in a jiffy."

"I don't know. He was in pretty bad shape when they took off," the taller of the two warned before closing his door.

The comment made Sara feel like vomiting. "Hurry," she mumbled. "We need to leave."

Emma started her car and waited for the men to turn the ambulance around. As the vehicles left the property, she caught Sara staring at her.

"What? Why are you looking at me like that?"

"You were supposed to be gone all day," Sara said. "Why did you come back to the farm?"

"Something told me to turn around. I know that must sound downright loony, but honestly, I had this gut feeling that I had to come back. Usually I would have chalked it up to hunger, but not this time. It was different, almost overwhelming. Damn good thing I did. Did you call David yet? He has to come home."

"No. He's on a plane flying to San Diego."

The two drove on in silence for a while. Sara stared out the window while nervously chewing on her fingernails. The hospital where Jack was flown was over an hour away. Lingering under the surface was the fear that he could die without a parent there by his side. After about 15 minutes Sara needed to share her thoughts; the mental clutter percolating from the morning's accident had been unceasingly streaming through her head. She wanted another opinion on these multiple visions.

"Emma. I think I'm in trouble. No, I think my entire family may be in trouble."

"What do you mean?" Emma asked.

"Do you remember when I told you that I thought the house was haunted? Remember the whole incident on my birthday with the dogs and the mirror?" Sara asked.

"Yes. But Sara, come now. You're taking what James said to heart. You're not cursed."

"I don't know about that. There have been other unexplainable events. Today a foxhunt rode through the property but no one was there. The sounds and sensations were, but no horses, no riders, no hounds! Gale Force and Gremlin reacted to it too. That's what prompted them to bolt. Then…then I saw a redheaded little girl riding my horse. It had to be Katy, but she was racing after Jack as if she was chasing Michael. It had to be some kind of weird psychic memory. She was calling to him, yelling for him to stop. Hell, for all I know, it was Michael. It must be either he or his father haunting the farm. Shoot, it could be both."

"Sara, I don't know what to say. Are you sure you weren't seeing things? Letting your imagination take over under stress? I can't imagine how this could be happening or…why."

"Wait, there's more. Try to explain this coincidence. Before she died, my mother recorded her dreams, dreams that may have contributed to her heart attack and dreams that are similar to what I've been experiencing. You know I'm adopted. In my mother's papers I found the document recording the adoption. It listed my birth mother. Her name was Grace, the same name as my daughter and the same name as one of the girls that grew up on our farm."

"Sara, hold on now. Don't jump to conclusions. Was her name Grace McHugh?"

"No, but maybe she was using another name. Heck, maybe she was married. Mr. Sullivan said those two girls had a zillion kids each. Maybe they started giving them away."

By the time they reached the hospital, Sara was convinced that Emma finally grasped the gravity of the situation.

"According to Mr. Sullivan, Michael didn't die right away. He actually lived for several days, almost a week. He believes that history is repeating itself. If he's right, you only have a few days to figure this out. If the doctors are able to stabilize Jack, you better get yourself over to see that priest you mentioned about doing an exorcism. Plus, Lester Brown should be able to have visitors by now. He's probably the only one able to verify your suspicions," Emma said as she shut off the car's engine.

"You're right," Sara said, forcing a thin smile. "Thanks, I'm glad you don't think I'm nuts."

"At first, I was quite sure that you had gone batty, but frankly, the evidence is pointing to something much scarier," the pretty British woman said. "Let's go in. Your son needs you to be with him, maybe more than either one of us can fathom."

CHAPTER THIRTEEN

By the time Sara and Emma arrived at the hospital, Jack had already been whisked off for a CAT scan. The attending physician, a slender, gray-haired man, came out to speak to Sara. "Mrs. Miller?" he inquired with an outstretched hand.

"Yes, I'm Sara Miller," she answered.

"Hello, I'm Dr. Garrison."

"Are you the doctor helping my son? Is he going to be all right?"

"I've been in charge of his care since he arrived. However, there will be a number of specialists working with him. Your son is in critical condition. He has sustained a compound fracture of his right arm, a trauma to his brain, a bruised liver and kidney, as well as two fractured ribs. The good news is that there are no signs of internal bleeding, bleeding into his brain or damage to his lungs."

"He'll be fine, right?" Sara asked, hoping for a confirmation.

"Of course he'll be," Emma added before the doctor could answer.

"As I said, his condition is quite serious. I must warn you, your son is in grave danger due to the brain injury. It's bi-frontal, which is the best kind to have if you are going to have one, but he is unconscious. The medical team will be closely monitoring the intracranial pressure in his brain. He has been started on a hypertonic saline IV in an effort to reduce the chances of brain swelling, which could mean the possibility of brain damage or in the worst case, death. Fortunately, we have been able to avoid putting him on a ventilator. However, the longer he stays in a coma, the poorer his prognosis. Over the next several days, we want to see Jack's GCS level, which measures neurological responsiveness, increase while the pressure on his brain decreases."

"His what? Can you explain that in plain language without the lingo?" Sara asked.

"The bottom line is we want his ability to respond to us to improve as the pressure exerted on his brain from the swelling decreases or stays steady. We're going to be closely monitoring these things. It's as simple as that," the doctor said.

Sara tried to understand as best she could. Ultimately she got the picture.

"Can I see him?" she asked. "I want to be with him. Please. He needs his mother."

"Briefly. We're still working on him."

The doctor escorted Sara to the trauma room, where Jack lay helpless. She was taken aback at the sight of him. There were tubes running to his left arm, his right arm still had a grotesque unnatural bend, and, although he wasn't on a ventilator, he had a mask over his face, delivering oxygen. She could see his head had been shaved to insert the ventricular catheter into his skull in order to monitor his brain pressure. A male nurse led her over to Jack's side. A single tear slid down her left cheek as she bent over to kiss him on the forehead.

"Jack, it's Mom. Oh, baby…I'm so sorry you got hurt. I wanted to let you know I'm here. You went for a ride in a helicopter. You're at a hospital with wonderful doctors who are taking good care of you. They won't let me stay with you right now because they are going to fix your arm, but I promise I won't be far away."

Sara wanted to touch him, to hold him, to turn back the clock and make all the pain go away. She thought about Maureen and Patrick McHugh keeping a vigil at their son's bedside, terrified that he would die. Sara was horrified by the prospect that she and David could be facing the same outcome. Threads of fear, anger, and desperation wound around her like persistent, creeping vines, threatening to strangle the hope she was using to survive. She wasn't going to let those fears take hold. She was determined that there could only be one outcome: He would get better. She would not lose another child.

"You need to wake up now, Jack. Try to wake up. I know it's really hard, but try to follow my voice back from wherever you are," Sara urged, hoping a piece of him would grab hold and fight to come back to her.

The nurse put his hand on her shoulder, alerting her that she needed to leave. "One more minute, please," she begged of the man dressed in blue scrubs. "I promise, I won't be long." He relented, giving her a few more precious moments. There was a strong possibility that these minutes might have to last her a lifetime.

Sara bent down close to Jack and whispered. "Sweetie, you need to fight. Don't give in to them. You are not Michael. I promise you that I won't stop until I find a way to bring you back. You are my son, not theirs. I love you. Hang on."

"Mrs. Miller, you need to go. We'll take good care of him."

This time Sara knew there was no room for negotiation.

Back in the small room where other family members waited in tortured limbo, Sara joined Emma, who was on the phone, wrapping up a conversation with Leila.

"Sara just walked in. We'll expect you then straight away…very good. I'll tell her," Emma said, severing the connection before turning her attention to Sara. "How is he?"

"He looks terrible, but he's alive. What did Leila say?" she asked, falling into a chair.

"She's on her way."

"Did you call Carlos?"

"That's next on the agenda. Do you want to do it yourself?"

"No," Sara answered. "You can call. Tell him that David doesn't know about the accident yet. He was on his way to San Diego. If he calls home, have him call my cell phone or try us here." Sara was lost in her own thoughts, barely aware of the conversation taking place next to her. The accident replayed in her mind over and over again. She was shaken back into the moment when she felt Emma's hand on her back.

"Carlos said he'll stay at the farm for as long as he's needed, not to worry," Emma said. "He was quite choked up, promised to say a prayer for poor little Jack."

Sara wiped away a tear and nodded. She had made up her mind that the young man's prayers needed to be reinforced by some big guns. She intended to enlist the help of the closest priest.

"Emma, I need your help," she said. "Can you drive me to a church? I think I have to arrange for some divine intervention. We should wait for Leila to get here, then we can briefly run out."

"No problem. I'm at your service."

When Leila arrived, Sara was relieved by her oldest friend's presence. They hugged, releasing a floodgate of nervous tears. After regaining some composure, Sara brought Leila up to speed on Jack's condition and her plan. "Christ! We're lucky he's still with us. It happened so fast."

"Are we allowed in to see him?"

"The doctor let me in for a few minutes, but I was in the way. They're still working on him."

"That's crap! You should be by his side," Leila protested with a scowl. "I'm going to talk to the nurses. You wouldn't be in the way." Leila made a beeline for the door.

"No. Wait," Sara said grabbing her arm. "I have to run out anyway. We were waiting for you. Emma is going to drive me over to a nearby church. I need to talk to a priest. I would really appreciate it if you would stay here with Jack. If the little guy wakes up or, God forbid, he takes a turn for the worse, I don't want him to face it without family, and you qualify as family under any circumstances. I was told that access to him will be limited for at least the next hour or two, which gives us a brief window to work in. I'll have my cell phone with me in case his condition changes. We can get back here in no time."

Leila put her hands on Sara's shoulders and stared her straight in the eyes. "Fine. Do whatever you need to make this better."

Sara nodded.

"Come on, the clock is ticking," Emma said, holding the door in one hand and a page out of the phone book in the other. "I'm resourceful. I found you a church. Now let's go!"

It took about 20 minutes driving back toward the farm to reach the closest church, St. Thomas' Catholic Church.

"Let me come in with you," Emma suggested. "I don't think you should do this alone."

"Thanks, but I would prefer to do this on my own," she replied, handing her cell to Emma. "Come in and get me if Leila or the doctor calls."

The sign out front listed three Sunday Mass times. The last one had let out about an hour earlier. This worried Sara, since she didn't know how long the priests remained at the church after the final service was complete. The names of the two priests stenciled on the board at the front door were Father Thomas O'Connor and Father Sean Kennedy. Sara squinted as she stepped through the heavy outer door. As her eyes adjusted to the change in lighting, she scanned the pews. A few devoted parishioners lingered in prayer. Hesitant to interrupt those kneeling in worship, Sara surveyed the interior of the church in hopes of finding someone who could tell her where to find a priest. Flanking the altar were rows of small candles. A plump, gray-haired woman sporting the signature hump molded by osteoporosis was busy lighting a string of blue glass votives. A statue of the Virgin Mary glowed from the cumulative light cast by the steady flames. Sara, pressured by time, had found her target. The old woman wrinkled up her face as she noticed the approaching intruder.

"Excuse me. I hate to bother you, but I was wondering if you could direct me to the church office?" Sara asked, sensing the woman's uneasiness.

"I don't recall ever seeing you at this church," came a suspicious reply. "Why do you need to see Father Kennedy?"

"I don't belong to this church," Sara explained, finding herself caught off guard by the question. "I've come because my son has been severely injured and this is the closest church to the hospital. I was hoping to speak to one of the priests, either one, it doesn't matter. Could you please direct me to the office? My time is very limited."

The woman eyed her up and down, as if assessing the level of desperation in Sara's face. An old hand reached out and took hold of Sara's crossed arms. The aged voice crackled as she spoke. "You've been without faith, closed off to it by a deep fissure in your heritage. You need to find it, believe in the miracles of the Lord. There is a reason for everything. Right now God is challenging you to find his purpose. Even tragedies have hidden opportunities, hidden meanings. Open your heart and you will see the truth."

Sara didn't know what to say. The woman's eyes seemed to bore right through her, directly tapping into her injured soul.

Looking away to hide her embarrassment, she repeated the question. "Please, I have very little time to waste. Can you direct me to the office?"

A frail voice delivered the answer she needed. "Take that corridor to the side of the altar. The path will wind around, but near the end, you will find what you are looking for."

Sara didn't have the courage to look back as she said, "Thank you."

Following the directions down the side hallway, she eventually located a door with black letters etched into a brass nameplate. It read, Father O'Connor. Holding her breath, Sara knocked three times.

"Come in," responded a deep male voice.

Sara inched the door back, catching sight of a young man in his early thirties with shiny black hair. He was seated behind a worn desk and looked up when he heard her enter. He had piercing blue eyes encircled by the metal rims of glasses. He smiled as she approached, showing off a row of perfect teeth, no doubt the product of several years spent trapped in braces.

"Can I help you?" he said, the deep baritone of his voice reminiscent of a radio personality. Sara found him remarkably attractive...for a priest.

"Would you like to sit down?" he asked.

"Yes, thank you. I'm desperate and hoping you can help me. My name is Sara Miller and I need the church's—no, God's help," she said lowering her body into the chair facing this now bewildered man.

"And you need this why exactly, Ms. Miller?" he said, frowning.

Sara quickly described Jack's accident and her theory on unsettled spirits having a hand in it. "I'm not sure what you call the procedure for getting rid of ghosts, but I'm begging you to help me," Sara implored leaning forward with both hands gripping the edge of the young priest's desk. "Do you have any experience with something like this?"

Sara recognized the look that was traversing this man's face. She had seen it with David, Leila, and Emma at one time or other since these psychic events started building. Hell, she even saw it on her own face as she peered into a mirror only to gaze into another woman's eyes.

"Let me get this right. You're telling me that your house is haunted?" Father O'Connor asked.

"Yes, absolutely. But I'm not sure if it's haunted by Michael or Patrick or both. You see, they both died there, one by accident, the other by suicide. I guess it could also be Maureen, since she had red hair, but I don't think she died violently like the other two," Sara said.

"And somehow you think this Michael or Patrick or Maureen is trying to kill your son?"

"I'm not certain that they know he's Jack. To be honest, I think it's a repeat of what happened to Michael. As a matter of fact, I am almost 100 percent sure. You see, I saw it; I watched the whole horrible accident happen this morning," Sara said, realizing that this man must be thinking along the lines of heavy psychotropic sedation by now.

"Your son's accident?" he said patiently, as if trying to ferret out reality from hallucination.

"Yes. Well, yes…and no. He was Jack at first," Sara said, struggling to make him understand the convoluted nature of her predicament. "How do I explain it?"

"Maybe starting at the beginning would help both of us," he said, resting his cleanly shaven chin on the entwined fingers of his propped up hands.

Sara stared at him. She found something about his peaceful demeanor to be soothing.

"The beginning. I don't know if we have time to start at the beginning. I feel like I've broken some seal that contained these tormented memories, and now that they are loose, they're lapping over into the present. And my gut is telling me that time is running out. I have seen, felt, and heard things that should be impossible, and I'm not alone. If I'm crazy, so is everyone else around me. My mother in New York died almost two weeks ago after being haunted by events and images taking place at our farm located about a half hour away from here. My husband was with me the night our dogs returned bathed in blood. To this day, we cannot find an explanation. And both my son and I have seen a mysterious woman in a mirror I bought on my birthday. It all started that day. My birthday was the catalyst and I don't know why. This morning I watched as my son's pony galloped away. Behind him raced a red-haired girl on my horse calling for Michael to stop. That ghostly image intervened, stopped the pony, then poof…disappeared into thin air. Please, please help me," Sara begged.

Father O'Connor leaned back from his hands without taking his eyes off Sara. Slowly and thoughtfully he pieced together his thoughts for her. "Mrs. Miller, it seems to me that you have quite an unusual situation manifesting itself at your home. I'll gladly do what I can, but you may want to consider locating a psychic in this instance. Let me explain. An exorcism is done when a person is possessed, and your situation doesn't appear to include this rare phenomenon, but I can come out with holy water to bless your farm. That may reduce some of the activity you're having. And I will certainly pray for your son's recovery. Wednesday evening's mass can be dedicated to him, harnessing the prayers of all the parishioners."

"Thank you, Father," Sara said with limited relief. She glanced down at her watch, noticing that she had been gone from the hospital for an hour. "If you give me the phone number here, I'll call to let you know when I can make it back to the farm to meet you. I need to return to the hospital, but I may be able to get away sometime tomorrow."

"My dear, you need to be with your son. He needs to hear your voice and feel the touch of your hand on his. Go and be with him. I can manage alone. Write down the directions to your farm and I'll leave immediately," he said with the voice of someone accustomed to providing comfort and direction. He pulled a legal pad and pen from his desk. "You are welcome back anytime to join us in prayer. Sometimes reaching deep into one's faith awakens dormant truths, something that may guide you through the darkness of these difficult times."

These comments ricocheted in her brain. The content of their message held a striking similarity to the one delivered by the humped-over older woman. Sara took the pad from him and wrote out the directions to their farm. "You can expect to meet a young man there. He works for us. His name is Carlos. He will lead you through the house and around the property. This is my cell phone number in case you get lost or run into any problems."

Rising to leave, Sara had one more question for Father O'Connor. "There was an older woman in the chapel who directed me to you. She was terribly hunched over from age. Do you know her?"

"I'm sorry, I don't recognize the description. Interesting, though. I thought I had met everyone who attends mass regularly. The seniors are particularly eager to introduce themselves. I would have anticipated that a woman with such a noticeable hump would have stood out in my mind. I'll need to make an effort to meet her," he replied, scratching the side of his head.

He took both her hands in his to offer a brief prayer before accompanying her to the office door. "May God bless you and your son. May the Lord shower him with his love and in doing so heal his wounds and deliver him back to your waiting arms. In the name of the Father, Son, and Holy Spirit. Amen."

"Good-bye, Father. Thank you."

"Good-bye and may peace be with you."

Sara was anxious to get back to Jack's side. She looked down at her watch again, thinking that David should be trying to call home soon. The last thing she wanted to do was leave a message telling him to hop back on a plane because his son was in critical condition. She quickened her pace as she followed the hallway back toward the front of the church. She slammed head on into an older man, who had rounded a corner from a side passage. The man's collar identified him as the second resident priest, Father Kennedy. He had to grab hold of her shoulders to avoid tumbling to the ground.

"Oh gosh, I'm so sorry," Sara apologized. She was thoroughly embarrassed by the fact that she nearly tackled the poor man. "Are you all right?"

"Yes, my dear. I'm fine," he said, letting go of her as he regained his balance. "We clearly need to post a new speed limit or perhaps put in a traffic light here."

Sara forced an awkward smile as she peered into the elderly priest's face. She could tell that he had been quite good-looking in his youth. He retained a chiseled jaw, dimples, and an imposing presence. The priest had at least six inches in height on Sara, with a full head of silver hair. She noticed that his eyes were deep pools of aquamarine, the kind that seem to change with the light or color of clothing worn.

"Excuse me," he said and dodged around the stunned woman.

Something was gnawing at the back of Sara's mind as she fell back into a slower gait. Stopping, she closed her eyes to try to recover a memory. It was right there...she could almost visualize a scene. Sara turned around to look at the man to try to jog it loose. Father Kennedy had stopped in front of Father O'Connor's door. The young man that had haunted her sleep materialized. As he turned the knob, he looked back in Sara's direction. For an instant their eyes locked, creating the sensation of being pulled down a tunnel. Dizziness wrapped its enticing arms around Sara's consciousness, making her steady herself by leaning against the wall with her left hand. The man's facial expression showed no change as he stepped into the office, lost from her critical eye. She began to hyperventilate as claustrophobia trapped her briefly in a snapshot stolen from the past.

Sara had to escape. She ran down the corridor and from the

church. Grabbing hold of the wrought iron railing leading down the church's front steps, she bent over and vomited. Emma witnessed this from the car and darted to her aid.

"Goodness, are you all right? Lovely donation you're leaving on their front steps," Emma commented as she took hold of Sara's arm for support. "Did he agree to help you?"

Sara looked up and nodded before bringing up the remaining contents of her gut.

"Father O'Connor offered to go out to the farm today. We need to alert Carlos. Tell him to give the man complete access to the property," she added, wiping her sleeve across her mouth.

"Can you make it back to the car? I think we've been gone long enough. Leila just called to update us that Jack can have limited visitation. I was about to run in to get you. Seems the doctor's definition of immediate family and yours is at odds. They won't let Leila in to see him," Emma explained as she started guiding Sara down the steps.

As the two women pulled out onto the road, the scenes from a recent dream danced in Sara's head. She recognized this man in spite of the inevitable disguise that age would provide. Glancing back at the church, the words of an old woman and young priest clawed out from the depths of her depleted soul.

"I'm getting closer. I need to have faith," Sara whispered to herself.

CHAPTER FOURTEEN

Leila's hovering presence brought Sara back from the shallow level of sleep she was able to achieve. Glancing at her watch, she worked hard to uncurl her stiffened limbs from the confines of a blue vinyl waiting room chair. It had been a torturous night, with Jack's brain pressure initially rising, but then, thankfully leveling off.

"Has the doctor been in again?" Sara asked. "Did I miss him?"

"Haven't seen him since three o'clock. I think he would have woken us up if there was anything significant," Leila said, handing her one of two paper cups filled with coffee.

"Thanks," she muttered, peeling back the plastic on the lid to take a sip. The heat from the dark liquid traveled right through the cup, scorching the skin on her palm. "Wow! Could they make it any hotter?"

"Next time I'll put some ice in it for you," Leila said, blowing across her cup.

"It's eight o'clock. I think I'll check if they'll let me in to see Jack for a few minutes. I still can't believe they wouldn't let me stay next to him through the night," Sara said, stinging from her run-in with the intensive care nurses.

"They were just doing their job," Leila stressed. "He's so fragile right now they must think you would be in the way if he started to go into distress. It was probably safer for him that way. Come on, drink up so you're coherent when the doctor comes to give us an update."

Sara left to go freshen up in the ladies room. When she returned, Leila was on her feet, anxiously waiting.

"The doctor stopped by. He said he was going to check on Jack and then come back to talk to you," Leila explained.

"Good. Maybe we can go see him then," Sara said, returning to her chair. "I'll try to reach David after we talk to the doctor. It's awful waiting. I can't even imagine how terrible it is for David, being so far away and unable to do anything. I can't tell you how horrible the conversation was last night. Then when he couldn't get on a flight until this morning, he was torn up. All he wants is to be by his son's side."

Leila sat down in the chair next to her. "Don't worry. Jack is as tough as nails, just like his mom. He's going to make it through this and be fine!" she said, making Sara smile.

"Thanks again for staying with me. You, Emma and Carlos have been wonderful. I better check in with them. I know that Emma wants to come back later this morning. I told her she didn't need to, but you know that stubborn British streak. She wouldn't hear of it."

Twenty minutes passed before the doctor reappeared. His broad smile brought both women to their feet.

"Is he awake?" Sara asked.

"No, not yet," Dr. Garrison reported, "but he is slowly improving. We've seen a decrease in his brain pressure in the past two hours. That's a very good sign. The rest of his vitals are holding steady, and there is good circulation down at the fingertips of the badly broken arm."

"Can we see him?" Sara begged.

"Yes, one at a time, but for no more than 15 minutes per visit. If he continues to show progress in the next several hours, we can loosen that up. He's not completely out of the woods. We need to see him wake up and have some level of awareness. You need to be prepared for residual problems with his memory and decision-making skills. But the good news is that children are usually more resilient and therefore have a better prognosis than an adult with this type of brain injury," the doctor cautioned with a reassuring nod.

When the man left, Sara and Leila each did their own version of a happy dance. They pulled up short when a nurse poked her head in the room to see if Sara was ready to visit with her son.

Jack looked so peaceful in spite of the numerous tubes and

monitors attached to him. Leaning over and kissing his cheek, Sara could tell that his color was a little better than the day before. The cast of his right arm ran from below his shoulder to his fingers. The other hand was taped, holding an IV needle in place. She wanted to touch him, to hug him, to hold his hand, but his condition limited her physical contact. Sara had to settle for stroking his cheek as she spoke.

"Jack, you're doing great," she said. "The boo-boo in your head is getting better. The swelling is going down so it's going to be easier for you to wake up and talk to Mommy. Auntie Leila stayed with me all night in the waiting room. She can't wait for you to open your eyes. Daddy will be here soon. How about if you wake up before he gets here? That would be the best gift in the whole wide world."

Sara watched as Jack's chest rose and fell in a consistent rhythm, its regularity instilling in her a sense of security that he would get through this ordeal. When her father died, that was how she marked his passage from this world. His breaths had been irregular, gradually lengthening until a final prolonged exhale.

"Time's up, Mrs. Miller," a chubby nurse announced, startling Sara.

She nodded in her direction, stood up, and kissed Jack's cheek. "Honey-bunny, I promise I'll be back in a little while. Auntie Leila wants to see you too. Hang in there and keep fighting. I love you so much."

Walking out of the room, Sara looked at her watch. It was nearing the time that David would be departing for the airport. She figured she could catch him en route on his cell. He would have a better flight home knowing that there had been improvement. As Leila went in, Sara ran outside to make her calls. She dialed David's number, counting the number of rings until he answered.

"Hello," David answered.

"Hey, it's me," Sara replied. "The situation is encouraging this morning. The pressure on Jack's brain has started to drop. The doctor said this is a positive sign. We're just waiting for him to wake up. I told Jack to open his eyes by the time you get back."

"Thank God," David rejoiced. The heavy tone in his voice was lightened by the good news. "I'm so relieved. I knew I never should have left the two of you alone."

"It's not your fault. It was an accident. A priest was supposed to be out at the farm yesterday. I haven't had an opportunity to speak with Carlos to see how it went, but I think we're on the right track. If Jack's progress remains steady this morning, I'm going over to the nursing home to visit with Lester. He's the old guy who used to work for the McHugh family. I'm hoping he can put some of this craziness to rest. I just need to sneak past the guard dogs that try to pass themselves off as nurses."

"If you go anywhere, make sure Leila stays at the hospital. I'm not scheduled to land until around four-thirty this afternoon, so by the time I get to you, it will be after six. And that's if there aren't any delays. He needs to have someone there in case he wakes up," David said.

"I'm not an idiot. I know that. Call home if you run into flight problems. I'll have my cell off, but Emma can relay the message when she shows up."

"Will do," David said. "I love you."

"Me too," Sara answered. She pressed "end," then dialed her barn number.

"Hello?" The unmistakable Spanish accent resonated across the line.

"Good morning, Carlos," Sara responded. "How's everything there?"

"All the animals are good. How is Jack?" he asked.

Sara could hear Emma impatiently asking the same question in the background. Sara repeated what she had just told David about Jack's condition, then asked, "Did Father O'Connor make it out yesterday as promised?"

"*Sí.* He came and blessed the house. But you didn't tell me you were sending two priests. The dogs went *loco* when the second man drove in. They had him pinned against the car. By the time I pulled them into a stall, he was gone. Sped away. I think the dogs really scared the poop out of him," Carlos explained.

"What? That makes no sense. I only spoke to Father O'Connor about what had happened. Did this other priest have gray hair?" Sara asked, disturbed by the older priest's unexpected and uninvited presence at their home. The small hairs on the back of her neck felt electric. The image of puking on the church's front steps had not left her.

"*Si.* He was much older than the first man. Do you know him?"

"I'm pretty sure he's the other priest from the church, but frankly, I don't know what he wanted. Maybe there was an emergency and he was trying to track down Father O'Connor."

"Maybe."

"What time is Emma coming over?" Sara inquired. "I need to use her taxi skills again."

"Around noon," Carlos answered.

"Perfect. Tell her I'll see her then and take good care of everyone. I'll check in later. Thanks." Sara returned to the waiting room where Leila had resumed her position in a yellow chair.

Over the next few hours, Jack's condition remained stable. This allowed him to have increased visitation. Sara spent most of the morning by his side. He seemed to reach a plateau, neither improving dramatically nor worsening any further.

When Emma arrived at twelve-fifteen, she delivered bad news about David. "Hello, ladies. Hate to curdle the cream, but Sara, your husband called. Apparently storms are sweeping through the Midwest, causing delays and cancellations across the board. The airlines are pushing back their timetables. The first flights out are tentatively set for late afternoon," she reported.

"Oh...he must be as angry as a bear," Sara surmised aloud.

"You guessed correctly," Emma said lifting both eyebrows in exaggeration.

"Considering things haven't changed much here, I think we should take that ride out to visit good ol' Lester," she suggested. "Leila, would you mind hanging around here?"

"Please...you couldn't pry me away from the little guy if you tried. I'll ring you if there's any change, but according to his doc, progress could be slow. Remember, he told us it could take three to four days for him to come around."

"I know. I heard that too," Sara replied.

"Well, since you're totally convinced that this old geezer can help Jack, get going! Sooner you're there, the sooner you're back," Leila said, giving her friend a symbolic push.

"You're a doll, Auntie Leila," Sara said, blowing her a kiss.

The nursing home was 45 minutes away from the hospital. Sara had been mulling over the information that Carlos had told her during their phone conversation. Why would that older priest, Father Kennedy, show up at the farm? She had recognized him from her dreams but didn't think he had ever seen her before. This development solidified her suspicion that he had some sort of tie to the fractured family that once dwelled there.

"Emma, we may need to stop by that church again," Sara said. "Carlos told me that Father Kennedy showed up at the farm yesterday."

"I thought that was the point. You had them drive the nasty spirits away. Is there a problem?" Emma asked, her eyes glued to the treacherous country roads.

"The problem is that I think I recognized him. I ran into him, quite literally in the hallway. I didn't talk to him for more than a second and that was to apologize. Emma, he's been in my dreams. He was younger then, decades younger, but his face is still the same. I don't have a clue why he would have showed up at the farm yesterday," Sara explained.

"Perhaps the other guy told him he needed help, inexperienced with trapped souls. Two priests are better than one. Are you sure you saw this bloke in your dream?"

"I was 99 percent sure before, but now, knowing he showed up out of nowhere and then left without a word, I would bump that up to 100 percent. I think he's connected to the McHugh family. In my dream he's arguing with another man while some red-haired lady is crying nearby. Maybe he tried to intervene with Patrick and Maureen. She supposedly had red hair. Maybe she was distraught because Patrick had turned into such an ogre. This guy could be feeling guilty because he could have done something differently that would have changed the course of events for everyone involved. I mean, in the end, Patrick killed himself," Sara said in an effort to make sense out of the presence of this new character in the scenario.

By the time the women reached their destination, a light rain had started to fall. The nursing home parking lot was void of life except for a flock of Canadian geese waddling their way toward a pond on the other side of the property. It was still early for the arrival of seasonal birds, but Sara chose to think of it as a sign that winter was saying goodbye. As she and Emma crossed the lobby, Sara was surprised that the receptionist actually looked up from reading an issue of *The Star* to acknowledge their presence. The woman hidden behind the celebrity-splashed pages only stopped long enough to utter a nearly incomprehensible question: "Oo you gonna see?"

"Lester Brown," Sara said.

"Okay, turd flawe," the woman replied, vanishing behind the paper.

"So far so good. If he still had health problems, she would have stopped us or at least tried to," Emma said.

"I wouldn't bet on it. I have a hunch that her incompetence runs pretty deep," Sara said, rolling her eyes.

Lester wasn't in his room when they arrived. This sent Sara into a moment of panic as she considered the prospect that he had passed away. "See? I told you she was incompetent. The poor guy is probably dead already," Sara said as she gazed at his empty bed.

"That would be awful," Emma murmured.

"What should we do?"

Almost simultaneously, a woman's voice startled them. They turned around to face Lester Brown in a wheelchair, being pushed by the same unpleasant nurse who had chased Sara out of the home a few days earlier.

"Excuse me. Wait a minute. It's you! What are you doing back here?" the large pink-clad nurse said as she wheeled Lester past them to his bed.

"I'm here to visit with Mr. Brown. You said I could come back when he had recovered from his surgery. The receptionist told us he was well and it was safe to come up," Sara said, stretching the truth a little.

As the woman repositioned the old man onto his bed, she spoke loudly and slowly to him. "Lester, you have visitors. Are you feeling up to it? If not, I can send them away," she suggested.

"No. I have to stay. I really need to talk to him. My son's life may depend on it," Sara insisted.

As the nurse gave her a skeptical glance, Sara had the distinct impression that she was looking into the mug of a bloodhound. The folds of this woman's face and neck were dangling from the force of gravity, making her look remarkably like a canine cousin. Sara shook this image from her head to refocus on gaining full access to her target.

"Please. We are not going to take up very much of his time," Sara said calmly.

"Let her stay, Margaret. I never get to talk to anyone but you or Lamar over there, and half the time he's asleep," the old black man said, motioning for her to leave.

"Make it quick and don't upset him," the nurse said through tightly pursed lips as she pushed past them.

"Come sit over here, young lady. My eyes are bad and I can't see but a few feet in front of me. Do I know you?" he asked.

Sara moved around the room, taking up position in the chair next to the old man. Emma moved closer to the foot of the bed. Lester pushed himself up on his left elbow. With a fair amount of effort, he leaned in close to Sara to try to make out this mysterious visitor.

"No, sir," she explained loudly, "you don't actually know me. My name is Sara Miller. I came to visit you last week. You had just returned from your eye operation and your watchdog nurse wouldn't let me stay. Do you remember me stopping in to speak with you?"

"I recall there being some commotion here last week. Was that you? I thought the good Lord had sent an angel to come take me home. Why are you here?" Lester asked with a strong, slow Virginia twang. He collapsed back on his pillow; the effort of pulling himself up was too much to sustain for more than a moment. "If it's not the eyes failing me, it's the body. I apologize. I have no right to be complaining now. I've had a good life."

"Mr. Brown, could I please ask you some questions? I believe you are the only one that can help me," Sara said.

"How's that, if I don't even know you?" Lester asked, rightly confused.

"My family moved into the farm where you used to live. It's been a couple of months now. Initially, we couldn't have been happier, but sir, you see, there have been a number of very strange incidents that have taken place, and now my 7-year-old son is lying in a hospital bed, unconscious, as a direct result of one of these. I believe that the farm is haunted, if not by a ghost, then by the memories of the tragedies that the McHugh family experienced," Sara explained.

Lester closed his eyes, making Sara think that he drifted off to sleep. The two women looked at each other. Emma shrugged her shoulders and silently motioned for Sara to shake the old man. Just as she was reaching out to take hold of his arm, he spoke.

"It was a long time ago. The dead should be left to be. The McHughs were good folk. They took good care of me my whole life, gave me a job and a place to live. I will not sully their reputation now," he said opening his eyes to stare straight ahead.

Sara's heart sank, but she persisted in trying to sway the old man. "Mr. Brown, I believe the dead should be left to be, as well. They should rest in peace. The problem is, that's not what's happening out at the farm. Yesterday morning, I watched a little girl with long red hair race after my son's runaway pony. She was riding my horse, a horse that had gotten away from me before I could mount him. This girl was calling after Michael to stop. She caught my son's pony and he fell to the ground. She then vanished. My son, Jack, is in critical condition with broken bones, injured internal organs, and a very serious head injury. Now if you can convince me that the dead are resting in peace, I'll go away, and you'll never be bothered by me again. But Mr. Brown, I have to ask you something before you do. Do you really believe that your loyalty to this family is worth more than the life of another little boy?"

Lester's head turned so he was facing Sara. He was obviously torn. Through trembling lips he spoke as he relived each 40-year old detail. "Michael had gotten a pony for his birthday, a 6-year-old bay stallion. God only knows why Patrick bought the boy a stallion, but he did. The boy wasn't supposed to ride him without his pa's supervision. I came out from the shed house and there they were, Katy and Michael. The boy was racing through the field, Katy was close behind on her gray mare. I heard some yelling but couldn't make out what they were saying. Next thing I saw was Michael's pony make a sharp turn and head for the stone wall. He lost his balance. The boy's head smashed on the rocks. Katy's horse pulled up in time to avoid trampling him. I ran out to them. I don't think I ever ran so fast. When I got there, Katy was rocking her brother in her arms. I could see where his skull was pushed in and blood was oozing out. She looked up at me and said it was her fault. By the time the ambulance arrived, Patrick had ridden back in from hunting. He shook Katy hard, demanding to know what happened. She would only repeat over and over that it was her fault. Michael died a few days later, but it really killed all of them."

Sara listened intently while watching the tears stream down Lester's leathery face. By the time he finished telling this story, he could barely speak. The old man dropped his head into his bony hands and sobbed.

Sara waited for him to regain his composure before speaking. "It wasn't her fault. She was calling out for him to stop. Michael had raced out after the hunt that had galloped through the property minutes earlier. He had blatantly ignored his father, and Katy knew he was going to get into trouble. She tried desperately to reach him. I know because I stood witness to it yesterday. I'm not sure how or why this was shown to me, but it was. She only thought she was responsible because of failing to catch her brother before his fall. Yesterday morning, she didn't fail. In fact, she may have saved Jack's life," Sara explained.

A look of shock had weaved itself through Lester's worn features.

Emma had remained silent up until now. "Could this be it? That she was unfairly blamed?"

"I don't know. Maybe," Sara answered, however her gut was telling her there was more to it. "Mr. Brown, can you tell me about the three girls? What happened to them after Michael died? I know that the two older girls moved away and Katy became a nun. But where are they and why didn't they come back to settle the estate?"

"Grace, the oldest went off and married herself a doctor and had a boatload of young'uns. I think eight in all. They were up in New York City. Never cared to come back. Memories of Michael dying haunted them all. Eileen was a couple of years younger. She moved up to the Boston area, not really sure where. She wanted to see the world, but she gave that up when she got married. I think he was a fireman or policeman. I can't recall exactly. The two of them had about a dozen kids. Patrick used to say she was crazy with all those kids. It was a real shame 'cause he and Maureen never saw any of their grandbabies," he explained.

"What about Katy?" Emma asked.

A transformation swept over the old man's face as he spoke; his friendly features turned hard and distant. "Katy had it rough. As far as any of us knew, the accident was her fault. I mean, that's what she told us. And Pat, well, he lost his son and just couldn't forgive her. There isn't anything more to say about her. She found her peace with the Lord. What happened, happened."

"So Katy is off in a convent somewhere? Do you have any idea where?" Sara asked.

"I don't have anything else to say about Katy other than she suffered the most," the old man said in as firm a tone as he could muster.

"I see," Sara said, sensing his reluctance to speak anymore about this particular daughter.

"Mr. Brown, you said that the McHughs never saw any of their grandchildren. Did I hear you correctly?" Emma asked.

Sara wasn't sure where her British friend was going with this.

"Yes, that's right. I think it would have done them some good after losing Michael—given them a way to climb out of the past and grab hold of the future," he answered.

"I find that very peculiar because James Sullivan told us he saw one of those girls carrying a baby out of the house in the company of her father, Patrick. How would you explain that?" Emma asked, cocking her head.

"Sullivan must be out of his mind or maybe drinking too much alcohol," he said.

"Maybe. Or maybe you aren't being completely forthcoming, sir. It makes me wonder why," Emma said.

"Are you calling me a liar? You have some nerve calling an old man you never met a liar. Let me tell you a thing or two, young missy. I have never done anything that wasn't in the McHugh family's best interest," he exclaimed growing increasingly agitated.

Sara responded by trying to calm him down. "I'm so sorry for my friend's rude accusation. I'm sure she didn't mean to disparage you in any way. We appreciate your willingness to speak with us about the past. Believe me, we are not trying to taint the McHugh family's good name. You've been so kind, and we certainly don't want to upset you."

"That's right! I am being very kind," he said shaking his finger in Emma's direction.

"Mr. Brown, if you don't mind, do you happen to know Grace and Eileen's married names?" Sara asked, hoping he hadn't shut down on them.

Lester shifted his eyes from Emma back to Sara. "I don't know why it would matter to you. They haven't been back to the farm since they were youngsters."

"Please, Mr. Brown. Humor a mother whose child is somewhere between life and…and a place I can't say," she implored, taking hold of one of his hands.

He softened his demeanor, squinting to try to bring her face into focus, "Eileen Finnegan and Grace McCarthy. That's their names now."

Sara felt a shot of adrenaline burn through her veins. She looked over at Emma and grinned. She felt as if she had just won the lottery. "Thank you," Sara said. "Thank you so much, Mr. Brown. You know, this may seem odd, but I'd like to pay a visit to Michael, Maureen and Patrick's graves. I'm convinced that Katy wasn't responsible for her brother's accident. I'm hoping my theory will put their souls at ease."

"You would bring them flowers?" he asked, prompting Sara to nod her head. "That's nice of you, Sara. You're a good girl. Michael is buried over in the cemetery at St. Thomas' Catholic Church. But Patrick and Maureen, they became embittered with.... Well, let's just say they stopped going up to the Catholic Church is all. They're buried in the Lutheran cemetery over in Warrenton," he revealed.

"Thank you, again. I'll visit soon and let you know how my son is faring." Sara patted his arm as she stood up to leave. Following Emma across the cramped room, she turned to ask Lester one final question. "I'm sorry, this kind of stuck in my head. Did the McHughs happen to know Father Kennedy over at St. Thomas' Church?"

Lester's face grew serious. "That man is not what he seems. He's a devil in disguise. You'd best stay away from him."

"I see. I certainly will. Bye-bye for now."

As they were about to get on the elevator, Margaret bulldozed down the hall toward them. When the doors slid open, they made a quick escape, choosing to avoid another confrontation with the cranky nurse.

"What did you think?" Emma asked.

Sara smiled. She was sure she was on the right track. "I think I've discovered the hidden connection. The adoption documents I found in my mother's safety deposit box revealed that a Grace Anne McCarthy was my biological mother. Grace McHugh got married and became Grace McCarthy, which makes me seriously question whether I could be a descendant of this insane family. Consider all the strange visions and dreams that I've been having. Could my presence in the house have opened some sort of weird window into the past? Maybe Michael wanted to set the record straight about his sister's involvement in his death and his spirit was able to channel that through me."

"Sounds a tad bit far-fetched, but going on the assumption that your hunch is valid, what now?" Emma asked.

"Now? Now we find Grace McHugh-McCarthy. She's going to fill in the rest of the story," Sara said as they traipsed through the lobby.

"Isn't it strange that Lester claims that they never saw a grandchild? What was that about?" Emma commented.

"He wasn't lying. The baby wouldn't be their grandchild if that child was put up for adoption. Think about it. The woman was already overflowing with kids. Another baby could have put unbearable stress on her marriage. Who knows? I could have been the product of an affair. Grace could have come down here to give the baby up, possibly through Catholic Charities. It would explain why Patrick and Maureen were so angry with the church. They may have felt that the one grandkid they got to meet was being shipped off to someone else. Heck, that may explain the dreams I've had of that priest, Father Kennedy, arguing with another man. It must have been Patrick. Who but the devil would tear another child from their family? That devil is Father Kennedy. The woman crying was Maureen, the lady with red hair. And the baby crying? It had to be me. With how twisted the whole thing appears, it's likely that Katy was somehow involved in the whole process. It didn't sound like their opinion of her improved over time," Sara said with a rush of energy.

"Damn!" Emma exclaimed. "I'm amazed at how complete the pieces fit together."

"We need to get back to the hospital. I have a special job for Leila. With her connections and computer expertise, she'll have Grace McCarthy tracked down by the end of the day," Sara said with confidence.

CHAPTER FIFTEEN

Sara bounded into the waiting room, with Emma following closely on her heels. She found Leila reading a magazine in the corner of the room.

"How is Jack doing?" Sara asked, standing squarely in front of the seated woman.

"He's improving a little. His levels are moving in the right direction. The doctor is cautiously optimistic," Leila replied.

"Great! I'm going to keep my fingers and toes crossed that he heard me and wakes up by the time his father arrives."

"That would be a miracle, wouldn't it?" Emma commented, clasping her hands together. "Another fantastic development."

"God, yes! It sure would top the day off," Sara answered, giving the girl a knowing glance.

"I caught that," Leila said. "What did Lester tell you? Spill the dirt."

"It turns out that Mr. Brown was very informative and tremendously helpful at shedding some light on the McHugh family. You see, he was able to tell me one vitally important detail—one he doesn't even know he gave me. It just so happens that my birth mother's name and the married name of the oldest daughter are the same. Quite a coincidence, wouldn't you say?"

Leila's jaw dropped as she gasped. "That's unbelievable. How creepy is it that you moved into that house? When you were looking at the house, you kept telling David that you felt like you were home. Apparently you were right. It's too weird!"

"I need your help. You have all sorts of connections. All those high-powered men you've slept with will finally come in handy. Run through your memory. Is there anyone who stands out that you can squeeze a favor out of? Someone who may have the means to track Grace down? Lester told us she was married to a doctor in New York. I think we should go on the assumption that they're still living there. So it would be Dr. and Mrs. McCarthy. Grace's middle name was Anne, Grace Anne McCarthy."

"Hell, yes!" Leila screeched. "There have to be at least a half-dozen guys that I can tap into for help. Off the top of my head I can think of a congressman from New York, a couple of lawyers, a computer wizard, and some docs. There's probably an American Medical Association database they could scan. Do you know the doc's first name?"

"No. He didn't give us that," Sara answered.

"I'll probably be able to locate her myself. You would be amazed at what a computer search will pull up. We know her maiden and married names and most likely location. Anything else that could be pertinent?" Leila asked.

"What about her sister, Eileen?" Emma added. "She was married to a cop or fireman."

"She's up in New England. I would check Boston first. Last name was Finnegan," Sara said.

"How about her age? Any clues?" Leila asked.

Sara and Emma looked at each other. Neither Lester nor James Sullivan ever mentioned how old she could be.

"I'm thirty-five. I'm guessing that I was probably her last child. She had eight other kids, and women usually married in their early twenties back then. Figuring a year or two between each child would make her sixty-five to seventy-five years old. Wow, I never really thought about her being old. She could even be dead by now. That would be an unanticipated complication, huh?" Sara said, suddenly concerned.

"She had nine kids?" Leila clarified, looking completely revolted by the thought. "Are you sure you're related? You're not exactly the best whelper in town. Let's not think negatively. I'll head home, make some calls, punch some info into the computer, and we'll see who gets dredged up. With any luck, I'll come back with an address and phone number."

"You're an angel," Sara said.

Leila picked up her coat and purse to leave. "Check in with me in a couple of hours. Keep me posted on Jack."

"Thanks," Sara added.

"Why don't you visit with your son while I check in with Carlos at home?" Emma offered.

"That sounds like a wonderful idea," Sara agreed. "I'll be back in half an hour."

Time seemed to evaporate for Sara as each precious minute ticked by with Jack. She was surprised when Emma stuck her head in the room and motioned for her to step out. There was news about David. The weather conditions that had delayed or cancelled the majority of flights west of the Mississippi were starting to improve. It looked like the stranded father was going to get a break. "I spoke with Carlos. He said David called back with a revised flight plan. Your husband is about to board. If all goes as scheduled, he will get in around midnight and then come straight over to meet you here in the wee hours of the morning."

"That's a relief," Sara commented. "He'll be glad to finally be underway."

"How's Jack?" Emma asked.

"About the same. I've tried willing him to wake up, but no luck. It kills me to see him like this…rips my heart right out of my chest. He looks so vulnerable. I know he's getting better, but it still scares the hell out of me. I'd gladly trade places with him. I feel so damn powerless."

"He's going to get better," Emma assured Sara. "You'll see."

Sara was impatient in spite of knowing that she had to give Leila time to get home to set things in motion. The hands on the wall clock inched toward seven in the evening. She noticed that Emma had fallen asleep while reading a magazine. Caving into her mounting curiosity, Sara quietly left the room to phone her appointed detective. She was directed immediately into voice mail that told her Leila was on the other line.

"It's me. I'm biting my fingers into bloody nubs waiting to find out if you've uncovered anything. I'll call back in a little while. Ciao."

Killing time between calls, Sara walked around the lobby and gift shop. There, tucked among a pile of stuffed animals, was a goofy-looking puppy dog resembling a Great Dane. She purchased it, thinking that Jack would find it comical when he woke up. After signing her credit card receipt, she rechecked the time. It was now seven forty-five. With bag in hand, she returned to the darkened parking lot to try Leila again. This time she answered.

"Hey. What do you have for me?" Leila asked.

"What? I don't know what you're talking about," Sara responded. "Have you found Grace?"

"Sorry. I was expecting Brian to call back. Dr. Brian Toone. He's a plastic surgeon in New York. Did some liposuction for me a while back, very handy with his tools—if you get my drift. He's following up on a lead for me. If the phone beeps with another call, I need to take it. Sara, we may have our girl." Leila was on the verge of being giddy.

"You are shittin' me! You've only worked on this for a couple of hours."

"I told you I could deliver," Leila said proudly.

"But I don't understand how this Dr. Whoever is going to help us," Sara asked.

"Dr. Toone. He recognized the name—Dr. McCarthy. He was pretty sure his wife sees an OB/GYN by that name. Anyway, he had to go down to her bedroom to ask. He warned me that there are probably a gazillion docs with that name and to not get my hopes too high. I guess it's a pretty common Irish-American surname. But I have to tell you, I have a good feeling about it. He's supposed to call right back."

The call-waiting signal beeped twice just as Leila finished her sentence.

"Perfect timing. Hold on."

As Sara paced up and down the sidewalk, she could feel her heart racing. Minutes passed, making her want to crawl out of her own skin. By the time she heard Leila again, she felt lightheaded and had to take a seat on the curb.

"Dr. Dennis McCarthy, OB/GYN, is still practicing in New York. He's in his early seventies, set to retire later this year. And his lovely wife, Grace, has worked in the office as the receptionist for more than a decade, setting up appointments. She didn't like being home alone after the last of her eight children went off to college. Sara my dear, we may have found your biological parents," Leila announced triumphantly.

"You're amazing!" Sara screamed. "I knew you could do it. Did you get their address?" She was completely in awe of her friend's abilities.

"What do you think I am—an incompetent spy? I have the office address and phone number, as well as their home address and number. I think I'll call in one more favor and secure us some upscale private jet transportation. When do you want to leave?"

"I'm not sure. David won't get here until sometime around two in the morning. I haven't had a chance to tell him any of this. He is going to freak. Could life be any more bizarre?"

"You never cease to provide me with a reason to appreciate my comparatively normal life," Leila said, laughing aloud.

"Your life is anything but normal," Sara replied.

"My point exactly, my friend," Leila stressed, still finding humor where Sara found little.

"Humph! Back to the matter at hand, I know David will want to stay with Jack. If you can blackmail someone into letting us use their plane, let's try to take off tomorrow morning around nine o'clock. I'll need to get a shower and clean clothes. Can I come to your place before leaving for the airport?"

"No problem," Leila concurred. "In fact, I would insist on it. You don't want your first impression with Grace and Dennis to be that you've turned into some sort of disheveled homeless woman. If I get us a nine o'clock take off time, you should try to arrive at my place no later than six. Of course, I'm assuming you'll abscond with David's vehicle."

"Shouldn't be an issue," Sara said. "Do you want me to call

back to confirm the flight time?"

"Just be here tomorrow morning. New York, here we come!"

Sara pushed herself up from the edge of the sidewalk. Looking up at the concrete building rising in front of her, she spoke to herself. "You hang in there, my little man. The planets are aligning in our favor."

The elevator opened on the floor housing Intensive Care. Sara returned to the family waiting room and found Emma awake, flipping through a two-inch thick fashion magazine. Her short blonde locks were pressed flat against one side of her head. It was like having half a head with hat hair while the other was normal.

"Hey," Sara said.

"And where did you sneak off to?" Emma asked, taking the paper bag from Sara's hand to examine the contents. "I see you're carrying some sort of fluffy pup there. I presume you raided the gift shop?"

"Sure did. Then I called Leila. She found them, Dr. and Mrs. Dennis McCarthy. I guess it pays to have friends in low places that have friends in high places. She's arranging for us to fly to New York in the morning on one of her ex or current lover's private jets."

"You must be, um...I'm not sure exactly what you must be, but I'm sure you are," Emma bumbled out.

"Well put, my English friend. Explains my emotions exactly."

"I believe this is evidence that I'm in need of lessons from that girl because obviously I must be doing something wrong. The only blokes I attract are poor and without prospect. Do you think she could direct some of her cast-offs in my direction?" Emma asked in a semi-joking manner.

"Ah, you don't want any of them. They're usually married and old," Sara answered.

"Mmm, you're right there. You wouldn't mind the taste of prunes if you harvested them as plums, but to go straight to prunes...it would make me lose my pucker," Emma said pursing her lips like she had just bitten into a sour lemon.

The description uncorked laughter from both of them. After several minutes, they were able to pull together enough composure to speak.

"My funny friend, you should head home for the night," Sara suggested. "You have been a valiant trooper. Get a good night's rest."

"Are you sure you don't want me to stay? I really don't mind. Carlos has everything well in hand at the farm."

"I think you've far surpassed your job description over the last couple of days...hell, the last few weeks. I can't even begin to tell you how much I appreciate all you've done. I don't see any reason for you to spend the night slumped in a chair. Jack is stable. David will be here in a few hours. Then I'm off on a mission come morning. Get out of here! Go crawl into a real bed. With the grace of God, Jack will emerge from his coma at any time now and then we can all go home to get a good night's sleep."

Emma smiled and patted Sara on the knee. "You're the boss. Off I go. Let me know how tomorrow pans out, and kisses for Jack."

Sara watched as the door swung shut. She picked up the stuffed dog and held it tightly against her chest. This was the first time since Jack's accident that she was alone standing vigil, waiting for him to come back from the edge. Laughing with Emma had been good medicine for her soul. She was lost in her thoughts when a pretty nurse stuck her head in to find her.

"Mrs. Miller, you may want to come sit with Jack. We've had some signs that he may be getting closer to coming around. It's important for someone to be with him."

"Oh, my God! That's great. Thank you," Sara said, rushing past the woman.

When she got to Jack's bedside, she was surprised to see that he appeared the same as before. Somehow she thought he would have looked different. She dragged the chair out of the corner and sat down next to him. She gently held the fingers on his left hand. "Hi honey-bunny. It's Mommy. I know you can hear me. I love you. The nurse said you're going to wake up any minute now. I can't wait. I've missed your smile so much. Your dad will be here in a couple of hours. He's going to be so happy. We both are. I knew you were trying to wake up before your father arrived. You are one tough cookie. I'm right here and I'm not leaving," Sara said. She squeezed the plush puppy she still had in her hand. "Oh I forgot to give you this. I bought you a little present. I can't wait for you to see it. He'll be beside your pillow." She carefully positioned the stuffed dog to the side of Jack's head.

Sara chatted away for hours, hoping her son would open his eyes. It was close to midnight when exhaustion crept up on her. She fought to stay awake but eventually succumbed to sleep. It was three o'clock in the morning when a noise jerked her awake. It took her a moment to register that David was nowhere in sight. Concern flooded her semi-conscious state and fueled her movements. Thinking he should have been there close to an hour ago, she found herself standing at the ICU nurse's station. Sara glanced at the name on the nurse's badge before addressing her.

"Excuse me, Carol. I was wondering if you've seen my husband, David?" Sara asked, pushing her disheveled hair behind one ear. "I thought he would have gotten here by now."

"He walked in about 10 minutes ago," the nurse answered. "We updated him on your son's condition before he went in. He made it to the entrance, took one look and had to step out to compose himself. I think he's in the hall."

"I fell asleep. Are there any changes?"

"No. He's stable," Carol reported. "That's good. He hasn't shown any additional indicators that he's emerging from the coma. I know it's terribly frustrating when it appears there's progress and then it seems to stall. Try to be patient; his brain needs time to recover from the trauma. There's a lot to hope for."

Sara nodded, although she longed for quicker progress. She wanted to find David. She was worried that he didn't wake her. She located him slumped against a wall in the hallway. He had his eyes closed and was pinching the bridge of his nose. She could tell he had been crying. Sara cleared her throat to draw her husband's attention. Glancing in the direction of the sound, he immediately straightened up and went to her.

"I'm glad you're back," Sara said, meeting him halfway. The couple embraced for several tension-filled minutes. "Are you ready to go in?"

"I think so. I thought I had been prepared but I wasn't. Seeing him lying there like that, I…I didn't want to fall apart in front of him."

"I understand."

As Sara escorted David back into the ICU, they could see the motionless boy through the glass that divided the room from the nurses' monitoring area. Jack was hooked up to monitors, oxygen, and IV lines. Sara stood by her husband's side, painfully aware of how shocking the picture was. Putting her hand on his shoulder, she felt an unexpected shudder. David turned and looked at her. Tears were lining the rims of his eyes. His composure was quickly deteriorating. He held her hand. Husband and wife, father and mother, stood there in silence, desperately clinging to one another, giving each other permission to feel the flood of emotions they had fought to suppress until now, emotions that would have engulfed each of them and rendered them useless to aid their ailing son. Neither needed words to express the heartache and terror plaguing them. David let go of her hand and went to Jack's side.

"Hey, buddy. It's Dad. Sorry I couldn't get here sooner. Gosh, I missed you. The nurses told me you've been a super patient. Your boo-boos are almost healed up and it's time to go home. So wake up, bud. Your mom and I are here and ready to see your silly grin," the shaken father said.

Sara noticed the time. It was close to three-thirty, less than two hours before she needed to drive to Leila's house. She was feeling pressured to talk to David about the theory she had concocted about her suspected birth parents and the plan to go to New York.

"David, I need to talk to you," she said.

"About Jack?" he asked, an uneasiness littering his question as his gaze focused in on the beeping monitors.

"No. The doctors have said he's doing exceptionally well. In fact, we thought he was coming around a few hours ago," Sara explained.

"That's a relief. You scared the crap out of me. So what's the problem?"

"I need to talk to you about something else. It's important. Maybe we should step out so we don't disturb Jack or the other patients."

"What? Can't it wait until later?"

"It can't. Please, you'll understand as soon as you hear what I have to say."

"Sara, forget it," he adamantly replied. "I'm not leaving. If you have something to say you'll have to tell me here."

She sighed with resignation and then spent the next 15 minutes giving him a complete run down of the conversation with Lester and the results of Leila's search. She also shared her suspicions about Father Kennedy. David listened intently, asking for little additional detail until she was done.

"What's your take on this little soap opera? Any ideas or comments from my security consultant husband?" she asked, truly wanting him to agree with her convoluted conclusions.

"I...I don't even know what to say. You want to take off for New York to pursue some far-fetched idea that this woman, who may or may not be your birth mother, can somehow heal our son who is lying here in a hospital bed with titanium hardware sticking out of his head. I'm not sure if the stress has caused you to lose your mind or if you were always this nuts and I've overlooked it," David angrily said.

"I'm not crazy! It's no coincidence that we found this house, that my birth mother grew up within its walls, or our son had an accident that almost duplicates the one that killed Michael. I think we were lured here to set the record straight, to expose the truth," Sara replied.

"You're putting your trust in a fantasy," he insisted. "For God's sake, think about what you're suggesting. It's beyond ridiculous. I swear I never should have left the two of you alone. I should have known that your mother's death was too big a blow for you to absorb. You couldn't handle losing the baby. Hell, you were non-functional for months. We ended up moving because of it, and look what's happened now. You're worse than ever!" David rubbed his temples in frustration.

"That's not fair! It's not the same."

"Really? Seems to me that you're just as obsessed and unable to face reality."

"At least I didn't act like nothing happened—like our daughter didn't matter."

"Now who's being unfair? I grieved for Grace, but we had another child to take care of, one that needed us. I kept on living."

An uncomfortable silence filled the room. Sara realized that they had spent more than a year skillfully masking the tension that stewed dangerously under the surface of their "happy" marriage. She knew that the majority of couples that bury a child end up divorcing from the strain.

"It's my fault Jack is lying in a hospital bed. I shouldn't have gone to California."

"Don't you understand? It wouldn't have mattered. We've been set on this course by a force that knows no bounds. Its parameters extend beyond the confines of the property. We didn't initiate this game or contribute to the rules, but destiny dictates that we'll be the ones to end it. I will be the one to end it," Sara explained.

"You're seriously scaring me when you talk like that. You realize that, don't you?" He studied Sara's face, absorbing the full intensity of her being. "I can see it in your face: You're completely consumed by the unlikely possibility of this incredible scenario being true."

"David, I need to go to New York. I have to leave. Leila will have a flight for us in a few hours. I'm sorry you can't support me."

"You're going to leave Jack again. Bad enough you've been running off interrogating some old man in a nursing home. Now you want to abandon your son to chase after this delusion. I can't lose you to this insanity. I won't," David said, taking hold of her hands.

An irritated nurse interrupted their exchange. "Excuse me! There are very sick patients on this floor. We can hear you arguing at the desk. You need to keep it down or take it outside."

"Sorry. It won't happen again," David apologized.

The nurse spun on her heels and left the couple to stare at one another. Sara's eyes pleaded her case in silence, forcing David to turn away. It felt as if those she loved the most dangled by a fraying and tenuous thread. If he was right, she must be slipping into madness. If she was, a more ominous threat was looming. And at the very least their marriage was in danger of dissolving underneath their feet.

"I'm coming back—back with the truth to set us all free from the past," Sara insisted. "The key that unlocks the final clue is in New York. I feel it."

"I can't do this anymore. Do what you want. I'm tired of fighting with you."

Sara kissed Jack on the cheek and whispered, "I promise, I will not fail you or my family."

CHAPTER SIXTEEN

The limo driver met the two women at ten-thirty in the morning as they disembarked from the luxurious private jet. Sara had assumed that they would fly into LaGuardia, but the plane brought them into a private airstrip in Westchester County.

"Welcome to New York. Do you have any luggage with you?" the driver asked.

"No baggage needed this time," Leila answered, slipping him a piece of paper with two addresses scribbled across it. "Here are our destinations. How long do you think it will take us?"

"That depends on which one you want to go to first?" he asked.

Leila looked over at Sara who had begun to climb into the rear seat. "What do you think?"

"Should we try his office first?" Sara asked, nervously. "I'm guessing they would be at work this time of day."

Leila agreed and then turned to the driver "Let's head to the doctor's office on Park Avenue," she said, getting in the car. "I'll update you if we need to change the plan."

He nodded in acknowledgement and closed the door. Sara watched him walk to the front and get in. Leila slid up the privacy divider, blocking out his view of the back.

"Do you want to call to make sure they are there or do you want me to do it?" Leila asked.

"I don't think I can," Sara said. "What if Grace answers the phone? I'm not sure I could talk."

"No problem. I have it covered." Leila took out her cell phone, hit speaker mode and then dialed the number she had copied onto a second slip of paper.

A recording answered, directing the caller to hit one to make an appointment, two to speak to a nurse, three to be connected to billing, or zero for all other inquiries.

"I'm guessing that tracking down your birth parents would fall into the 'all other inquiries' category," Leila said, pressing the zero.

"Very funny," Sara replied.

"Hello, Drs. McCarthy, Meadows, and Paine's office. How can I help you?" the female receptionist inquired.

"Hi. I was wondering if Dr. McCarthy is in today?" Leila asked.

"Are you a patient?"

"Not exactly. I'm an old friend of the family," Leila said, stretching the truth like it was Silly Putty. "I'm in town for a convention and was hoping to swing by to surprise Dennis and Grace. Are they in today?"

"No. I'm sorry. They aren't. They've been on vacation for the past two weeks. Dr. McCarthy isn't expected back in the office until tomorrow," the voice informed her apologetically.

"Do you know if they're at home?" Leila asked. "I could stop by their place."

"I think they were scheduled to get in late last night."

"Perfect. I'll try them there. Thank you very much." Leila disconnected the call before the receptionist could say another word.

"So we're off to their house. You better tell the driver up front to alter his course," Sara said.

Leila picked up the phone linking the back to the front of the limo and relayed the change of plans. It would be another 45 minutes before they could weave their way to the McCarthy's brownstone on Charlton Street in lower Manhattan. When the car finally pulled up to the curb and stopped, Sara felt dizzy. She took a compact out of her purse to check her make-up and realized that all the color had drained from her face. She was now a frightening shade of gray. Sara added a little blush to her cheeks, but didn't think it helped conceal how she was feeling.

"Here," Leila said, pushing a glass with some clear liquid into her friend's hand.

"What's that?" Sara asked, bringing it up to her nose to smell. The aroma of alcohol burned her nostrils. She momentarily considered handing it back but decided a shot of vodka or whatever it was would help to put the bones and muscles back in her now rubbery legs. She downed it and held the glass out for a refill.

Leila accommodated her, adding at least one more shot of Grey Goose to the crystal tumbler. The driver came around and opened the rear door as Sara finished up the second round. He held out a hand, encouraging her step out onto the sidewalk.

"Okay, kiddo. Here we go," Leila said, pushing her from behind.

Sara and Leila found themselves in front of a four-story, rust-colored building. Stone steps led up to the main doorway. The grip of winter had not yet released the city. Piles of blackened snow lined the street, with puddles of gray slush rimming the edges. Explosive gusts of air whipped between the buildings, creating a wind tunnel. Sara's hair took flight in all directions, stinging her cheeks as it lashed against her vulnerable skin.

"Hell, I guess he's done well for himself as a doctor. These are worth a fortune," Leila commented, swiping a stray strand of hair from the corner of her perfectly painted lips.

"What is he, an OB/GYN? I thought the high cost of mal-practice insurance was putting them all out of business," Sara added.

"Maybe he works in the fertility field. They make mega bucks. I don't think insurance covers test tube babies and those other procedures," Leila concluded.

"Possible. So, any good ideas about what I say to them? You know, like…Hello, I'm Sara, the daughter you didn't keep. Can you tell me the deal with the haunted house? Oh, and by the way, your sister, Katy, wasn't to blame for Michael's accident."

"Works for me. I'd give them a minute or two after they come around from passing out to add the last little tidbit. You want to make sure they get it all." Leila squinted through locks of dark hair tangled in with her eyelashes. She put her arm around Sara and squeezed. "Come on, I've got your back. If they give you a hard time, I'll just open a can of 'Leila whoop ass' on them."

"I'll hold you to it. Deep breath and here we go."

The brownstone's exterior door allowed visitors to enter a

vestibule. On the wall were three buzzers that coincided with three names. Typed out neatly next to the one on the top were Dr. and Mrs. Dennis McCarthy. Leila reached out and pressed the button.

A few moments later a man's voice streamed through the intercom. "Hello. Who is it?"

The two women froze. Neither uttered a sound.

"Hello? Is someone there?" came the voice again.

"Yes. I'm sorry. My name is Sara Miller. I've come to speak to Grace McCarthy about the farm in Virginia. The one she grew up on. I hate to disturb you. I understand you've just returned from vacation, but this is very important. Please, I won't take much of your time."

"What's this about?" he asked suspiciously. "Why would you be interested in what Grace could tell you? She hasn't lived there in 40 years."

"I would like to talk to her about her sister Katy…and the baby. The baby given up for adoption," Sara said, concerned that she may have played her hand too soon.

There was a moment of silence. Sara and Leila eyed each other and held their breath.

"Please wait," the male voice echoed.

The seconds painstakingly ticked by as they indulged his request. Leila examined the expensive wallpaper while Sara shifted her weight nervously from side to side. She couldn't face being turned away. She jumped when the intercom crackled.

"I'll buzz you through," the man said. "We're on the third floor."

The two climbed the steep stairway up to the top floor. At the door stood a distinguished older gentleman whose expression remained unchanged as his eyes examined the approaching women. He backed against the frame, allowing them to pass into the residence. They stopped to wait for his direction, taking in the breathtaking fourteen-foot ceilings and ornate crown moldings.

"I didn't realize there were two of you," he said after closing the door.

"I'm Sara Miller and this is my friend, Leila Collins. Is your wife here?" she asked.

"Yes. She's waiting for you in the study. Follow me please," Dr. McCarthy said, gesturing for them to fall in behind.

Sara could tell that Leila would have loved to have spent the day going through the McCarthy's home. The traditionally elegant furnishings reeked of good taste. At one point she fell behind when she stuck her head through a door that was slightly ajar. She caught up as they reached the threshold of the study. The room was paneled in walnut, with bookcases running the length of one wall. Off to the side of the room, a petite older woman with silver hair drawn up tightly in a bun stood looking down at an old black and white framed photograph. She placed it carefully back down on an end table when her husband entered with Sara and Leila.

"My dear, this is Sara Miller and her friend, Leila," he announced.

Before the doctor had time to finish his introductions, Grace walked directly over to Sara to look her straight in the eye. Sara felt unnerved, unsure of what to do or say. The moment's intensity was far more than what she could have imagined. Old hands reached up, cradling Sara's face, as a wispy voice broke free of the confines of its aged owner.

"Kathleen. My God. Dennis. It's Kathleen," the woman said without breaking eye contact.

"Grace, this woman is not Kathleen. Dear, she's gone. You know that," he said, going over to gently remove his wife's hands.

"You're Kathleen. I'm convinced of it," Grace repeated.

"Sara, wasn't your birth name Kathleen?" Leila asked.

Hearing Leila seemed to break Sara free of the trance she was in. "Yes, yes. You're right. That was my name. Kathleen was the name you gave me. That's the name on my adoption papers. You gave me up 35 years ago," Sara said, speaking to the woman facing her now, the same woman listed as her birth mother.

"You look just like her. I knew it was you. You have the same face, but your hair is different. Yours is brown," she said, stroking Sara's long locks.

"How did you find us?" Dr. McCarthy asked.

"Are you my father?" Sara zeroed in on the balding man standing behind his wife.

"You don't understand," he said, shaking his head.

"There's an understatement," Leila mumbled.

"I think we should sit down, all of us. I'm afraid that you may be in for a shock," the man said as he led his wife to the sofa.

Sara and Leila each took a chair. They glanced at one another, confused by his last comment. The couple facing them held hands as they searched for the right words.

"You're correct. Your birth name was Kathleen—Kathleen Teresa. And I was listed as your mother. I did give you up for adoption. But my dear child, we are not your parents. I am not your mother," Grace explained in a barely audible volume.

"What?" Sara asked. "What the hell do you mean that you're not my parents? Why else would you be on the adoption papers?"

"To protect you and…," Grace said as tears started to fill her eyes. "…and to protect your mother. There was no choice."

"If you're not my birth mother, than who the heck is?" Sara asked, feeling sick to her stomach.

"I named you after her. Your mother was my sister, Kathleen," Grace revealed.

Sara's head was spinning. She felt Leila's hand reach across to touch her arm.

"It's Katy. Katy is your mother," her friend said with a mixture of excitement and alarm.

"How did you know that we called her Katy?" Grace asked, surprised by hearing the shortened version of her sister's name.

"We know an awful lot about the McHugh family. I bought your parents' farm," Sara said softly, still reeling from the revelation.

"What?" Grace asked, turning ashen in color. "You bought the farm. Why would you do that? What would possess you to go back there?"

"That's the key word: possess. It was definitely unintentional," Sara murmured. "How can this be? I don't understand. Katy was a nun." She blankly stared at the couple across from her.

"This must be a very difficult situation for you to digest. Here you arrived, thinking we were your biological parents," Dr. McCarthy said with the kind of compassion and gentleness a doctor would use when delivering bad news. "Grace, I think you should share what details we have," he suggested to his wife.

"Yes, she deserves to know. Sara, you're right. Katy was a nun. She never told me who your father was. I didn't even know she was pregnant until shortly before you were born. My mother called me to ask us to make the arrangements. She knew that Dennis would be able to find parents for you. His group specialized in helping women with fertility problems. Your adoptive mother was a patient of Dennis' old partner, Dr. Peter Vitale. You see, under the circumstances, they couldn't go through Catholic Charities. This way everything was handled privately, discreetly," she explained.

Sara felt as if she were in a dreamlike bubble. All movements and speech seemed to take place out of synch, like a movie whose audio is a second behind the visuals. Flashes of a young red-headed girl on a white horse danced across her mind. She understood now that she had seen her biological mother, not once, but several times. "Where is she now?" Sara asked sensing the answer. "Did she go back to being a nun?"

Husband and wife ominously locked eyes. As they shifted their attention back to Sara, her gut rolled, making her wonder if she was going to throw up.

"We don't know what happened to her. The last I ever saw or spoke to her was when I picked you up at the house. I've always feared the worst. Amazing that 35 years can dissolve in an instant," Grace said, shaking her head.

"Go on, Gracie. Tell her about your father," her husband urged.

"We received the call that Katy had gone into labor. Mother and Pa had taken her in during her unfortunate circumstance. When I arrived at the farm, you were about to be born. My father, your grandfather, had not been well for a long time. He drank too much after my brother died, and frankly, this situation, his daughter, a nun, having a bastard child, drove him over the edge. Katy was weak and bleeding profusely. I begged them to take her to a hospital, but he wouldn't hear of it. Pa was crazy drunk that night and in a rage. He said I was interfering in the Lord's punishment. Mother helped me to wrap you up and get you out of there. Katy made me promise to find you loving parents. I've always felt terribly guilty because she gave me something to give to you, but I dropped it when Pa ripped you out of my arms. By the time my mother and I got you away from him, it was clear there was no going back to retrieve it. I had to run while there was a chance," she recounted, taking a deep breath before continuing with the rest of her tale, tears in her eyes.

Sara and Leila exchanged a sideways glance as they tried to comprehend the significance of what she was conveying.

"After you were safe, after you were with your new parents, I called the farm to let Katy know. Pa answered. He told me that she was gone and I was dead to him. He warned me never to call or step foot in Virginia again. And the same went for my sister, Eileen. She wasn't even involved, but he refused to talk to her as well. I never heard from Katy. She never called or tried to reach me. The day you were born was the last time I ever saw her, my mother, or my father," Grace said, pushing tears away.

Sara leaned back in the chair and closed her eyes for an instant. Picturing Jack's playroom, she recalled how her birthday triggered the first vision from the past. "I was born on the third floor, in a little room carved out of the attic," she said, staring off. "Katy, my mother, had red hair, and green eyes just like mine. As a little girl, she blamed herself for your brother's death. And it was easy for everyone to blame her too. No one understood that she felt responsible because she didn't catch him in time, not because she was racing with him. Your father blamed her most all of because he couldn't live with his own guilt over giving Michael that pony. She wanted me to know all this. She wanted you to know. The truth needs to come out. The record stands corrected." Sara stared directly into her aunt's eyes.

"How do you know all this?" Grace asked.

"I've seen it all. You see…she's dead. And I'm almost positive that her spirit is still on the property," Sara declared, knowing now who had been speaking to and through her.

Grace covered her mouth with her slim age-spot-covered hand at the thought. She looked at her husband, then back to Sara. Leila was speechless for the first time in her life. Sara stood up. Silently she walked through the room, examining photographs that were set out on shelves and tables. Smiling faces of unknown cousins with features resembling her own jumped out from pictures large and small. In a black leather frame, she found what she was searching for: an old photo of a little boy with his three older sisters. There in black and white she laid eyes on the little girl who saved Jack's life. She spotted another photo of the girls when they were older. Michael was gone. The face of the youngest girl had started to mature into someone she recognized—a woman trapped in another place in time, whose memories of human failings haunted her in death as they had during her life, a tortured soul perpetually suspended, serving an unjust punishment.

Sara's calm demeanor cracked. She turned away as tears rolled down her cheeks. She felt as if she had been punched in the stomach. Anger and sorrow violently twisted in her gut, threatening to rip her apart. Sara fought to surface from the oppressive pain by taking long deep breaths. As she dried her face with the cuff of her sleeve, she gazed into her mother's frozen image. She felt as if she were in the middle of an emotional hurricane.

"What were you supposed to give Sara?" Leila asked Grace, who had been intently watching her niece wander from picture to picture.

"A necklace," she answered.

This caught Sara's attention. Putting down the frame she was clutching, she moved in front of her aunt. "Was it a gold chain with a little key?" she asked.

"Yes, it was. I dropped it somewhere in the house. I think in the upstairs bedroom," Grace replied with astonishment.

"Do you know what it was for?" Sara quizzed. "What did the key open?"

"I don't know for certain, but I have my suspicions. She never told me. All Katy said was that someday it would unlock the truth for you," she explained.

"And you didn't ask how?" Leila asked. "Why the heck not?"

"No. You don't understand. There was no time for conversation. I had to get that baby out of there. Plus, I assumed it was for her diary. She had always kept a diary, and even there in that one picture you can see a key hanging around her neck. I'm ashamed to admit this, but she didn't trust us. Eileen or I surely would have peeked if she had left it in the lock, so she was never without it. It never left her until you were born," she answered.

Sara laid a hand on her chest but it was bare. The key was sitting in the jewelry box in her bedroom. They had to go back. All was not finished. They had to find Katy, which meant making one more stop along the way. Someone knew where to find her, someone who was the keeper of this dirty little secret.

"We have to go," Sara said catching all three by surprise. "We have to get back to Virginia."

"Oh, no, not yet. Why the rush? At long last we've had the chance to meet you. I want to know everything about you, what your life has been like. Please. Stay and visit," Grace begged, looking panicked by the prospect of this girl being lost to them again.

Sara smiled at this lovely old woman who was sincerely reaching out to her. Under different circumstances, she would have loved to linger in conversation. "I truly appreciate your offer. I promise to be in touch with you very soon. We have something very pressing to attend to. I have a little boy, Jack. He was in an accident, one very similar to what happened to Michael. He's fighting for his life. I need to get back. Your sister is calling, demanding my immediate attention and I don't think there is any other way to save my son," Sara said, leaning over to give her new-found aunt a kiss on the cheek.

"Godspeed," Grace called out as the two women left.

CHAPTER SEVENTEEN

Upon leaving the brownstone in Manhattan, Sara settled into the limo and immediately called David at the hospital.

"Sara, is that you?" he said.

"Yes. How's Jack?" she asked.

"Things couldn't be better! Jack is beginning to come out of the coma. He opened his eyes about half an hour ago. He hasn't spoken yet, but he turned toward me when he heard my voice. I swear it's a miracle."

Happy tears rolled down Sara's cheeks as she listened. "Thank God."

"What's happening?" Leila asked impatiently.

Sara held up a finger for her to wait until she was done talking to David.

"Where are you?" David asked. "Are you on your way back? Is that Grace woman your mother? Did you find what you were looking for?"

"We're on our way to the plane as we speak. We met Grace McCarthy. And no, she isn't my mother. Turns out she's my biological aunt. Katy was my mother. David, I was born in the house, our house, in Jack's playroom."

"What? No way," he answered.

"The necklace with the little gold key was my mother's. She had wanted me to have it. Honey, I know you're convinced that I've lost my mind, but there's a whole lot more to this story than you think. Grace told us that her sister, my mother, was never heard from after the night I was born. David, Katy is the one who's been haunting my dreams and visions. I'm certain of that now. I think she died the night I was born and she's still there. The entire scandal was covered up by her family because she was a nun. I think her soul is trapped at the farm."

"I can't believe it. Are you sure this woman was telling you the truth? Could you really have been born there? It's…it's…. I don't know what it is," David stammered, trying to make sense out of what she had shared. "Sara, do you realize what you're saying? You're suggesting that your mother—wait, did I hear you say she was a nun?"

"Yes," Sara answered patiently. "That's right. Kathleen McHugh was a nun."

"It's not adding up. You're willing to take this woman's word without any hard evidence."

"David, I saw her picture—my mother's picture. We have the same face. It was unnerving. That is how Grace recognized me. Plus, why would anyone make up such a grotesque story?"

"Okay, the whole thing just keeps getting weirder and weirder. And you think she is buried somewhere on the farm? That sounds pretty over the line to me."

"I think so, but I'm not one hundred percent sure. Leila and I will be taking off in about 30 minutes. We were planning on talking to Lester Brown before going over to the hospital, but with Jack coming around now, I'm not sure what to do. If anyone knows what happened to Katy, it's him. The old guy's demeanor changed, becoming abrupt and elusive, when I asked about her during our last conversation. He's hiding the truth. David, we are so close to getting to the bottom of all this. I really think it could be valuable."

"I don't know, Sara. I don't like the idea, but since it appears that I may have been wrong about your ties to the McHugh family, I'll keep my mouth shut. Oh, and one more thing…I'm sorry I said such mean things to you before you left. We've been through more in the last couple of years than most couples face in a lifetime together. I don't want to lose you or our family. You drive me absolutely crazy, but I love you more than I could ever tell you."

Sara was crying again. She wiped away the tears with the back of her hand. Leila pulled a tissue from her purse and handed it to her. Sara was balancing on a fine emotional ledge. She blew her nose and cleared her throat before answering David.

"I'm sorry, too," she replied. "We've had a lot of crap thrown our way lately. It appears that we're finally turning a corner. I'm thrilled about Jack. I guess I could postpone seeing Lester for a few days."

"No, don't. Get it over with so we can focus solely on Jack. It shouldn't take you long."

"Are you sure?" Sara asked. "I should be there."

"Yeah. But your head won't be until this is resolved once and for all. And I've learned my lesson about trying to get you to take the rational road. Go. And hurry back!" David said.

Lester Brown was about to receive a shockingly familiar visitor. It was early evening before the travel weary friends pulled into the nursing home's parking lot. Even though the availability of the limo and private plane hastened her return home, Sara was starting to feel the effects of the sleepless nights with Jack and the twisting turn of events.

"I'm telling you one thing—that old man better come clean and quick because my 'patience meter' is on empty," Sara said, slamming the car door as they headed for the building.

"You and me both," Leila concurred.

The lobby was empty. There wasn't a person in sight. Apparently the home didn't bother having a receptionist at the front desk in the evenings. The aroma of the day's dinner overtook the usually foul smells that permeated every fiber of the place. When they reached Lester's floor, Sara saw the food service staff wheeling a large metal cart down the hall as they delivered the plastic trays to the residents.

"Looks appetizing," Leila said sarcastically.

Lester and his roommate where sitting up in bed, eating, while watching The Wheel of Fortune. They didn't appreciate being disturbed during their favorite program.

"We are here to talk to Mr. Brown," Sara explained.

"Now you girls get out of the way of the television," Lamar, his roommate, cried as creamed corn exploded out of the corner of his mouth.

"Believe me, we'll make it quick," Leila added.

"Hush up. This is the good part," the upset man complained as he swayed back and forth trying to see the picture.

Leila took the opportunity to shut the television off to get Lester's full attention.

"Hey! What are you doing?" Lester objected, his roommate repeating the same, only with many expletives thrown in at the end.

"Mr. Brown, do you remember me? I visited you yesterday. Sara Miller. Remember? We need to chat again. Seems that there was something you left out about the McHugh family—something about Katy. As soon as you tell me what I want to know, I'll have my friend put your program back on. I promise." She walked over to the man who was hovering over a dry piece of meatloaf and a lump of mashed potatoes.

"I remember you. I told you everything I know. I thought you were a nice girl. Now look at you, disturbing a couple of senior citizens trying to eat their dinner and watch some TV," he said, quite perturbed.

"The only enjoyment we have left at our age," Lamar snorted.

"Mr. Brown, how is your eyesight today?" Sara inquired, moving even closer.

"A little better. Why?" he asked, squinting in her direction.

"I want you to take a really good look at me. Up close. I want you to see who I am," she said, leaning across his bed. "Lester, I visited Grace today. Grace McHugh. She recognized me right away. Do you?" she asked, climbing onto the bed so she was a mere eight inches from the man's face. Sara felt as if her gaze bore straight into Lester's soul as she waited, with unwavering resolve, for that flicker of recognition.

"No! No! Can't be. Who are you? Can't be. Oh Lord, you're playing evil tricks on me," the man cried out, cringing as if seeing the living dead.

"Who am I? I'll tell you who I am. I am Kathleen McHugh's

daughter, that's who. And I want to know where she was buried," Sara said, without giving him an inch of wiggle room.

"What are you talking about? Katy was a nun. She had no baby. You're not right in the head is what you are," he said, pressing his body back against the elevated mattress.

"Mr. Brown. I have been up since before dawn. I have flown to New York and back with a stop at Grace and Dennis McCarthy's house thrown in the middle. Believe me when I tell you that I am tired and cranky. Grace told me what happened to her sister, Kathleen. When Katy got pregnant, she went to stay with her parents. She gave birth to me in her parent's home and was never heard from again. I want to know what happened to her."

"Jesus. Sweet, Jesus. Deliver me," he started to call out.

"He's not going to help you. Just spill your guts. It's been a long day," Leila said, moaning with increasing impatience.

Lester started to tremble. "O' right. O' right. I'll tell ya."

"She died, didn't she? Did Patrick bury her in some unmarked grave?"

"She passed, but I swear she wasn't buried without a marker. It's there. You just have to know what it is. It was the worst day of my life. I didn't know she was even in the house for all those months. They had her hidden away in the attic. Poor girl. I didn't find out until she died. Bled to death up there givin' birth is what they told me. I never saw the baby. Grace took the bastard away. Never told me if you was a girl or boy. If Patrick wasn't crazy before, he was after. I dug a hole out front near where Michael had his accident. I figured she might rest in peace out there. Took me a long time to dig the grave. Field was frozen somethin' terrible, being winter and all. Patrick was passed out from whiskey by the time I finished. Just Maureen and I set her in the ground. We wrapped her in a horse blanket to carry her out there," he said, tears spilling freely down his wrinkled face.

"Can you imagine losing two of your babies? Then giving your grandbaby away? Maureen was lost after that. Didn't talk much. Would look right through Pat as if he was dead too. I guess he was," Lester said, shaking his head in agony over their shattered lives. "It haunted him. That girl never left his head. Swore he saw her. He would insist that Katy was alive, still up in that prison of a room. Guilt drove him to suicide. Shot himself in the head over the top of her grave 32 years to the day after she died. In hindsight, I'm surprised he hung on as long as he did."

"You're saying she's buried in the front pasture near the stone wall, beside that really big oak tree, right?" Sara asked wanting to be sure of the location.

"Yes 'um, that's right," Lester confirmed with a nod. "Look for the big rock that has a swirly thing carved out of it."

"What do you mean by a 'swirly' thing?" Sara asked.

"Maureen said Kathleen couldn't have a cross, being that she was a sinner and all, givin' birth to that illegitimate baby. But she had me chip out some Irish pattern she had in a book. Took me a month. Almost took a finger off. I laid that stone on the girl's grave. Patrick told me he would kill me if I ever breathed a word to anyone. And I didn't. Not until now. You find that stone and that's where little Miss Katy is." Lester Brown bowed his head in shame.

Sara and Leila let out a sigh at the same time. They accomplished what they came for.

"Thank you for telling me the truth. You did the right thing… finally."

"I'm sorry," Lester said. "Shouldn't have been like that."

"Do you know who my biological father is? Did Patrick or Maureen ever tell you his name?"

"Never uttered a word to me and I knew better than to ask. Don't know how she got into that predicament. She had been a good girl, a religious girl. I can't imagine her whorin' around," he said in a vain attempt to defend her honor.

"Goodbye, Mr. Brown. We'll let you finish your dinner now," Sara said, getting up to leave.

Leila turned on the television. Wheel of Fortune was still on. As the two women left the room, they heard a contestant blurt out, "The answer is a woman's intuition." Sara smiled.

The next morning, Sara, Leila, Emma, and Carlos scoured the front pasture, looking for the marker. Sara found it exactly where she thought it would be: right where Jack fell off Gremlin. Sara shook her head as she recalled the other misunderstood signs. It was the very same spot where the three dogs charged out to on the night of her birthday. Not long after, Buster furiously dug at the ground, as if trying to unearth a lost treasure. And she realized it was the precise location where the miniature key sent a searing pain ripping through her chest.

The stone was flipped over, exposing its smooth side. It was probably turned as a result of hay being harvested at some point in the past. Sara knelt down and pried the boulder loose from its earthen nest. The Celtic pattern was filled in with dirt but still visible. Without warning, she was drowning in tears. Feelings of satisfaction and relief were quickly swept aside by overwhelming sadness and regret. A hand touched her shoulder, bringing her back to the present. She looked up into the faces of her three loyal comrades.

"I think we'll need to call the police," Sara stated, brushing her cheeks dry with her dirty palm. "We are talking about digging up a body. What do you think?"

"Bloody 'ell, yes! I'm not crawling down there to scrape out some bones," Emma declared, her hands planted firmly on her hips and her head shaking back and forth.

"Who else would you call? Is there a government agency for this sort of thing? I think the police would be best. They'll bring in the appropriate equipment for a recovery like this," Leila agreed more diplomatically.

"That's right. And if it's not their department, they'll know who to ring," Emma added.

"You sure, Miss Sara? I can dig your mama up for you," Carlos offered so casually that they all looked at him and laughed.

"I'm sure. Thank you for offering to go the extra mile, Carlos," Sara said, standing up with the large stone in her hands.

"What are you going to do with that?" Leila asked.

Sara looked down at the filthy relic. "I think I'll have the funeral home order a headstone with the same pattern. It's the only shred of acknowledgement that she was given, and I think it should be honored and stay with her."

"I think she would like that," Leila said.

Initially, the police must have suspected that Sara was one egg short of a dozen. When she called to ask the authorities to come out to her farm to dig up a body that had been secretly buried for more than three decades, it took several attempts with various levels of law enforcement before anyone took her seriously. By mid-afternoon, she had heavy equipment scooping up large metal baskets full of Virginia clay. Sara, Leila, Emma, and Carlos each had to give a statement before being shuffled out of the way. From the other side of the wall they watched as a mountain of dirt was piled next to the large pit. Eventually the officer assigned to monitoring the progress that the monster shovel was making started waving his hands for the backhoe operator to stop.

"Hold up, Fred. I can see a skull," he yelled.

A ladder was lowered into the hole as three guys grabbed shovels to finish the recovery. Sara turned away when a black vinyl body bag was lowered down to the soiled hand of one of the men, only to be passed back up in a matter of minutes. Leila put her arm around the shoulders of her shaken friend. Sara noticed Carlos making the sign of the cross and bowing his head in silent prayer. She wished she could remember one to offer but she was drawing a blank.

The four of them followed Katy's bones to the waiting van. The group watched as her remains were slid into the back.

Sara stepped forward to touch the thick black casing just as they were about to close the doors. "Can you give me a second?" she asked looking around at the small crowd standing in the immediate area. "Please."

The police officer in charge nodded, sending his men off to collect the remaining tools. Leila, Emma, and Carlos walked toward the barn, stopping about a hundred feet back, uncertain of whether to wait or go. Sara stood alone with what remained of the woman who gave birth to her, the woman who maneuvered her to buy the farm, and the woman whose memories haunted her own mind.

"You can go now," Sara whispered, laying her hands on the bag. "See. I found you. Just like you wanted. You're no longer a terrible secret stashed away to protect some ridiculous name and sense of honor. I promise you'll have a proper burial. It's all over."

She felt the bulge of a skull and other bones through the cold vinyl. The sensation was jolting, causing her to take a step back. The realization of what she had felt in her hand made her want to vomit. She lurched sideways, bumping into an officer who had silently appeared by her side. His presence made her shriek in panic, eliciting a sympathetic smile from the burly man. Sara blushed from embarrassment over being so easily spooked.

"I guess it has to be creepy having a dead body pulled out of your front yard. Wouldn't be surprised if you have nightmares for a while," he said to Sara.

"Actually, I think they'll stop now," Sara said, turning to walk toward her waiting friends. As she did so, she could hear doors slamming, followed by the start of multiple engines. Sara thought about what he had said. Nightmares? He had no idea.

"Are you okay?" Leila asked as she approached.

"I could be better, but at least it's over. All I want now is for my son to get well, come home, and for us all to live happily ever after. You think that's too much to ask for in one lifetime?"

"Not for a normal person, but then again, when have you ever been normal?"

"Leila! I don't think that's the most constructive thing to say at the moment!" Emma added with British flair.

Sara chuckled at the exchange, causing them all to look at her as if she had lost it. "It's fine, Emma. Leila's right. I don't do 'normal.' I think I'll aim in that direction, though, and see what happens. Can't say life has ever been dull."

"How about next time finding an adventure with a gorgeous guy in it for me? I'm getting tired of this eerie stuff. I think it's given me a wrinkle," Leila said, smoothing the outside corner of her right eye, making the rest of them roll their own.

Emma and Carlos veered off toward the barn to attend to the daily farm chores, something that had been put on hold for most of the day.

Leila stopped short of the stairs leading into the house. "If you're really okay, would you mind if I cut out? It's been a wild couple of days and I'm guessing you're going to be leaving for the hospital shortly."

"Go ahead. I'll be fine. I have some things to do here first. I'm sure I'll catch up with you later. Oh…and Leila, thanks again for the trip to New York, hunting down Lester, and hanging around while the cops dug up Katy. What can I say? You're one in a million," Sara said, watching her friend crawl behind the wheel of her car.

"You're right. I am. Don't sweat it. I'll be sure to figure out some way for you to repay me," she promised, waving as she pulled down the gravel drive toward the few official vehicles lingering on the property.

Watching the procession pull out onto the road, Sara knew her responsibilities weren't over. Though she was Katy's biological daughter, she didn't qualify as the next of kin because of the adoption. She telephoned her newly discovered aunt in New York. Sara was forced to rehash the gut-wrenching events of the day as she described what had taken place.

"I'll speak to the funeral home director to transfer all authority over to you. I want you to have the power to make the final arrangements. Sara, without…without you, we never would have found her or known the truth," the frail and quivering voice stammered. "I'll call Eileen. I'll make all the arrangements for us to travel home to attend Katy's service."

Sara had one more phone call to make. David had been keeping her abreast of Jack's progress, but his condition was changing rapidly. She longed for some good news. She hadn't seen her son in about 36 hours and she ached for him. The phone rang at the ICU nurse's station. She recognized the voice of the nurse named Carol.

"Hi, Carol. This is Sara Miller. How's Jack, and is David around?" Sara asked, dropping into a chair at their kitchen table.

"Jack is good. I'll let your husband tell you. Wait on the line and I'll go get him," she said, leaving Sara hanging on the other end in silence.

"Sara! I'm so glad you called. I tried reaching you on your cell a little while ago. Jack is completely awake! He's back, Sara! He's a little groggy and not sure where he is, but he's talking clearly, knows who he is, who I am, and most of all, wants his mom!" David blurted out.

Hearing the news made Sara weep with joy. After a few moments she was able to garble out a few words. "I'll be right over. Tell him I'm on my way and I love him. I knew he had angels standing watch over him."

On her way out the driveway, Sara stopped to look toward Katy's grave. The sky was illuminated in shades of purple and orange from the sun falling behind the treetops. Laser-like rays of light sliced through the branches, creating an image of fingers reaching out to scoop up the newly unearthed soul. Sara silently prayed for her biological mother. Maybe now she could find her way to a better place, a place free from disappointment, sadness, and guilt.

"Thank you. Thank you for saving your grandson," Sara whispered as she pulled away.

CHAPTER EIGHTEEN

By the time Sara reached the hospital, Jack was asking for ice cream and soda. The sound of his voice made her heart jump.

"Please. I'm starving. I want a big bowl of rocky road covered in syrup with some whipped cream and a root beer. Come on, Dad. You can sneak it in," Jack begged. When Sara entered the room he cried out, "Mommy! Mommy, I missed you." A smile the size of Texas spread across his face. "Can I go home now? I'm really hungry."

Sara bent down and kissed Jack on both cheeks. David joined her as she stood by their son's bed, winding his arm around her shoulders to hug her tightly. Thankfulness mixed with pure delight filled her heart as she gazed down at Jack.

"It's over, Honey," Sara whispered as she took the little boy's hand. "Do you remember what happened? Do you know why you're here?"

"Um, not really. Are we still in New York? I got hurt but I'm not sure how. Look at this big cast on my arm. It's neat. I'm gonna have everyone sign it. The nurse lady said the doctor is going to take some measurer out of my head. I'm not supposed to touch anywhere above my face but it feels funny—kinda itchy," he said with more animation than Sara would have expected.

A nurse wielding a clipboard smiled with approval as she squeezed into the cramped room. "That's right. You're being a super patient," she said, marking something down in his chart.

"Will he at some point recall what happened?" Sara asked the busy woman.

"Maybe. We can't really predict. Some people never get the whole series of events back. He is doing exceptionally well. The neurologist will be in to see him in a little bit. I'm guessing that the doctor will remove the catheter tomorrow morning. It's going to depend on the results of Jack's test," the nurse answered.

"Will he stay in the ICU much longer?" David asked

"The doctor will transfer him over to the pediatric unit as long as he remains stable for the next 12 to 24 hours. You'll like it better over there. It's more comfortable. Plus, he'll be free of a lot of these monitors," the nurse said, redirecting her attention to Jack.

"Do they have good food over there, 'cause I'm real hungry," he asked.

"It's six-thirty. I'll see about ordering you up some dinner. Hang on," the nurse promised, winking at the famished boy.

While they waited for his meal to arrive, Jack entertained his parents by cracking jokes and humming a tune they didn't recognize. "The diary fits the key. The truth is in the diary," he sang.

David and Sara looked quizzically at one another. Jack's words had ignited their curiosity. "Jack, where did you come up with that line?" David asked uneasily.

"My friend Katy told me it. She told me over and over so I wouldn't forget it when I woke up. Hmm, that's kinda funny. I wonder where she went to?" Jack looked around the room for her.

"Who is Katy?" Sara asked, intrigued by the possibility that Jack had passed in and out of her birth mother's ethereal prison. "How do you know her?"

"She's my friend. She's real pretty. She has green eyes like us, Mom, and long, long red hair. I've been with her the whole time. We sang and played hide and seek. You were playing too, Mom. I saw you. You were looking out in the field for us. You found Katy. Remember? She was hiding under the rock you picked up. That's when she told me I had to wake up. We couldn't play anymore because you found her. She wanted me to tell you to open the diary. If you open it she can see her brother Michael again. She really wants to do that," Jack said as casually as if he had spent the afternoon with a classmate.

David looked at Sara. "What's he talking about?"

"I think he means where I found Katy's remains. Her grave was marked by a large carved stone. I picked it up, but I'm not sure about the rest," Sara answered.

"How can that be? He couldn't have known that. Heck, I didn't know about it," David replied.

Sara shook her head in disbelief and shrugged. "Jack, honey, I don't have Katy's diary. Did she tell you where it is? Where can I find it? Did she hide it someplace?"

"Mom, you're so silly. Yes, you do have it." The little boy giggled as if she was honestly pulling his leg on purpose.

"No, Sweetie. I don't," she said, trying to get him to understand her dilemma.

"Yes, you do. It's in the library. You were going to cut it open and I wouldn't let you because you didn't have permission. But now you do. Katy said it was okay. She said to use the tiny key on your necklace and it will open up. She gave you permission to read it," he explained.

A candy striper arrived with a tray of food.

"Yippee!" Jack hooted, drawing his attention away from Sara. The bland selections set before him instantaneously deflated his excitement. He poked his finger at the jiggling yellow and green gelatin cubes. "At least there's some Jell-O."

"Jack, would you mind if I left for a short time? Dad will stay with you while you eat. I'll come back later tonight," Sara promised apologetically.

"Why, Mom? Are you going to go get Katy's diary? She would like that. She told me Michael has waited a really long time for her to come," Jack said, while trying to balance a wiggly green square on his spoon.

"I'm going to run home to get it so she can be happy. She should be with her family. The way we are," Sara said, squeezing his left arm affectionately.

"We are her family. She told me she's proud of how smart you are. You've almost figured everything out," Jack declared as he dropped the first morsel of food in his mouth.

Sara kissed her son on the side of the head. David escorted her out of the room.

"Unbelievable! He can't remember what happened but has full details on the ghost living in our house," David exclaimed.

"She guarded him," Sara replied.

"That's questionable. I wish you would think twice about running off to peel back another layer in this demented saga. How do you know that this diary won't trigger some other tragedy? You shouldn't be charging off to do this alone. Wait a couple of days and we can do it together, when Jack is out of the woods," he urged.

"Don't you see? That's why I need to go now. Katy needs to move on and leave us alone. I thought we accomplished that by finding her body, but now I'm not so sure. There's another piece to what happened. Something she wants me to know, and it's locked away in her diary."

"You are the most stubborn and aggravating woman I've ever met. We've been through this before. You're going to do whatever you want anyway. Go."

"David, come on. Don't be like that."

"Call me as soon as you're done. Phone the nurse's station and I'll get back to you on my cell." He strode back toward Jack's room in frustration.

Sara sped up the driveway and skidded to a stop, leaving a deep trough of displaced gravel in the car's wake. Emma had witnessed her boss's premature return home and dashed out of the tenant house to meet her. She barely caught up with Sara, who was bounding up the stone steps two at a time.

"Sara, I saw your lights coming up the lane," Emma called from the far side of the car, prompting her friend's sprinting form to awkwardly skid to a stop. "What are you doing back so soon? Is Jack all right?"

"Geez, Emma, you scared me! I didn't see you there. Sorry. Jack is fine. Actually, he's better than fine—he's great!" Sara announced.

"Fantastic! But then why are you here?"

"I would say you wouldn't believe it, but in light of all we've been through, I'm sure you will. Jack is awake now and told us he was with Katy while he was in a coma. He knew about us finding the stone marker. He told me that I have her diary, so…I'm here to read it. It's the last thing she wants me to do. Whatever is in there won't let her go," Sara explained.

"I thought we were through with all this when they hauled her bones away. Now I see where you get your stubborn streak."

"Seems to be a theme tonight."

The dogs heard Sara drive in. She had left them inside without a light on. Waves of unhappy howls filled the night air and thundered across the open fields. The moonlit outline of the dark house's massive structure made her uneasy.

"Do you want to come in?" Sara asked, motioning to the door. "You can get a first-hand account of Kathleen McHugh's horrid life."

"Why not? It's not like I'll be able to sleep tonight anyway. Finding a secretly buried body isn't exactly on my everyday chore list. I may as well be privy to the rest of the nastiness," Emma replied, hopping up the steps.

Sara opened the back door and slid her hand up the wall, feeling for the light switch. The bright illumination of the ceiling's incandescent bulb immediately took the edge off the spookiness. The dogs greeted them with exuberance, making it difficult for the women to walk in.

"Settle down already!" Sara commanded, which had little if any effect on their behavior.

"How do you go through this every time you have to move about? It's like scaling a wall. Try pushing Madison's rump out of the way," Emma suggested, dodging a swinging tail.

"You get used to it," Sara answered, breaking through the bottleneck.

"Where is this infamous diary?" Emma asked, following the parade through the kitchen.

"In the library, but I need to get the key to open it. It's in my bedroom. Do you want to wait for me in there?" She pointed in the direction of David's office.

"Don't be long," Emma said, the two briefly parting ways. She was palming the old leather journal when Sara returned, brandishing the key.

"Is this it? Tell me it hasn't been sitting here on the desk for the entire time you lived here. You wouldn't have had to jump through all those hoops like a trained circus poodle if you had just read the bloody thing already." Emma's tone conveyed her utter disbelief over the irony of the unfolding circumstance.

Sara snatched the book from the Englishwoman's hands. "You don't think I've realized that? Now is not the time to spell out the obvious."

"Understood. My lips are sealed." Emma plopped down into one of David's oversized armchairs.

Sara placed the journal on the desk, took hold of the key, and slid the shaft into the tiny hole. With a turn to the right, the claws of the lock sprung open. She slid off the leather arm protecting her mother's secrets from unwelcome eyes. Sara's hands shook, from a combination of excitement and apprehension, as she pressed back the front cover. Taped inside was a gold cross. Sara closed her eyes, filtering images that flooded her mind. This was the same gold cross that hung around the neck of the red-haired woman from her dream. Sara shook her head, trying to clear this memory from her head, a memory that escaped from the past and belonged to someone else.

The date on the first page read January 1, 1971. Sara flipped to the last page. It was the last day of that same year, a few weeks shy of her birth. She fanned back through the pages, thinking about what the entries must contain.

"It covers the year she was pregnant with me. It doesn't go into January at all. I wonder if she wrote anything during those last few weeks," Sara considered aloud.

"What was that in the front?" the English girl, asked pointing at the diary's cover.

"That was her cross. I guess she no longer wanted to wear it after getting pregnant. I've seen it before…in one of my dreams. She was wearing it the night I was conceived," Sara said, without realizing the impact of this statement.

"What? You're telling me you saw your parents doing the deed? That's utterly disgusting," Emma said with a screwed up face.

"Ah…I guess you're right. I hadn't really thought about it, but that is kind of gross. Yuck," Sara agreed.

"Well, what does she say? I guess she would still be in the convent in the beginning," Emma said, leaning forward to get a glance of the neatly written script.

"Give me a minute to read." Several minutes passed as Sara skimmed over the first month's entries. "They're all pretty much the same. She writes about her life being a first grade teacher in a Catholic school, Mother of Angels. How she loved the children, yet in spite of this, how she felt empty and lost. There was the monotony of living in a convent, with its routines and methodical prayers. It sounds to me like she realized that she had chosen the wrong path." Sara empathized with her mother's sadness.

"Skip ahead to when you were conceived. You were born in January, so look at the end of March and beginning of April," Emma impatiently instructed.

Sara fingered through the end of March but didn't find anything until the last day, the 31st. "Wait a minute. She mentions a man here."

"What did she write? Does she name the man?"

I'm planning on visiting my parents for a few days when our children have their break. Since it's my parent's fortieth anniversary, I will be allowed to go. I'll be accompanied by one of the other Sisters. While we're there, I'm hoping to visit Sean. We haven't seen each other in a very long time, but I find myself finding sanctuary in the memory of our friendship. I must be a very wicked girl to have such sinful thoughts. I will say extra prayers for the salvation of my soul.

"Oh, my. Sounds like the girl had her mind on more than friendship. I wonder who Sean was. Locate the entry for when she goes home," Emma said.

"Let's see…still at the school. Here we go—April 9th. School is let out for a week and she packs to leave, blah, blah, blah…April

10th, she and her traveling companion arrive at the farm midday. She visits with her parents, finds them the same: mother cold and distant while father is belligerent. She writes that she was embarrassed by his drinking and cursing. Regardless, she bakes a cake for their anniversary. Now this is interesting. The nun that went with her gets drunk at dinner doing shots of whiskey with her father. Holy shit, that's funny," Sara says, chuckling as she related the anecdote.

"Really? Are nuns allowed to drink alcohol?" Emma asked, both amazed and confused.

"Hell, I think that's about the only thing they are allowed to do, then or now. I had an acquaintance once tell me that her sister left the convent because she was appalled by the fact that the convent's electric bill was less than the booze bill each month. Come to think of it, I'd stay pretty loaded if I had to spend my life chaste," Sara added with a shrug.

"Go on. Then what happens?" Emma asked.

April 11th —This is a day of shame. I have betrayed my vows and am the worst of all sinners.

"I'm guessing this is the day I was conceived," Sara said before returning to the entry. "She sees an opportunity to go see Sean alone because the other nun, Anna, is busy puking from a hangover. Wow, that's bad."

"Not pretty!" Emma agrees.

"Back to her story. It's Sunday. She went to mass over at St. Thomas' Catholic Church. Neither of her parents joined her. Father was hung over. Caught him mixing booze into his morning tea and dear old Mum locked herself in her room," Sara reported, taking a breath. "Here we go! After mass, she lingered in prayer, hoping to talk to Sean. He noticed her and came over to greet her. Told her it had been too long and confided that he missed their childhood antics. He convinced her to go with him for some refreshments so they could spend time visiting with one another." For the most part, Sara had been paraphrasing for Emma up until this point, but she switched over to reading directly from the text.

At first we spoke about our friendship, but I knew in my heart that there was always something more, a tension just below the surface. I should never have gone today. It was unfair to both of us. Sean made it clear that it was I who chose the path for both of us, I who led us into this unnatural arrangement and I who now came to tease him with the possibility of changing the rules, which I had single-handedly imposed so many years ago. I am ashamed at who I have become. When he came to me and led me to the bedroom, I did not protest. When he slid the clothing off my body, I did not protest. When he kissed me and laid his hands upon my naked breasts, my body burned for him. I watched as he transformed into a hungry animal, lusting for the taste of my flesh. My own wicked desire surprised and shamed me. How could I, a bride of Christ, allow this violation with such ease? My protests were half-hearted as he thrust into me, forever staining me, forever leaving my soul branded. How can I ever ask forgiveness for my sin? Sean told me I will be his forever. Did this fill my empty heart or lighten my burden? I think not. I fear that I have merely exchanged one for another. He gave me his cross with his flesh. We have both fallen from grace. I return to life in the convent, an imposter among my sisters. Sean will have his own demons to overcome; his vows to the Lord are as broken as mine. Father Sean Kennedy, as you deliver communion, will you consider who will claim your soul now? Will it be the Lord, our Heavenly Father, or the Devil? In the end, I'm sure we will be there together.

Sara looked across the desk at Emma, whose hand was drawn up across her mouth in shock.

"Un-fucking-believable! Your father was a priest and your mother a nun!" Emma said, enunciating each syllable.

"Holy crap. I've met him. Well…we were not exactly introduced. I ran into him. Remember the other day at the church? I bumped into him in the hallway. Looked right into his eyes. He was so familiar. I recognized him from a dream, but I didn't know how he was connected. I feel sick." Sara wasn't certain how to recover from this unexpected blow; her head was reeling.

"You didn't put it together because you didn't know your mother was a nun! You thought she was Grace McHugh, not Kathleen McHugh. This is the most convoluted turn of events I ever could have imagined."

The women tried to make sense out of the account, to spin the encounter into something more palatable. The alternative that Katy and Sean were simply horny was way too disturbing.

"It's clear they knew each other when they were children. Maybe he fancied her, even wanted to marry her. She could have chosen religious life over his love, but then, years later, had a moment of doubt. What do you think?" Emma asked.

"That was quite a moment of doubt!" Sara replied. "You could be right. She does say that she had made the decision for both of them. I guess he either wanted her or no one. Do you really think it's possible that he became a priest because he didn't want anyone else? After she broke his heart, the priesthood was the only future he could envision?"

"Can you come up with a better explanation? What did she do next? Katy ended up back here at her parents' home. Did she tell him? Did he know he got her pregnant? Look ahead."

Sara flipped through the pages of the diary, summarizing the entries as she went. "She returned to the convent the following day. Sounds like the guilt ate away at her. She vowed to spend an extra hour each day praying for forgiveness. School resumed and she tried to put it out of her mind. In May she doesn't appear to write about anything but her normal routine. Then here in the first week of June she started feeling sick, she threw up and thought she caught a stomach bug. Yuck! Sounds like she did a boatload of puking for the next several weeks. July 1st she was hospitalized for dehydration from being so ill for the past month. It's during the exam that the doctor noticed her bulging middle and asked her if she could be pregnant. She confessed to him. They tested her and lo and behold—I'm on the way. Of course now she has a pretty serious dilemma. She considers her options and realizes she doesn't really have any. She had to leave the convent. It looks like she told them she wanted out but didn't reveal the real reason. On July 15th she returned home. When she told her parents about her predicament, her mother broke down in tears. Maureen was horrified and couldn't look at her. Shit, this is just awful. Good old Dad smacked her across the face, knocking her to the floor. He called her 'the devil's whore' and told her she could stay but would not be allowed to leave her room except to use the bathroom. He declared that his home would be her prison, not her sanctuary. Boy, that Patrick was a really sensitive and wonderful man, wasn't he?" Sara quipped sarcastically.

"I can't imagine why she came back here knowing what he was like. Why didn't she go to stay with one of her sisters?" Emma wondered.

"Here she wrote that she wished she could have turned to Eileen or Grace, but she knew that they each had several small children. She believed that her presence would have been a burden. Plus, she planned to tell Sean that he was going to be a father. Oh and listen to this—this is horribly sad," Sara said.

Sean will now have what he always wanted—me as his wife and children of his own. This was his one true desire. I never should have turned my back on him when he begged me to choose him. But at the time I had a debt to pay for failing Michael. This will be a new beginning. I feel the life we created growing inside me, an innocent life born from our emptiness, our desperation, our need, and weakness. Out of sin comes goodness, a chance for us to start over. Sean will deliver me from this hell.

"We were right about the two of them having some history. See what happens when she tells him." Emma encouraged Sara to read faster.

"Hold on. Give me a chance to find it. Here…the next day Katy called him and asked him to meet her at the house. She explained that she didn't have transportation and she had to see him immediately. He was curious about her call, but she didn't reveal anything over the phone. He told her he would drive out the following day."

Sara turned the page and continued to reading.

I have been betrayed! How can he do this to me? How can he do this to his child, his flesh and blood? It is awful. Sean denied ever touching me. He told me that I was nothing more than a common prostitute, that I had opened my legs, giving my virginity to others. He claims that the sisters found me with workmen, that I had been cast from their walls in disgrace. It was now, heavy with child, imprisoned in my father's house, that I sought refuge in his past feelings for me. Sneering, he looked straight into my eyes and told me that I alone created this situation and I alone would suffer the consequences. I sobbed, groveled at his feet, and begged him to be truthful. My father apologized to Sean for my evil wickedness as he led him to the door. He reminded him that I was to blame for his own son's death, and that the devil was my only companion. I find that this was the only truth spoken. The face of the devil is the face of Father Sean Kennedy.

"My God!" Emma exclaimed sitting back.

"What a bastard! This was what she wanted me to know, that she was betrayed by that hypocritical son of a bitch. It has to be," Sara said, staring down at the open diary.

For several minutes, Sara scanned page after page. She stopped to read another passage about three quarters of the way through the journal. "It looks like her mother started to speak to her in October. Can you imagine? Prior to this, they barely acknowledged her! It was like she was already a ghost. Maureen wanted to know what she was going to do once the baby was born. How she would support herself as a single mother. She suggested giving the baby up for adoption."

"We know how that bloody well turned out, now don't we?" Emma replied.

Sara turned the page and read on.

Mother spoke to me again about giving up the baby. I find myself considering this option, regardless of my feelings. I have nothing to offer a child. I cannot believe my life has turned out as it has. I told mother that Sean is this baby's father. I swore to it on Michael's soul. Sean was the only one, ever. I trusted him. I believed that in the end he would come to me and make amends for his betrayal, but I have been wrong. Mother looked at me, looked into my eyes, and asked why? Why did I seek out Sean? Why did I allow him to have what was not rightfully his? He a priest, I a nun—how could we have faltered so badly?

When Michael lay dying in my arms, I died. I tried so very hard to stop him, to catch him, but I couldn't. Becoming a nun was a way to try and run from myself, to devote myself to others so I didn't have to admit how broken I was. It worked for a while, but then the emptiness swallowed me. I needed to feel alive, to feel needed, to feel loved, to feel whole. I thought Sean was my salvation. I thought we could find that in each other, for one moment in time, forever frozen, a memory to sustain us. I was so wrong, so naïve. I never considered that I would get pregnant. I never considered that Sean would turn away in disgust. How is it that he finds pleasure in my humiliation and revels in abandoning me? He claimed to love me. Is he a coward or just spiteful? I turned from him once, telling him to dismantle his feelings for me. I always knew that becoming a nun drove him to the priesthood. Ultimately, we both sought God for the wrong reason. We were not there to exalt the Holy Father; we were there to hide from ourselves. We went years without seeing one another, without speaking, without touching. Was it fair of me to go to him, to seek him out, to offer myself? I shifted the relationship, but he obliged, he took part. So does he choose the priesthood over me now? I suspect not. I believe he is punishing me, making me suffer for a decision I made years ago. The trouble is that neither one of us can turn back the clock. Neither one of us can change the past nor undo the choices that we have made.

Sara stopped for a moment and stared at the ceiling. She blinked over and over, trying to hold back the tears filling her eyes. The enormity of Katy's pain transcended decades. The diary's revelations were overwhelming, using up what little was left of Sara's emotional reserves.

"Do you want to stop for a bit?" Emma asked, with sincere concern in her voice. "This has to be miserable for you."

"On one hand, it's like watching a movie. I'm in the audience, a passive observer to the events unfolding. But in another way, I have the lead role. One I didn't audition for, mind you. So there I am, pushed out on stage, with no script or idea about what scene comes next, and I'm told to wing it, to improvise. I don't know what to feel—sadness, fear, anger. I don't have a clue," Sara said, dropping her chin back down so she could look at her friend as she spoke.

"I'm really sorry this has happened to you. I'm sorry it happened to all of you."

"Thanks. I guess I'm sorry it happened to me too. Overall though, I have no right to bitch about my life. I had parents who loved and wanted me, who did a good job nurturing me so I would land on my feet. That's a heck of a lot more than Katy got."

"That's for sure," Emma concurred.

"Onward. The sooner we finish, the sooner I get to nail that bastard to the wall," Sara said, picking up the diary again. "She wrote that her mother was starting to be kinder to her, while the opposite was true for her father. He appeared more menacing the bigger her belly got. More than once he burst into her room, raging incoherently. It sounds like Katy was growing more and more terrified that he would hurt the baby. He threatened to kill me once I was born—a truly loving grandpa. This was the final straw that convinced Katy to give her mother the okay to contact Grace. However, she made Maureen promise to not tell her sister how she became pregnant. Katy was relieved when she heard that her sister agreed to make all the arrangements for the adoption. It would be handled privately. Grace would say the baby was hers."

Sara jumped ahead, looking for anything that stood out. Most of Katy's writing in November and December dealt with coming to terms with giving her baby up. She read a passage from December 20th.

I cannot believe how tremendous my girth is becoming. I am much larger than I ever anticipated, making it harder and harder to move around. I spend most of my days reading or in prayer. At long last, I am at peace with my decision to give this baby up for adoption. I am certain that Grace will do her best to find good people who will whole-heartedly love him or her. I have so many regrets, too many to name. With this child goes my last chance for happiness. It is the punishment that I deserve. Perseverance is my only companion now. I do not doubt that I will leave this earth alone.

The December 25th passage caught Sara's eye. It was a short entry. She read it to Emma.

He may be the devil, but my child is God's. I will not rest until the truth comes out. This baby will not pay the price for our sins or for Sean's cowardice. There will be a day of reckoning, a day when the liar is held accountable.

"I guess you have your work set out for you," Emma surmised.

"He knows I'm coming. That's why he drove out here. I am my mother's daughter, the spitting image. In me he saw a ghost that will not let him escape his past. The dogs knew what sort of monster he was; that's why they wouldn't even let him get out of his car. I think I'll need David to come with me when I confront him. I don't want to give the weasel any opportunities to squirm out of this and bolt."

"What a bum!" Emma said.

"The day of reckoning has arrived for Father Kennedy, you can be sure of it," Sara exclaimed.

The last page, December 31st, held an ominous sign. Sara shivered as she read it, understanding the foreshadowing of what was to come.

I am starting to have contractions and bleed a little. Mother has told me to stay in bed to avoid going into premature labor. Two hearts beating in synch, beating as one. How soon they will be parted. Will they ever be reunited? I can only hope. But right now there are other worries. I am frightened. Something doesn't feel right, but Mother has told me that having early contractions is normal. I asked about going to the hospital, but she has said that Pa would never let us out. He is crazed by the thought that I have brought shame to our family. He told me that I will have this child and go or he will take care of the bastard himself. I worry that Grace will not make it in time and he will rip the baby from my arms. If given the chance, he would take both our lives.

As I have been trapped here, Mother has ferreted out books from our library. These stories have been my only company and means of escape.

When I am done with this day, my words will be mixed in with the stories that buoyed me. My tale will be hidden away, camouflaged from those who deserve no explanation. Someday, somehow, all will be known.

Sara pulled the cross from the inside of the front cover before pressing the book closed. Sliding loose the key from the lock, she dangled it from the delicate chain. The light glinted and danced off its angular prongs. Sara opened the clasp, snaking the cross onto the thin gold rope. The two metal objects clinked as they struck one another. As she fastened the key and its old companion around her neck, she felt stronger.

"Shall we?" Sara asked rising to leave, journal in hand.

"Oh Lord, that man doesn't have any idea what level of hell is about to descend upon him," Emma mumbled under her breath as she followed Sara out to the car.

CHAPTER NINETEEN

Jack's eyes were closed when Sara returned to the hospital later that evening. Panic toyed with her senses as her thoughts landed on the worst possible scenario: having sins from the past break through to the present to claim her son. She found her answer in David's calm demeanor. He rose to meet her, bringing a finger to his lips to silence her pending question. The couple huddled together beyond the door's threshold, leaving the boy to dream peacefully.

"Shush. It's fine. He fell asleep. The burst of activity and a full belly wore him out. The doctor said he's doing great, better than anticipated. Of course Jack still isn't sure why he's here. He's convinced that he was simply out playing hide and seek with his new friend," David said in a half whisper, cognizant of the very late hour.

"I swear I can't take another loop in this rollercoaster. He freaked me out. I thought he went back into a coma," Sara whimpered, falling against her husband's chest.

"He's stable. I swear," he promised, hugging her increasingly thin frame.

Sara had not eaten in days. She needed some food before she collapsed from the combined effects of hunger and exhaustion. It was closing in on midnight, and the hospital cafeteria would be closed for several more hours. Vending machine snack food was the only thing available.

"Honey, the stress you've been under is making you melt away," he warned. "Please, let me get you something to eat—a granola bar, pretzels. What do you want? Seriously, you need energy or you're going to be in a bed next to Jack."

"I appreciate your concern, but I couldn't stomach anything. It would come right back up. I promise I'll try tomorrow," she pledged halfheartedly.

"I won't push it...yet."

David changed the subject. "Leila came by. She went home to shower, change, and nap after leaving you at the farm this afternoon. She sauntered in right after you left. Was elated when she saw that her 'little man' was back from nowhere land, then bawled like a baby. That woman really is nothing but a needy mess underneath that icy cold princess façade. The nurse had to tell her to get it together, because Jack was trying to comfort her!"

"Did she rush out to empty the nearest toy store? I can picture her skipping through the hospital followed by a string of butlers carrying wrapped boxes of every size." The vision brought a smile to Sara's worn face.

"She promised she would be back by eleven o'clock in the morning. She'll probably lose her business and we'll end up having to support her." A horrified look tarnished his features.

"If she does, we can think of it as having our own private designer on staff." The joke was apparently lost on him since she found herself being met with a scowl.

However, Leila's anticipated return gave Sara a needed window of time for hijacking David. She knew that in spite of her husband's increasing curiosity about the journal, he would patiently wait for her to broach the subject. This seemed like as good a time as any to bring up the visit to Father Kennedy.

"I'm glad Leila will be back tomorrow because I want you by my side for what's coming up next. I need your muscle and...your heart. Please." Sara hoped her request had sufficiently whet his appetite. He provided her one safe haven, the place where she always belonged. She understood that no matter what, he would never lie to her or leave. There wasn't anyone else in the world that she trusted like that, no one, ever. In her heart, Sara knew he would never deny her anything. And she wanted him by her side more than ever.

"Now what?" he asked, arching an eyebrow. "I don't want to

leave Jack. Whatever it is can wait. You found Katy and read her diary. Enough already!"

"Believe me. I wouldn't ask you unless I needed you," she begged.

"Sara, one of us should be here," David answered. "No, both of us should be here. You're all set to run off chasing after another clue or whatever. Give me a break. Our son needs us. Put him first this time."

Sara was stung by his words. Pushing back tears, she lashed out. "No wonder you get paid so well as a security analyst. You have it all figured out. You're right. I've been nothing but a selfish, delusional, and negligent mother."

"That's not what I was saying."

"Really? Isn't that exactly what you're implying? After everything that has happened and all that I've discovered about my life, you still don't trust my instincts. You can't even take the time to ask why I need you. I know you've been torn up about Jack. So have I! Don't you think it would have to be pretty damn important for me to even ask you this?"

"True, you got me there. I'm sorry. I never meant that you were a bad mother. So what do you think is so darn critical that we can't wait until Jack is out of the hospital?"

"Katy's diary was an eye opener. Turns out I have a naughty and quite unholy priest for a daddy. He has a serious problem with lying while hiding behind that finely pressed collar of his. He hung Katy out to dry. The good Father denied any and all responsibility for my creation. And this tops it all off: It seems he took some sadistic pleasure in telling Patrick, Katy's already angry, violent, and persistently drunk father, that she had been tossed from the convent for having sex with a bunch of workmen. Not true, but worth throwing into the mix for entertainment value."

"How do you know all this is true?" David asked, pulling her bony body toward him and engulfing her in his arms.

"Who would make something like this up? Katy's diary was one page after another of shame, guilt, and regret. I believe her account of what happened. And, it turns out I met dear old Dad the other day. He is the senior priest over at St. Thomas' Catholic Church. Looking into his face I felt chills. There was definitely some kind of uncomfortable connection that happened. Tomorrow, the good Father 'fesses up. What do you think? Will you come with me? Please."

"What do I think? I think I'm skeptical, but I'll come. Leila can stay with Jack."

"Thanks," she said with a weak smile. Sara could always count on the guy she fell in love with. It spoke volumes about how she was raised. She had enough self-worth to choose a man who would love and respect her, even when she drove him nuts.

Patrick and Maureen had failed terribly at instilling that in their youngest daughter. Through a veil of sadness, Sara realized that the best thing that ever happened to her was being given up. She was freed from the destructive cycle that crippled the McHugh family.

"Hello. Are you in there?" David asked.

"I'm here. I'll always be here," Sara answered.

They wove their fingers together, joining hands. Together they would wait for the breaking light of dawn to chase the shadows of the past from their lives. In the meantime, Jack's bedside was where they wanted to be. He would have their undivided attention.

Leila made a grand entrance bearing an obscene number of gifts at exactly eleven o'clock the following morning. She carried several stuffed animals under each arm and deposited her bounty around the elated little boy. He giggled as he picked up each gift to examine it closely. It was a regular safari with a stuffed lion, elephant, gorilla, giraffe, and tiger.

Sara could tell that Leila was satisfied by his reaction. David squeezed her leg and smiled. Joy filled Sara's heart as she watched her son. It was truly a miracle. She wondered how much credit belonged to the skill of the doctors versus the protection offered by his grandmother watching over him. Katy came to him as a child herself but seemed to intervene with maternal instinct. Sara's train of thought was interrupted when David leaned over to ask her a question.

"Do you want to pull Leila into the hall for a minute to ask her to stay with Jack while we go on this errand?" he asked in a hushed voice. "They seem completely enamored with each other. I don't think he'll get around to missing us for a couple of hours."

Sara motioned for her friend to follow her.

"Hey, Kiddo. I'll be right back. Your mom wants to see if I brought her a gift," Leila said, winking at the boy.

"I'll be back in a minute, Pumpkin," Sara promised.

Sara was silent as they walked to the waiting room. She knew she had to be sending up a red flag that something else was wrong.

"How are you holding up? It's not every day that you dig up a body from your property," Leila asked. "Anything else happen after I left yesterday? I mean, not that you haven't had enough manure land in your lap in the last few days. Sorry I split on you, but I needed sleep badly. I had hit empty and fumes weren't cutting it. When I stopped by last night, David told me you went back to read that ratty old diary you found in the used bookstore."

"I'm glad you left. Just because I'm bogged down in this mess doesn't mean that everyone around me should share the wealth. However, I am going to take advantage of you one more time. I would swear this is it, but I've learned to avoid making promises that I may not be able to keep," Sara admitted.

"What is it now? You found out you were the product of immaculate conception?" she joked.

"Not quite. But I do need you to stay with Jack so David and I can run out to St. Thomas' Church," Sara started to explain.

"Are you going to make the arrangements for Katy to get reburied in their graveyard? Do you think they'll let her in, you know, 'cause of being a naughty nun and all?"

"No. We're heading over there so I can confront my biological father," Sara replied as anger and resentment rose up, threatening to choke her. "Seems that I have the incredible good fortune of being the product of a wayward nun and an unscrupulous priest. Turns out, he refused to own up to plowing the field, if you get my drift. Implied she was whoring around. She declared that she would never rest until the day he admitted his sins. My dear, that day has cometh. I think the good Sister deserves a "Get Out of Purgatory Free" card. I'm bringing David with me. From what I can tell, Dad is a pretty slimy character."

"This is downright delectable...in a really sick kind of way. We definitely have to find you a publisher. There has to be some way to profit from your outrageous life. I can see it now; you'll be cruising through the talk show circuit in a matter of months. Can I come?" Leila pleaded.

"One thing at time. Can you stay with Jack for a couple of hours?"

"Of course," Leila said. "I was planning on being here until after lunch anyway. I have a decorating appointment at one o'clock out at Sara Miller's farm. Oh wait—that's you. I'm guessing you won't care if I'm late. Of course, I'll still be billing by the hour. Chop-chop. Go get your hubby. Your daddy is waiting."

It was twelve-thirty by the time Sara and David pulled up to the church. The previous chance meeting with Father Kennedy was seared into her memory. David turned the ignition off, leaving the couple suspended in silence. He reached out to Sara and turned her face toward him.

"Honey, you don't have to do this. You can let it go. We'll give Katy a proper burial. I'm sure her soul will move into heaven...or wherever," David said.

She could tell he was really worried about her snapping from all the stress. But in her heart she understood that there was no other option. "Things are what they are, but it didn't have to be like this. I have to do this. I need to do this. Katy deserves to be at peace. I want to do this," Sara stated, as much to convince herself as David.

"Okay," he answered, leaning over to give her a kiss.

The church looked quiet, serene against the brilliant blue sky. Sara's churning gut felt as if it stood out in stark contrast to this lovely late winter's day. Against the side wall of the building, several crocus were already attempting to break free of their heavily mulched blanket.

"Are you ready?" David asked, watching her closely as she stared up at the entrance.

"Do you think he's here?" she questioned. "It looks empty. I wonder if we need to go over to the rectory. That's what they call his house, right?"

"You're talking to the wrong person. I don't know what Catholics do or call things. I was raised Methodist, strictly casual, without all the pomp and protocol."

"I think we should try the office first."

"After you, my dear. I don't have a clue where to go other than through those doors."

David followed Sara up the steps. They pulled on the iron handles.

"Locked!" David declared, stepping back to look in both directions for an alternate entrance. "Now what?"

"Let's walk around. There has to be a side door. Could be they bolt the front during off hours," Sara suggested, barely getting the words out before hearing the lock click. They looked at each other, then back to the lock. Father O'Connor pushed open the heavy doors.

"Mrs. Miller, I wasn't expecting you. Are you here to see me? Your son, is he doing better?" the flustered man asked.

"Yes. My son has come out of the coma. He is much better, thank you," Sara answered.

"Thank the Lord. A miracle," he responded, spreading his hands.

"Father O'Connor, I would like to introduce you to my husband, David. If you could help direct us, we would appreciate it. We're here to see Father Kennedy," Sara politely inquired.

"Very nice to meet you. I'm so relieved for both of you. I know you were so worried. I guess my blessing helped to remove whatever was haunting your farm," he answered, while making the sign of the cross.

"Actually, a backhoe seemed to work better," David interjected.

"Pardon me?" the priest asked, perplexed by such an odd statement.

"Father, please excuse my husband's flip comment. We discovered that one of the family members died at the farm and was buried on the property in an unmarked grave. As a matter of fact, I need to speak to you later about making arrangements for the body to be properly buried here next to her brother, Michael. The medical examiner won't be releasing the remains for a few more days. However, at the moment, we really need to speak to Father Kennedy."

Sara was getting anxious to get on with the task at hand. Her fingers were tapping nervously on the leather cover of Katy's journal.

"Is he in the office?" David asked, trying to move things along.

"Father Kennedy? Funny you should ask about him. He questioned me about you last time you were here. He was quite agitated after hearing that you had sought us out to conduct a blessing to rid your house of ghosts. I didn't realize the two of you knew one another."

"We don't…exactly. It's a very long story. My mother knew him very well. In fact, that's why we're here. I have a message from her that I need to deliver to him in person. Is he available?" Sara asked, trying to skirt the issue.

"Unfortunately that's going to be impossible, at least for today. He hasn't been himself lately. Apparently he's come down with a bug in the past week and has taken to his bed. He was supposed to conduct a funeral today but asked me to preside over the service in his place. I was shocked because he had known this woman a very long time. Wait a minute. I think you met her the last time you were here. If you recall, you described a badly hunched over older lady. You had asked me about her identity. I drew a blank—couldn't place her at the time. Coincidence is that she passed on to the Lord the following day," he explained.

"Another coincidence. Not surprising. They seem to follow me around like a lost puppy. Who was she?" Sara asked.

"The woman had been a nun in younger years, a school teacher over at Mother of Angels Elementary. She left the convent many years ago. Not sure why. Father Kennedy had known her all this time, 20 or 30 years, I suppose. I met her right before she died. She told me her job was done; the deliverer had arrived and justice was knocking on the door. I had no idea what she was talking about. She must have suffered from dementia," the priest said with an expression of pity.

Sara's heart skipped a beat. Astonished by what this man revealed, Katy seemed to swirl all around them as Sara tried to fit this new piece into the puzzle. "What was her name?" Sara asked with a bit too much intensity, making the young priest look at her with a curious expression.

"You said you didn't know this woman."

"I don't, or at least, I think I don't. The woman whose remains we found had been a nun and she had taught at the same school. Her name was Katy or Kathleen McHugh."

"The woman who was buried at your farm was a nun? That's outrageous. Someone would have missed her! The authorities would have been alerted," he said, clearly horrified.

"She died shortly after leaving the convent. Father, what was this other woman's name?" David asked, refocusing the conversation.

"Anna, Anna Harris. I never asked her religious name."

"Sara, does that name ring a bell?" David asked.

"Anna…I think that was the name of the other nun who accompanied Katy home," she said, flipping open the journal to April 11th. She skimmed down the page, finding the location of the name. "Anna. It was Anna. Would she have referred to another Sister by her given name or only by her religious name?"

The handsome young priest was craning his neck to read the writing upside-down. "It would depend. If they had been good friends, they may have conversed with each other off grounds by their given names. Was that Father Kennedy's name in there?"

Sara snapped the diary shut, not wanting to reveal anything more to this man. "Yes, he knew both Anna and Katy."

"It's urgent that we speak with him today. I'm sorry he hasn't been feeling well but it's imperative that we see him at once," David added, stretching out all six feet five inches of his imposing frame.

"He's sick in bed. It's simply impossible. Give it a few days and give us a call. I'm sure he would be interested in speaking with you, especially if your mother was an old friend," he explained as a hearse rolled up to the curb. They turned around to watch two men from the funeral home get out of the long black car. One opened the back hatch while the other came up to greet Father O'Connor.

"You'll have to excuse me. I need to direct these gentlemen where to bring Anna's casket. You're welcome to stay for the service. It should be starting in about half-an-hour," he offered, disappearing into the darkness of the church.

David put his arm around Sara and led her down the steps and halfway up the sidewalk. "I think we wait until Father O'Connor is tied up with sending the good Sister up to heaven and then make a beeline for Father Kennedy," David said, looking into Sara's weary eyes.

"I think that's the only way to do it. What do you make of Anna? Do you think she found out what happened to Katy?" Sara asked.

"Possibly. But why would she be hanging out with Kennedy? Maybe he was having an affair with her too. I mean, it's not like he was some sort of saint. She could have figured that he had a thing for nuns."

Sara shook her head. "I don't think so. Father O'Connor said she told him that 'her job' was done. The deliverer had arrived to tell the truth or set things right or something like that. I bet she felt responsible and was here to keep an eye on the good Father. She must have recognized me and knew it would be a matter of time until I forced him to 'fess up."

"So where do you think he's hiding out?" David asked, looking down at the old leather-bound book in Sara's hand.

The sound of the coffin being set out on a wheeled trolley prompted Sara and David to turn around. Men dressed in black suits pushed the polished oak box around to a ramp that led up the side of the building. "Let's take a walk," David urged when they were gone. He held out his arm to escort Sara up the path.

"Do you think Father O'Connor will come back out to look for us?" Sara asked with concern.

"I doubt it. People are already starting to arrive. He's going to be too busy to keep track of us," David said, nodding in the direction of two cars pulling into the driveway.

When they rounded the corner of the church, the cemetery spread out like a fan. A mausoleum sat in the center, with all shapes and sizes of headstones weaving patterns around two fountains set to either side. There were marble angels, huge crosses and pinnacles. Sara thought about Michael being buried somewhere out there, the child who forever shattered a family. She wanted to find his gravesite to let him know he would no longer be alone. But he would have to wait until they completed their mission.

Sara spotted a path leading up from a small prayer garden to a two-story brick house. She elbowed David as they approached. As they raised their eyes to the second floor, they saw an old man peering down at them. He abruptly pulled the curtains closed.

"I bet he has the doors locked and won't even come down when we knock," David said.

"He has no choice. He knows it's time," Sara answered.

They walked up the brick steps to the porch.

"Front or side door?" David asked.

"Good question. I've always been a backdoor secret, so why don't we go around to the front?"

They gazed through the etched glass double doors. As Sara reached out her hand to knock, a figure emerged on the top landing of the staircase. He took hold of the worn banister, appearing to need the support in order to make this journey down to these unwanted visitors. By the time his feet reached the bottom step, Sara's heart was pounding hard and fast. David took her hand, squeezing it tightly as the old priest stood face to face with them. No one dared to utter a sound or move. Father and daughter stared at each other while barely blinking.

Sara finally found her tongue. "Let us in," she said without any sense of emotion.

Father Kennedy silently nodded before turning the latch to unlock the deadbolt. They watched as he pivoted on his heels, then shuffled down the hall. David took hold of the worn brass knob, pushing open the door so they could follow. The priest entered a rear parlor with a window that framed the church cemetery.

"Why have you come?" he asked without looking at them.

"I think you know the answer to that, Father," Sara answered, her voice tinted with anger.

"I understand you were here about getting your house blessed after your son had an accident," he said.

"You know who I am. You knew from the very first time that our eyes met. You can see her in me. Admit it. That's why you don't have the courage to look at me now," Sara said with a sneer, walking in his direction.

"My dear child, you must be mistaken. I don't know what you are talking about," he said, shifting his weight as he leaned against the windowsill.

The anger that had been building inside Sara crumbled into despair. She started to shake as the reality of having him deny her yet again ravaged her already weak defenses. Tears streamed down her face as she turned to David, who protectively went to her side.

"Do you really want us all to go through this? Isn't it time to give your conscience a rest? Thirty-five years and you still don't have the guts to do the right thing. You are one sorry excuse for a man," David said, making no attempt to hide his disgust.

Sean Kennedy turned around to look at David, his eyes filled with the anguish of being torn in two. His legs faltered, but he caught himself.

"It has to end. The lie has to end here, today. My God, man! What does it feel like to be looking into the eyes of your own flesh and blood for the first time? To be talking to her, to have the opportunity to make amends for not having a spine for more than three decades? Because we all know, if you don't, you'll be rotting in hell till the end of time," David said, the urgency pressing through his message.

The man turned away again. Sara and David could see his eyes following the funeral procession out into the cemetery.

"Anna knew the truth. She went to her grave feeling partly to blame for Katy's tryst with you. If she had accompanied her Sister to church that morning, I would never be here. Was she waiting for me to save you or to send you on your chosen path?" Sara asked. "You tell me."

The old priest sighed and twisted his neck to take in the striking young woman standing defiantly before him. "You look just like her. I can't bear it," he admitted, his gaze dropping to the floor.

"Why did you betray her? You killed her. Did you know that? You killed her heart and soul, then you killed her body," she said, shaking the journal in his direction.

"I made a mistake, a terrible mistake. I...I didn't know what I was doing," he confessed, without lifting his eyes.

"Don't lie to me! For that matter, stop lying to yourself," Sara cried, spitting the words out at him. Tremors of anger shook her from head to toe as she stepped closer to the broken man.

"You don't understand. She left me. Not once, but twice. I asked her to marry me when we graduated from high school. I loved her more than life itself, but she wouldn't let herself give in to that promise of happiness. My darling, Katy, was haunted by Michael. She felt she owed him her life. I begged her not to leave me! I wasn't enough. She sealed both our fates," he recalled with tears welling up in his eyes as he raised them to face his accuser.

"But she came back to you. My God, she was carrying your child, the child both of you created. You had a chance to start over," Sara said, unrelenting in her need for his apology.

"That's not the whole story. I asked her not to return to the convent. I wanted her to choose me after we made love. I wanted her forever, each and every day. I told her that. She was the only thing in life I ever wanted, more than air, food, water, or my freedom. I was willing to leave religious life, the only life that I had envisioned without her by my side. But she did it again! She chose him. Guilt drove her back to him. Not God—Michael! For the second time she threw me aside. Katy fed off me, off my hopeful heart, then threw me away like a broken plate. She didn't value what we shared. I was devastated," the old man explained gazing out at the funeral service.

Sara was beginning to see this man, her father, as a man who suffered from human flaws and failings. The little boy buried out beyond these walls had destroyed so many lives. She wondered how many times this fractured man prayed at his gravesite to release the woman he loved. How he must have cursed him for his ever-lasting grip.

"What happened when you found out about the pregnancy?" David asked.

"I had made up my mind that I would never let her in again. I had steeled myself against her. Katy had left me half the man I once was, and I wasn't going to let her take the rest. When she called, I saw my opportunity to make her understand. She would know what she had done to me. She would feel the pain of aban-donment and isolation, the pain of losing my affection and my love. I sought revenge from the deep, dark place that my soul had fallen into. I left her there on her father's floor, belly full with child, sob-bing with fear over never having choices again," Father Kennedy shamefully explained.

"But as the months wore on, how could you live with your-self? You knew she was carrying your child. How could you leave your child? You knew Patrick had slipped into madness. How could you endanger your child's life—my life?" Sara asked.

"Katy wrote to Anna during the last few weeks of the preg-nancy telling her the real reason behind leaving the sisterhood. The letter explained what had happened between us. Anna contacted me. She talked to me and somehow found the piece of me that was still alive. I realized that I needed to make things right. I wanted to because I was still in love with her, in spite of everything," he said as he started to sob into his hands.

Tears lined Sara's face as she put a hand on her father's back. She now understood that she had accepted Katy's view of her father without realizing that his character had been distorted through her mother's own emotional prism.

"You are both a curse and a gift. When I look at you, my heart leaps, as I see her features in your face, the only woman I have ever loved. But this window into the past has a painfully sharp edge. I was too late. When I arrived at the farm, she was gone. You were gone. I told Patrick and Maureen that I was the baby's father. I admitted that I had behaved terribly, like a true scoundrel, but I had seen the error in my actions. I was there to ask his daughter to be my wife. He came after me, intending to kill me. He gave me a beating I will never forget. Lester pulled him off me as he was strangling the life out of me. I remember Maureen screaming at him, telling him that killing me wouldn't bring her back, that it wouldn't bring Michael back. I can see her face as she futilely pulled at those thick arms of his. I was nearly unconscious when Lester saved me. I shouldn't say saved me, because I died that day. I realized she was gone. At first, I didn't know where. I thought Patrick threw her out on her own with a newborn. When I came around, Maureen and Lester rushed me to the car. They told me to never step foot on the property again or they would let Patrick finish the job," he said, turning to face his daughter.

She could see the agony pouring from his eyes as she reminded him of her mother. The intensity of his gaze caused her to shiver.

"You could pass for twins, except for the hair. She had beautiful red hair. I remember a young girl with fire shooting out from her very core. To look at her you wouldn't have realized that the fire had died years before she did," he said, forcing a weak smile.

"So you knew she died. When did you find out?" David asked.

Father Kennedy turned to look back out the window. He was silent for a long while before composing himself enough to answer the question.

"The next day Maureen showed up here. I was a mess, bruised physically and mentally. I had decided to hire a private investigator to find her and the baby. I was going through a Washington D.C. phone book when she appeared in my doorway. She told me that Katy was dead. I couldn't believe it—wouldn't believe it. They had buried her, like a dead animal, out in the field. It was too awful to bear. This mother who had experienced the agony of losing two children sat before me, blaming me for her daughter's death and disgrace. The ultimate punishment was served to me on that day. I had to live with that knowledge. They would never let me back on the property. Not even to whisper a prayer for her. My life changed forever. Choices had to be made. Terrible choices. You were lost to me. Maureen told me that you had been taken by Grace to New York, that a wonderful, childless couple was holding you in their arms as we spoke. You were now their child, our fate written without my knowledge or consent," he said turning back to face Sara, his eyes pleading for her forgiveness.

"I'm so sorry," she said unable to find any other words.

"You shouldn't be. You were innocent," her father said, catching a glimpse for the first time at the chain around her neck. Tears fell freely as he held the key and cross in the palm of his old hand. He grabbed Sara's arm as he fell down to his knees. David rushed forward to help the man overcome by years of bearing the burden of his guilt.

"All I did was love her. What a terrible price we both paid. What a price we all paid," he considered as David lifted him while Sara pushed a chair underneath his limp body.

"We found her. She's free now. She's coming back to you— here," Sara told him gently.

"What?" Sean asked growing increasingly pale. "What do you mean?"

"When we moved to the farm, we had no idea about my connection to the place. I didn't know anything about the McHugh family or that Katy was my biological mother. But once we were there, she came to me. I would see her, feel her emotions and experience her torture. She brought us there so she could talk to you. She prayed for you to come, to have a change of heart, but she died believing that you had abandoned her. But she was wrong. You loved her till the end and clearly you love her still. I'm the vessel for her to finally understand this, to finally find the peace that had tragically eluded her in life as well as in death. She has been directing a series of events to bring me here to you today. All the secrecy is over."

"I'll be the first to admit that it sounds crazy," David chimed in. "I never bought into Sara's 'messages from the dead' scenario until today, until we met you. You were able to corroborate everything that she's been trying to pound into my thick head." He turned and looked apologetically at his wife. "I'm so sorry. I just couldn't accept that this stuff could have really happened until I heard it with my own ears. I should have trusted your instincts."

She smiled. "I know and…thanks. I think the most important thing we can all do is realize that Katy sent me here for a reason: to find my family and for us to forgive one another."

"She was too young. It wasn't her time. We should have been married. We could have been a family," Sean declared, taking both of Sara's hands in his.

"There's still time for us. You have a grandson that you have to meet. She saved his life and stayed with him while he was in a coma. She failed to stop Michael in time, but she didn't fail the son of her daughter," she said.

"Do you know where Katy's remains are?" he asked.

"The medical examiner has her," Sara said. "She should be cleared for reburial soon. I think it only fitting that she should come here. I think her final resting place should be alongside her brother, where you can watch over her."

He nodded in agreement, then stared out the window one more time. The trio watched as each mourner tossed a flower on Anna's casket as it was being lowered into the ground. Father O'Connor finished the service by making the sign of the cross.

"She was a good friend. She helped me move forward. I don't think I ever told her how much I appreciated her in those dark days right after I learned the truth. I listened to her guidance when I was lost—unable to care for myself or for another. The choice I was left with ate me alive. I understood what I put Katy through, how helpless she must have felt as the decision was made. But it was the right thing to do under the circumstances; it was the only thing," he said shifting his eyes back to his daughter.

"I'm not really following you here. Do you mean by letting me stay with my adoptive parents?" Sara asked, glancing at David.

"Yes…and no. You see, when Maureen sought me out the next day, she was not alone. She clutched a tightly swaddled babe to her chest. She brought me your brother, your twin," he said.

"What did you say?" David sputtered, his worried eyes immediately crossing to Sara.

Sara stopped breathing upon hearing this revelation. She felt what strength she had left drain away, as his statement started to register. As her thin limbs buckled, David caught her in his arms. Sara shook her head and blinked away the fuzziness that was threatening to consume her.

"I've got you! Do you want to sit down?" David asked, keeping an arm around her slim waist.

"No. I'll be fine," she answered, waving for her father to continue. "Please, go on."

"I'm sorry. I know this is shocking. It was to everyone involved. They didn't realize she was having twins. She never had any medical care, never saw a doctor. Grace left with you immediately after you were born. She had no idea another baby was on the way. Luckily, Maureen had stayed in the room with Katy. Patrick had stormed off after Grace pulled away to finish drinking himself into oblivion. She had no way to reach her eldest daughter to tell her to turn around," he explained.

"My God, I have a brother," Sara said with a mixture of excitement and sorrow.

"So where is he? What happened to him?" David asked.

The old priest rose from the chair and walked to the window. He was weakened from the encounter but steadied himself by holding onto the windowsill with both hands.

"Before Katy bled to death, she named him Michael Sean. Maureen told me that my Kathleen had a few minutes to nurse, kiss and hold him. I think that's what saved him from getting thrown in the hole with her. It broke my heart when that baby boy was handed to me, to think that she had held him in her arms. It was almost like touching her. I didn't know what to do after that. Here I had the chance of a lifetime, but I had nothing to offer him. If I kept him, I couldn't stay a priest. My own parents would have thrown me from their doorstep in shame. I would have had no job or place to live, no means of caring for him. When Anna called back to see if I had succeeded in begging Katy for forgiveness and another chance to make an honest woman out of her, she found a man in utter panic. We talked for a long time. She said what I could not bring myself to admit: that Baby Michael would be better off like his sister, put into a home with two parents who could love and raise him. We concocted the story that he had been abandoned at the church. The only trace of his identity was pinned to his blanket, a note with the name Michael Sean. He was placed through Catholic Charities in a local home. Through my position, I was able to learn where. Michael went to a family that attended services at our church. Through the years, I've been able to see him grow and develop into a wonderful man. Some may say I was a mentor to him, taking him under my wing from the time he was but a wee lad," he said, smiling at this small accomplishment.

"Where is he?" Sara said. Feeling stronger, she pushed David's arm aside so she could stand next to her father.

"He doesn't know. Michael lives a life free from this horrible truth," he said, staring off into the distance.

"He has a right to know. We have the right to know one another," Sara demanded in frustration. Most of her life she spent protected from "the truth" by her adoptive parents. Having a repeat of this situation was not an option now. Sara felt her temper starting to simmer in spite of the sympathy she felt for her father.

"Tell me, are you better off now that you know, or are you wounded to your core? Wouldn't you turn back the clock if you could? Honestly, wouldn't you jump at the chance to wipe this agonizing history from your past, to go back to blissful ignorance?" he asked.

Sara took but a minute to search the depths of her soul for the answer. Knowing her true identity didn't diminish or discolor the wonderful life she had experienced with her adoptive parents, nor did it harm her relationship with her husband and son. It was a lack of clarity and understanding that had endangered her and her families' lives. This new chapter of her life answered so many questions that had plagued her while growing up. "No, I wouldn't. This is who I am and it's okay," she said putting her hand over his.

"How is that possible?" he asked.

"I had a good life and still do. Discovering the truth behind my existence doesn't make me any less or any more of the person I am. My presence here is for a reason. I can see it now. Can you? You just need to be forthright, to claim the family that has eluded you for all these years. It's time to come home. It's time to be honest with your son. It's time to give Katy McHugh what she has long waited for over these past 35 years: vindication and reconciliation, with the chance to have her family reunited and whole."

The old man watched her face as she spoke, her green eyes piercing his heart like her mother's had so long ago. "You're offering me salvation when I'm not sure I deserve it. Your words are lifting me to a place I never thought I would allow myself to go, a place where hope has been tucked far away. The thought of having my children know and embrace me after all these years is too great a gift to imagine."

"It's time to forgive yourself," Sara urged.

"Maybe you're right," he said, looking out into the empty graveyard.

"Where's Michael now?" David asked. "We can take you to him. The two of you can talk to him together."

"No, no. I think it would be best if I told him privately. The boy has known me since he was a baby. He's considered me a trusted friend. This will be a shock for him. But he is a good man, a forgiving man, a much better man than I. There will be time for the two of you to become acquainted soon enough. Please, let me do this alone," Sean begged. He looked from Sara to David and back again with glassy eyes pleading his case.

Sara wondered if her father was showing natural paternal protectiveness of his son, or was he getting set to run from another uncomfortable confrontation? Searching his eyes, she realized that the desperation they saw in his face was coming from a fear of sustaining another loss, the possibility of having his son sever all ties after learning of this deception.

She was about to speak when another male voice broke the silence.

"Mr. and Mrs. Miller, what are you doing here? I told you that Father Kennedy was ill. You were not supposed to bother him today. I can't believe you forced your way in on a sick man. I'm so sorry, Father. I told them that you had been unavailable," Father O'Connor angrily stated.

Before Sara or David could say a word in their own defense, Sean motioned for the young priest to come to his side.

"Thomas, it's fine, really. I let them in. We had some important things to discuss. You see, Mrs. Miller's mother and I were very close friends some years ago, before you were born," he said to the obedient younger man.

"Sara, it was a true pleasure meeting you and your husband. I hope I can visit with your son sometime very soon. I know we have a great deal more catching up to do, but I need to speak with Father O'Connor. I hate to rush you off. I promise to be in touch," Father Kennedy added, looking intensely into his daughter's eyes.

Sara was unable to move. She wanted to continue getting to know her father and to discover more about her brother's identity.

"Sara, please," Father Kennedy whispered while squeezing her hand.

"Yes, of course. I'm sorry. I thought we weren't finished with our discussion, but I can see we are," she answered, scrambling to compose herself.

"Nice to see you again," the younger man said as the couple started heading toward the hall.

"Yes, you too, Father," David said, leading his wife toward the door.

"Father Kennedy, I hope to talk with you in the very near future," Sara added, looking over her shoulder. "You know how to contact me."

David escorted her out of the rectory. They were quiet until they reached the car.

"Should we stay? Wait until they finish talking? I can't believe this—I have a brother," Sara squealed like a child who was handed a present for no reason at all. "This hasn't turned out at all like I had expected. What do you think will happen now?" she asked, looking back in the direction of the house.

"I think your brother is about to have his world pulled out from underneath him. If he's half the man you are, he'll land on his feet," he teased.

Sara smirked, then leapt forward to hug him. "Thanks for standing by me. I can always count on you. No matter what."

"I meant what I said in there. I should have believed in you, in your crazy theory, but you know how I am. I needed proof, something tangible. I love you, Sara."

"I love you too. Do you think we should hang around?"

"I think our own son is missing us. We've been gone a long time. It's nearly three o'clock. Your father knows where you live. Give him some time. I'm sure he'll be as curious about you as you are about him," David said.

As Sara was climbing into the car, she could see the old man walking with his young counterpart into the cemetery. The scene made her wonder what her brother would look like. Would he take after Katy or their father? Would he look like her or someone totally different?

"Jack's waiting. Let's go," David said, starting up the car.

Sara's eyes lingered on the two men as they pulled away. "David?"

"Yes?"

"It's so strange. I never felt him. I never felt like I was missing a part of me, you know, like twins are supposed to. How is that possible? I should have known somehow. I should have sensed that he was out there. I picked up on all these other connections, but I missed this one," Sara said.

"Maybe twins only have that weird invisible tie if you're raised together or if you're identical," David replied with a shrug. "I don't think this should be one more thing to obsess over. Seems like you've done your part. You waded through the muck and got to the other side. Give it a rest. You deserve one."

"If he's living in this area, I could have met him and never even knew it."

"You're not going drop it, are you? Sara, did you ever consider that the reason your radar didn't go haywire may be because he's decent, happy, without serious mental illness or psychopathic tendencies? It seems like everyone else has been a tormented mess. That's how you've gotten sucked in. Whereas they've been the equivalent of a raging torrent of psychic angst, your brother could be more like a peaceful birdbath."

"Wow. When did you become so…philosophical?"

"I'm not. You must be rubbing off on me. Now cut yourself some slack! You need to get a break from this whirlwind you've been in. You haven't slept. You haven't eaten, and you're hanging on mentally by a fraying thread. I think you should go home after we check on Jack at the hospital. Go to sleep, put something in your mouth other than coffee, take a hot shower, and maybe ride a horse or two. It would be good mental therapy."

"Sounds great, but Jack needs me," Sara insisted.

"He needs a mother who is functional. I'm sure he would love to see you for an hour, but then leave. He's doing so well that the doctors will probably move him to the pediatric floor by later today, and he'll be home in a few days."

Sara leaned over and kissed David on the cheek. "You're a tough man to deny."

She thought about the word "home." They had found the farm that she had always dreamed about and desired. She wondered if it could ever be the safe haven that she had once envisioned, a place where her heart and soul could feel sheltered and secure.

CHAPTER TWENTY

Having listened to David, Sara returned home that afternoon and stayed through the night. She felt rejuvenated after getting eight hours of sleep. It was amazing what some protein and a little rest could do. While she got dressed, the sounds of the farm had sung so sweetly to her, she found herself changing into britches and boots. Sara hated to admit it, but David was right. She had desperately needed this mental break.

It wasn't long before Sara was mounted on Gale Force and guiding him through the front pasture and into the woods. She was carefully maneuvering around a fallen log, when she heard the honking of a horn echo across the open fields. The dogs sped off in the direction of the intruder at full cry. With a small squeeze from her lower leg, the horse sprang forward at a slow canter. Sara rose up from the saddle into a hand-gallop, allowing the gelding to use the muscles running along his back freely. The cool morning air had put a buck into the mount's repertoire, making her laugh with delight. It had seemed a lifetime ago that she had felt such simple pleasure, yet it was only a few weeks. By the time she trotted up to the barn, she realized it was to be short lived.

Standing next to an old blue sedan was Father O'Connor. Sara could see him shifting his weight awkwardly from one foot to the other as Emma tried to engage him in conversation. The feisty Brit offered to show him around, but he opted to stay near his car, probably for fear of being attacked by the dogs that had set up a perimeter. As Gale Force halted in front of them, Sara could tell that the priest was relieved to see her. She dismounted, and Emma stepped forward to take the horse's reins and lead him away.

"Hi, Mrs. Miller. Uh...Sara. Umm....Well, I guess I'm

here…. I'm here because…," the uncomfortable man attempted to say. "Because we…I…."

Sara sensed what his next words were going to be by his obvious stammering and discomfort. She felt her heart starting to race as she stared at the man standing before her. Electricity shot through her body, filling her with excitement. "Because you're my twin brother," Sara blurted out, finishing the sentence he was having so much trouble articulating.

"Well…yes. I guess that would be the case," he answered with a breath of relief.

Their eyes locked for several awkward moments, leaving them momentarily speechless.

"Please, why don't you come in so we can talk?" Sara offered, pulling off her helmet and riding gloves.

The priest followed her up to the house, the one he had blessed a few days earlier.

Once in the living room, Sara offered him a drink. "Can I get you something? Coffee, tea, a double scotch? We have it all."

"No, thank you," he replied, looking around the cavernous room he had sprinkled with holy water, as if seeing it now for the first time. The large space took on a new warmth, with its stone fireplace and overstuffed furniture.

"Please sit," she said, pointing to the couch as she sat in a chair across the room.

He lowered himself down into the deep cushions. An unnerving tension hung in the air between them as they scrambled for a way to break the silence.

Father O'Connor cleared his throat, as if trying to free the words that were lodged in his windpipe. "Father Kennedy, Sean, told me why you had needed to see him yesterday. He told me about Kathleen McHugh and the children she bore…. The words don't come easily. I don't know what to think or to feel," he admitted, looking down at his feet.

"Can I call you Thomas?" Sara asked. "I would feel awkward calling you Father O'Connor under the circumstances."

"Oh, yes. Of course." The man's radiant blue eyes wore the

marks left by pain and betrayal.

"Thomas, I'm sure that the past 24 hours have not been easy for you. I know they haven't been for me. But out of all the miserable details that have surfaced, finding out that I have a brother is a tremendous treasure, one completely unanticipated. Learning that you're my twin has been the one sliver of light in an otherwise black landscape," Sara said, making a pink hue spread across her brother's pale cheeks.

He had trouble meeting her gaze. Silence descended yet again as Sara waited for him to compose himself.

"I didn't know he was my father. I never suspected a thing. I always knew I was adopted, but I never questioned where I came from. I was told that I had been abandoned at the church—a package sent straight from God. My parents named me Thomas after the church where I was found. I thought I was one of the luckiest kids on earth. I had two parents who desperately wanted me and who truly loved me. Then there was Father Kennedy. He took a special interest in me, always making sure that I was involved in activities and taking time to tutor me whenever I needed it, being a positive presence in my life, like a second father. I had assumed it was because I had been abandoned in his church. I wanted to grow up to be just like him—and I did. Imagine that? My problem now is, exactly who did I grow up to be like?" A fissure had opened in his heart and the sorrow spilled out freely. Tears streamed down his cheeks, and when he looked up, Sara was standing in front of him, her soft hand ready to wipe them from his face.

"I'm so sorry. I wish I could say I understand what you're feeling, but I can't," Sara said, moving over to sit next to him on the couch. She had to fight back her own tears as she absorbed his emotions. She wanted to take his pain away, to shelter him from the agony she herself had felt. "Clearly he loves you. You were all he had left of a life that went careening out of control. It sounds like you have been blessed by having him in your life. I have no doubt he was. I would bet that you were probably the only thing that saved him."

This time Sara felt the connection. It was unmistakable. Maybe she was finally tuned into it, or maybe his raw turmoil made it more pronounced. Warmth showered down on her as she touched his hand. It was as if someone had wrapped a blanket snugly around her. She thought of a passage from Katy's diary. *"Two hearts beating in synch, beating as one. How soon they will be parted. Will they ever be reunited?"* Could her mother have known? Was she talking about her own heart beating in synch, or could she have known that there were two babies? Regardless, they were now reunited, together after 35 years apart. Two lives separated at birth, two lives brought back together by the restless soul of their long-dead mother.

"I think Katy, our mother, would have been pleased that we've found one another. Are you aware that she had named you Michael after her brother who was killed? I guess the planets are in perfect alignment: Michael and Kathleen together again on the family farm. Ironic," Sara stated.

"I'm not following you," he said sensing that he missed something in her comment.

"Grace, our Aunt, named me Kathleen before I was given up for adoption."

"That's a little unsettling," he said, letting out a tension-filled sigh. "Would you mind showing me where she was buried? I would like to spend a few minutes praying."

Sara had to turn away. The intensity of his gaze cut right through her. "It's out front. We can walk. Give me a minute to pull off my riding boots and change into some shoes," Sara said, standing up.

He caught her hand as she took a step. "No. Please. If you don't mind, I would prefer to go alone. I won't be long. I just need a few minutes by myself."

"That's fine. I understand. You drove by the field on your way in."

Thomas followed Sara through the front door down into the yard. She pointed toward the enormous mound of dirt deposited near the stone wall. The backhoe operator had left the grave uncovered until it was cleared by the police of being any sort of crime scene. She watched her brother stride off across the pasture. She thought he was younger the first time they met in his office. They didn't look anything alike, making her wonder if he resembled his namesake, Michael. She wondered if her brother was similar to her at all. Sara had abandoned religion, seeing only its flaws, while he had been drawn to it. It wasn't hard to imagine how different their lives would have been if Katy and Sean had chosen a different path.

So many different emotions washed over her as she thought about what lay ahead for all of them. She was incredibly excited and practically bursting with joy, but at the same time she felt scared and guarded. She wanted so much to claim her newly-discovered family and embrace them whole-heartedly, but she harbored a deep-seated gnawing fear of being rejected, of always being an outsider, the one who never fit in.

Sara was transfixed as she watched Thomas' shrinking figure being drawn to the gaping wound in the earth. The spell was broken when the phone rang. She trotted back through the house and picked up the receiver a split second before the answering machine had a chance to turn on.

"Hello," she said.

"Mrs. Miller, this is Ben Match from the medical examiner's office. I wanted to let you know that the remains of Kathleen McHugh have been released. You can contact the funeral home and they will arrange to have her picked up," he explained.

"Thanks. I'll take care of it right away. Goodbye."

Sara wondered who should conduct the memorial service. It definitely seemed inappropriate to ask Sean to do it, and now, with Thomas learning the truth, she suspected he too would decline. Sara returned to the front steps to wait for the priest, hoping he could offer some advice.

Fifteen minutes passed before her brother started back. He was wearing an emotionally torn and solemn expression as he approached.

"I can't accept it. How could any parent, even one that was angry, do that to their child? Dump her into the cold earth as if she never mattered or existed. What kind of people would do something so sinister? Please, help me understand," he said as he reached the bottom of the steps.

"They died along with her. Michael started them down that road when he didn't make it, and Katy finished them off. You know that Patrick killed himself on the very spot where they buried her. Put a gun to his head and pulled the trigger. I can't tell you if he did it out of guilt, cowardice, or loneliness. Grace and Eileen fared the best. They had more time with their parents before the bad times descended," Sara theorized.

Thomas took a place next to Sara on the second to last step. Taking her left hand in his right, their fingers curled together like the reeds of a basket. As they looked out toward Katy's grave, the bright sun warmed them. The farm seemed altered, like a veil had been lifted, making everything sharper and more beautiful.

"A new page has started for this family. A different history will be recorded from this day forward, one that finds healing through unity, coming together to celebrate our existence as the sum of all of our diverse parts. That's what Katy's memorial should be about—a new beginning for us. You, me, Sean and whoever remains from the McHugh family. It's the only way," Thomas declared with serene wisdom.

"The timing of your divine inspiration couldn't be better," she said, squeezing his hand. In his words she found the strength to take a leap of faith and trust him with her heart.

He grinned like a happy child as he looked into her face.

"We have a funeral that needs to be planned. I think she should be buried alongside Michael," Sara suggested. "Essentially she sacrificed her life for him."

"Agreed," he answered.

"I need to call Grace with the details. She'll be getting another surprise—a new nephew. If she wasn't willing to come down for the service before, I'm guessing she may be now."

"Will you walk me out to my car? I'd like to get back to the church. I have some arrangements to make," he said, winking as he pulled her up from where she was seated.

"I think I might like having a brother."

"I have to admit, it does feel pretty good knowing I'm not alone."

Sara waved as he drove away, feeling as if a little piece of her had vanished. Emma, who had been eavesdropping from inside the barn, appeared at her side full of questions.

"I've gathered that you've added onto your family tree again," Emma said with wide eyes. "How did that happen? No...I'm not sure I really want to know. It can't be good."

"Actually, it's the best thing that's happened yet," Sara answered beaming. "He's my twin. Katy had two babies."

"No! That's outrageous!"

"What did you think of him?"

"A little jumpy around the animals, but very nice. It's a damn shame that he's a priest. He's bloody hot," Emma added smartly as she elbowed her boss in the ribs.

"Are you taking lessons from Leila?"

"Don't I wish! So tell me, Mrs. Miller, what's it like to no longer be an only child?" she asked, fishing for details about their reunion.

"Well, Miss Emma Thatcher, I think it feels terrific," Sara answered.

"You don't have any other relations lurking about—maybe a sister or two tossed in for good measure?" she kidded as they both turned to go into the barn. The shadowy outlines of their bodies were stretched out in front of them as the bright sunshine followed from behind.

"I don't think so, but you never know. I guess we'll see if there are any more surprises in store for us at my mother's memorial service. I'll be holding my breath until Katy is laid to rest."

CHAPTER TWENTY-ONE

The flowers set around the simple oak casket greeted mourners with a fragrant scent. Colorful sprays of lilies, mums, gladiolas, and roses adorned vases and baskets. Sara and Thomas were huddled in a far corner when two petite old women with their aged spouses supporting them arrived. The white-haired foursome was accompanied by a parade of younger men and women. Sara immediately recognized Grace. The woman with her was almost certainly her other aunt, Eileen. They were practically identical. Seeing them standing next to one another sent Sara back to a comment made weeks earlier by the old blacksmith, James Sullivan. He remarked how hard it was to tell them apart as young girls. The older woman took her sister's hand and led her straight in their direction.

"Sara, my dear. I'm so happy to see you again," Grace said, hugging her niece.

"It's good to see you as well. I'm pleased you were able to make the trip. I know it's been difficult for you to face this," Sara replied with honest appreciation for her efforts.

"Yes, yes it has. But we couldn't have missed it. We owe our poor sister that much. Don't we?" she asked the frail woman standing next to her, who nodded in agreement.

"I'm sure Katy appreciates that you came," Sara added.

"I would like to introduce you to your other aunt. This is Eileen," she said, smiling.

"Oh goodness! The resemblance is uncanny. If you had red hair I would swear you were Katy standing here before me today. I can't get over it," Eileen said as she dabbed a crumpled tissue into the corner of her eye.

"It's wonderful to have the chance to meet you. Plus, there is someone else here I need to introduce. Aunt Grace, Aunt Eileen, this is my brother, Thomas. This is Katy's son," Sara said as she put her hand on her brother's back.

"Oh, my! I couldn't believe it when Sara told me that Katy had given birth to a second baby. I would have waited and taken you too. I never even considered that she could have had another one on the way. I'm so sorry. I never would have left without you," Grace insisted. She was ashamed that somehow she had failed him.

"There is no need for apologies. I had a good life with people who loved me as their own flesh and blood. And here I am reunited with my sister and my biological mother's family. I am blessed," he said, leaning over to kiss each woman on the cheek.

"True. I only wish we weren't here to bury our sister. She didn't deserve the fate that befell her. It wasn't right. She had more life to her than all of us combined. Katy was always sensitive and caring, but I can tell you that she was also brave and as stubborn as an overworked donkey. I think that's what got her in the end. That girl insisted that she was to blame for what happened to my brother. We knew Pa had bought him that crazy pony. If anyone was to blame, it was our father. She wasted her life trying to make up for an accident she neither caused nor could have prevented," Eileen painfully recalled.

Other mourners who were standing about started to filter over in their direction. The two sisters spent the next half an hour introducing Sara and Thomas to the mob that had made the trip to Virginia with them. Twelve of their children, along with their spouses and some thirty grandchildren, drove in from five different states to pay respects to a woman they had never met and knew little, if anything, about. Grace and Eileen had brought several pictures of Katy as a vibrant teenage girl, the last images captured before they moved away. After setting them out on a table next to her remains, the two frail ladies in their seventies took seats in the front row. The trip was difficult for them, having severed ties with their parents decades earlier. Sara was certain that the return to their childhood home inflamed wounds that had long been scarred over. She imagined their father rising from the dead to fulfill his quest for misguided revenge. Sara wondered if they were thinking the same.

When Sara saw her Aunt Donna, her adoptive mother's sister, and her two cousins, Laura and Isabella, come through the door of the church annex, she was pleasantly surprised.

"Sara, honey. How are you?" her Aunt Donna asked.

"Oh, my God!" she replied as she kissed each of them on the cheek. "What are the three of you doing here?"

"David called us," Laura responded with a heavy New York accent.

"We wanted you to know that even though you have found this family, you were my sister's child from the moment you were put into her arms," Donna explained.

"I love you guys! You're gonna make me cry," Sara said, extending her arms to hug the trio. "I'm so glad you came because I have someone I want you to meet. There are several people I want you to meet, but this someone is very special. He's my twin brother."

She released her grip to look around the room for the humble young priest who had been whisked away by one of Grace's sons.

"A twin brother!" Isabella exclaimed. "Who would have ever thought? Bring him over."

Sara briefly left the three women, returning arm in arm with the tall, dark-haired man dressed in his priestly attire, black pants and shirt topped with a rectangular white collar. David had failed to mention his occupation during the phone call days earlier. As the siblings stood side by side, they watched as the three women's jaws dropped in surprise.

"Thomas, I would like you to meet my Aunt Donna and my two cousins, Laura and Isabella. This is my brother, Father Thomas O'Connor."

"When you said twin, I expected the two of you to look more alike. Your hair is almost black and you have the most beautiful blue eyes," Donna commented, leaning forward to hug the surprised man.

"Bet the percentage of young female parishioners has skyrocketed since you started saying mass on Sundays," Laura added, making Thomas blush.

"It's nice to meet the three of you," he said, side-stepping the embarrassment of the last two comments.

"How long have you been a priest?" Isabella asked.

"I entered the seminary straight after college and, of course, I'm the same age as Sara, so it's been a number of years," he said, turning to look at his sister.

"You sure you're twins? You're kind of opposites when it comes to the whole religion thing," Laura added.

"True, I've had reservations about religion over the years," Sara said, "but finding out my mother was a nun, my father a priest, and my brother a priest has forced me to re-examine my thoughts about the church. This entire experience has helped me to better understand that all people are flawed, make mistakes, and struggle with doing the right thing. I think going to church, seeking out religion, and in some cases, entering religious life is a way to rise above these flaws, to serve someone other than yourself and your own needs. The past month has done more to make me believe in God than anything else has in the past 35 years. There had to be a divine power at work bringing everything out in the open, pulling a family back together that was so scattered and wounded," Sara explained.

"Amen," Thomas said.

David and Jack walked up behind Sara. Jack was still sporting a cast, but otherwise doing well enough to be sprung from the hospital. The little boy was having a hard time wrapping his head around the idea that the service was for the grown-up version of the little red-haired girl that had kept him company while he was unconscious. The situation was complicated for adults, let alone a child recovering from a brain injury. Sara and David had considered keeping him home, but he insisted on attending so he could say good-bye to his friend.

"Hi, Mom," Jack said poking his head around Sara's side.

"Oh my, God!" Donna cried as she bent over to kiss Jack. "There's my little doll! Look at you all banged up. We were so worried. I lit at least a dozen candles for you."

"What an angel!" Laura chimed in, kissing his other cheek. "You've been through so much. We're all so happy that you're better."

Isabella pushed her sister out of the way so she could hug him. "We were all praying for you. Did you get our get-well cards and balloons?"

Jack's face was covered in various shades of pink lipstick in seconds. "Yes, thanks," he answered as he fought to free himself from Isabella's tight embrace.

Leila arrived a few minutes later and made a beeline for Sara.

"How are you doing?" she asked, pulling her a few steps away from the boisterous trio.

"Okay," Sara sighed. "I think Jack would appreciate it if you could save him. He's a bit overwhelmed by all the attention. He's also having a rough time understanding how Katy could be dead. To him, she was a little girl. It would be great if you could help him sort things out."

"No problem," she replied. "Auntie Leila to the rescue."

"Hey, look," Sara said, nodding in the direction of the door. "Emma and Carlos just came in."

They waved from across the room, then took a couple of seats in the back row.

"I'll grab Jack and join them," Leila whispered before trotting off to collect him.

Sara watched as her friend skillfully lured the child away from the group. She saw David excuse himself from Donna and her daughters once Jack was free and clear.

"I see you sent in reinforcements," he kidded Sara as he came up and embraced her.

"I thought Jack needed a break. He looked a little ragged from all the loving."

"How about you?" he asked. "Are you fraying around the edges or are you hanging tough?"

Sara smiled. "You know me—calm and in complete control on the outside while I'm a mushy mess on the inside."

"That's what I figured. Remember to send up a flare if you need me." He squeezed her against his chest as he kissed her gently on the lips.

"Promise."

"It was nice of Donna, Laura, and Isabella to come," he said, nodding in their direction.

"They're pretty special," she agreed. "I can't believe how many people have come to pay their respects to Katy after all this time."

Sara let her eyes drift around the room. A tangled web of relations spanned the cramped church annex as old loved ones mingled with those newly anointed. Katy's memorial service was set to start in 10 minutes, with the funeral to immediately follow. In the shadows of the doorway she spotted Sean. Earlier, he had privately asked for forgiveness and said good-bye to his only love. Sara watched as he painfully turned to go. She wasn't the only one who had noticed him lurking in the hall. He was caught by surprise when a thin, almost transparent hand caught his arm. Grace had stopped him before he could leave. Sara grabbed David's arm and yanked him quickly in their direction.

"Is everything all right here?" Sara asked.

"I was asking your father to join us," Grace said. "I think he has avoided his responsibilities to my sister long enough. It's time he stands up and becomes part of this family once and for all. There have been enough examples of poor judgment and tragic mistakes to last a lifetime...for all of us. We are here to honor and say good-bye to a wonderful person. She would want us, all of us, to support one another and use that connection to heal," her poised aunt explained.

"I...I don't know what to say," Sean stammered.

"I agree. Please stay," Sara added.

Grace reached out and took Sean's hand. He was thunderstruck by her forgiving nature. Sara and David stepped aside as the petite woman led him into the room to meet the rest of the family.

"I thought she would have drawn and quartered him. Based on his reaction, I think he had the same idea," David commented.

"She's right. He's part of our family now."

When Thomas moved to the podium, signaling that the short service was about to start, all those who were standing took a seat. Sara motioned for Leila and Jack to join her and David in the four chairs that had been reserved for the immediate family in the front row. Thomas cleared his voice before starting to speak. He opened the service by offering a prayer and reading a lengthy passage from the Bible. Thomas had asked Sara to do the eulogy, but she had declined. What could she say about a woman she had never known except through haunting dreams? She left her brother to mine those words on his own. She was surprised by how he was able to magically transform the few personal anecdotes he had learned about their mother into a stirring description of her life.

"Kathleen McHugh was a spirit that touched so many and left a lingering mark on those whose hearts she came to know. She had been a brave and compassionate child whose worst offense seemed to be in holding herself to a standard that none could attain. She offered her life and service to the Holy Father and served him for many years as a beloved school teacher. She was a woman who suffered from human flaws and who could not forgive herself for them. Katy's search for wholeness and peace ended with the creation of two lives and the loss of her own. And it is now as we come together as a united family we send her to be joined with her brother and to sit at the feet of our Lord. She has achieved in death what she could not accomplish in life. God Bless her in the name of the Father, the Son, and the Holy Spirit. Amen."

Grace and Eileen dabbed tears from their eyes. Sean could not bring himself to look his son in the eye as the younger priest recited these words.

Thomas concluded the memorial with a final prayer after a soloist sang Ave Maria. "We can now make our way out to the cemetery for a brief service."

Sara, David, Leila and Jack led the way to the prepared gravesite. Michael's headstone sat to the right. Sara noticed the dates chiseled into the granite, marking his birth and death. He died not even a week beyond his ninth birthday. Chills ran up her spine as she realized that the haunting lullaby and vanishing bouquet of flowers appeared on the anniversary of his birthday while her son's return from the depths of his coma coincided with the day Michael died. Without doubt, they had barely skimmed through without losing Jack to the events that had plagued this family for nearly half a century. Sara pulled her son closer to her side.

"The stone cutters did a good job on that pattern you requested on Katy's headstone. *Separated Too Long, Together at Last*," David read.

"The funeral director told me he has the original stone in his car. I want to put it back in the field to mark where she was buried all these years," she answered.

"Good idea. What do you think they're talking about?" he asked, nodding in the direction of Grace and Eileen, who were looking very serious.

"Not a clue," Sara said.

They watched for a few minutes as the two women whispered back and forth. Curiosity getting the best of her, Sara walked over to them. "Hi, I couldn't help but notice that the two of you seem distressed by something. Can I help?"

"My dear, why did you choose to put that pattern on Kathleen's gravestone?" Eileen asked.

Sara was suddenly concerned that she had offended them.

"This is how I found her. Your mother had Lester carve this pattern into a stone from the nearby wall. He laid it over the spot where they buried her. It was the grave's only sign for all these years. I thought it would be appropriate. You seem to recognize it. Is there a problem with using it?" Sara asked.

"I would say it's perfect. According to Kathleen, it was our family's coat of arms, though not officially, of course. I recall when Katy was about 10 or 11 years old, she was looking through one of Mother's books on Irish heritage. She came across this pattern and dubbed it the McHugh family seal. The explanation she gave us was that the family is bound together through this never ending line that twists and turns but never breaks. Eventually it folds back and repeats itself over again, like being reborn or given a chance at redemption," Eileen sadly explained.

The funeral director arrived with the casket as Sara was about to offer a comment. The interruption gave her time to think more about the symbol's meaning and how it had woven itself so intricately through her life during the past few weeks. The funeral lasted 10 minutes. As the crowd was filing away, Thomas approached his sister. "You seem to have fared well through the day's events. Are they all returning to the house?" he asked, nodding in the direction of the mass of retreating relatives.

"Every last one of them. You are coming, aren't you?" Sara asked.

"Yes. However, I may be a little late. With your permission, I would like to invite Sean."

Sara smiled and took his hand. "I think that would be a wonderful idea. If Grace has the capacity to forgive him, then I guess we should extend the same generosity of heart."

"I'll offer him a ride. It's been strained between us. I would like to try and clear the air," he said, spotting the older priest standing alone near the church's side door. He kissed her hand and jogged over to their father.

She watched as the two of them disappeared inside the building.

As the crowd split off into their respective cars, Sara remembered something important that she had forgotten to do. David was helping to secure Jack's seatbelt as she turned to run back into the cemetery.

"I'll be right back," she called over her shoulder.

"What are you doing?" David yelled.

"I need to do something."

Sara was surprised that the bulldozer had already covered the casket with the mountain of dirt that had been set off to the side. The massive machine was slowly motoring away when she reached Katy's grave. She stuffed her hands inside her pockets and found what she was searching for. She cupped the gold cross and tiny key in the palm of her hand. Holding one end of the chain in the air, Sara allowed gravity to pull the shiny gold items down in a straight line.

"I believe these are yours. Rest in peace," she softly said as the chain slipped from her hand.

When Sara turned to go, she could hear a faint echo of children playing. Katy had found Michael at last. Smiling, Sara walked back to the car.